A Gryphon's Mercy

Kathryn Brown

The Quill and Claw Series

Book One: A Gryphon's Journey

Book Two: A Gryphon's Trial

Book Three: A Gryphon's Mercy

ACKNOWLEDGEMENTS

For my readers, who have shared in this incredible journey with me, and to all my loved ones.

CONTENTS

APPENDIX OF CREATURES

Gryphon: Diurnal, carnivorous predators that boast eagle-like heads and lion-like bodies. Possess wings and can live solitarily, in small units, or in large flocks.

Strigigryph: Nocturnal, carnivorous predators. May or not possess a crest. Have owl-like heads and lion-like bodies. Possess wings and are capable of nearly silent flight. Typically live in small groups, with larger flocks being extraordinary.

Ardeigryph: Crepuscular, piscivorous predators. Opportunistic feeders. Possess crested, heron-like heads, wings, long legs, and lion-like bodies. Typically live in large flocks.

Barbagryph: Diurnal scavengers, subsisting on mostly bone and marrow. Large, with vulture-like heads and heavy, lion-like bodies. Possess wings, but lack crests. Typically live in large flocks, with solitary members not extraordinary.

Alicorn: Diurnal herbivore possessing the body of an equine, with pale coats, wings, and a single horn. Have the innate ability to manipulate magick, and are long-lived and peaceable, with the tendency to live in herds.

Unicorn: Diurnal herbivore possessing the body of an equine. Possess pale or grey coats, and a single horn. Have the innate ability to manipulate magick, and are solitary in nature.

Basilisk: Crepuscular, serpentine carnivores
that are largely opportunistic in their feeding
habits. Capable of paralyzing prey with their
piercing gaze. Solitary and territorial, with most
living according to a basic hierarchy.

Aquila: Diurnal, predatory raptors possessing
the ability to form storm clouds and harness the
electricity therein. Typically live solitarily or in
pairs.

Fae: Diurnal, nocturnal, or crepuscular
depending on their type. Possess wings and a
basic ability to manipulate magick. Reserved and
aloof, they are typically peaceful and live in
colonies.

Tusker: Diurnal, mid-sized omnivores
possessing two tusks that curve upward on either
size of their snouts. Distinct for the grunting
sounds with which they communicate. Typically
live in small herds.

Peryton: Crepuscular, deer-like herbivores
possessing wings and cloven hooves. Males grow
antlers during their breeding season. Typically live
in small to large herds.

Longear: Crepuscular, small herbivores that
possess large ears and soft fur. Common in many
environments, and typically live in small colonies.

Pegasus: Diurnal herbivore possessing the
body of an equine, with pale coats and wings.
Live in herds and, while generally peaceable, are

highly territorial.

Pixie: Nocturnal carnivores that typically live in colonies. Possess wings, horns, and bright red hair. When able, forms a mutualistic bond with a host creature for both protection and increased chances of finding food.

Kirin: Diurnal herbivores possessing thick manes, cloven hooves, long, tufted tails, and bodies that are covered in scales. Have the innate ability to manipulate magick, and are long-lived and peaceable, with the tendency to live in herds.

Mermaid: Diurnal, aquatic, and piscivorous. Social. Possess a scaled body, sharp teeth, powerful tail, and webbed fingers, as well a pair of fins at the shoulders. Typically found in large bodies of salt water.

Kraken: Nocturnal, aquatic, piscivorous, and solitary. Possess eight tentacles, a sharp rostrum, and horizontal, rectangular pupils.

Daku: Crepuscular, carnivorous, and solitary. Possess powerful, forked tails, pointed dorsal fins, and rows of sharp teeth.

Selkie: Nocturnal, piscivorous, and social. Possess sleek, spotted fur and needle-sharp teeth. Typically found in large bodies of salt water.

Sea Serpent: Nocturnal, carnivorous, and solitary. Found in large bodies of salt water. Possess whiskers that help detect prey, a long, muscular body, fins, spines, and serrated teeth. Long lived, with the ability to continuously grow throughout their life span.

Phoenix: Diurnal, long lived, and typically solitary. Have the innate ability to manipulate magick, and to rebirth at the end of their life cycles. Raptor-like, with fiery plumage in varying shades of red, gold, or orange, as well as notably long tails.

Cockatrice: Nocturnal, solitary, and territorial. Capable of paralyzing prey with their piercing gaze. Large and unflighted, with an upright stance and the ability to run at great speeds. Possess both scales and feathers, and rely on stealth to track their prey.

Kelpie: Crepuscular, predatory shape-shifters that prey on the essence of others. Possess the ability to manipulate magick. Distinctly equine in appearance, with skeletal features in various stages of decay. Inhabit dark pools of water.

CHAPTER ONE

Arias dug his talons and paws into the warm sand, relishing the peace of the moment. The ever-present roaring of the surf made even the shrill cries of the Ardeigryph overhead sound muted, and Arias took in a deep breath of the salty air as he surveyed the grainy dunes surrounding him. It wasn't long before Larin loped up to join him, her black pelt and feathers a startling contrast to the bleached out sand surrounding them. She pricked her ears expectantly as she lay down with forelegs crossed, watching him. Larin was one of his most trusted friends, and had been with him nearly since the moment he'd begun interacting with other Gryphs. She never let her enthusiasm lag when she saw Arias heading out here, but he always had his doubts.

Arias picked his way across the beach, searching for the perfect place to test out the abilities of the seashell pendant he wore around his neck. The string of shells gleamed under the sunlight as though to mock him. They looked mundane enough, but according to the Mermaid he'd received them from, they evidently possessed potent properties. He'd never stopped worrying about his flockmates that had chosen to remain marooned on a tiny island in the middle of the ocean, and he knew that the journey to bring them here was too dangerous to take lightly. He didn't want to have to risk anyone else if he could help it… which is where the seashell pendant came in. If he could contact Naia, the Mermaid who'd given him the necklace, it was possible she knew of a way to reach them. After all, the briny abyss that stretched out before him was her home. But, there was a problem.

Arias had become adept at hiding his shortcomings, but Larin was keener than most. He'd already walked much closer the water's edge than he'd intended to, and he could feel himself stalling, just as he had every other time he'd come to experiment with the pendant. Larin knew, and he knew that she knew, but she didn't make a sound as she watched him pace the damp line that marked the furthest reach of the waves. Arias was aware that he'd never been afraid of water before. It was never his favorite thing, but he swam when he had to, even wading into the deeper reach of freshwater to avoid the stagnant, warm swill in small ponds when he went to drink. But ever since returning here from Dantzik, the very sight of the ocean had seized him with terror. It had taken long days before he'd been able to relax near the beach, let along come this close to the mass of water. Even then it was with a breathless expectation that something terrible could happen at any moment.

"Naia didn't mention how this thing works," Arias muttered. "It can't be that difficult. She wouldn't have given it to me without mentioning specific instructions if it was."

Larin tilted her head as she regarded the shell pendant, a soft croak rising from her throat. She waded out into the surf until it was up to her chest, bracing herself to keep the waves from dragging her further out with their aquatic claws. Arias took a step back when she gestured for him to do the same. It wasn't the first time she'd suggested that perhaps the ocean itself could somehow activate the pendant, but he always froze at the mention of going closer to the surging waves. He swallowed uneasily. "Why don't you take it?"

Larin dunked her head beneath the waves, then allowed the rest of her body to sink under. When she stayed under for longer than a few murms, Arias had to smother the panic that rose in his chest. Before the sensation could take hold of him, Larin resurfaced. He hoped the horror he'd felt at seeing her dive down wasn't apparent, and evidently it wasn't, as she frowned in response to his prior request and shook her head, then pointed at him with her sodden tail.

"Why not?" Arias asked. "What if it doesn't matter who is wearing it?"

Larin splashed at the water with her wings, and he scrambled backwards to avoid the spray.

She opened her beak, wrestling with what little of her tongue existed enough to say a short, "You." Like all Gryphons that had suffered the misfortune of living in the Arborochre flock, she'd had her tongue removed as part of the purported sacrifice of keeping her life and serving their deity of the night. In Arias's time spent with her and the others in her group, he had learned their more non-verbal ways of communicating quite well.

"I think that's enough time spent messing with this thing for today," he said. "Let's head back to the eyrie."

Larin shrugged her jet-black shoulders and pranced back onto the beach, falling into step with him as he hurried to distance himself from those terrifying waves. It wasn't until they left the salty landscape behind that he was able to relax again, tuning into the beauty of the season to distract himself. Summer had wrapped the land in its charm, having adorned plants with flowers, imbued the wind with warmth, and tempted the sun to rise earlier and set later.

"I think I have a taste for wriggler today," Arias said, more in conversation than with actual meaning. He'd been having less and less of an appetite for anything, and entire days slipped past in succession without the idea of preymeat ever crossing his mind. His short summer coat didn't do well to hide his rapidly appearing ribs, and he wasn't the best at avoiding the scrutiny of others. "What about you, Larin?"

The gryphoness made a face and shook her head. She'd never been a huge a fan of the seafare, a sentiment that he supposed he understood. When he'd first tasted the slimy, scaly prey, he hadn't been too excited about it either, but it had grown on him. They'd almost made it back to the eyrie when they spotted a silhouette streaking toward them, and Arias suppressed a sigh. Bala dipped his head amicably as he came to a stop, and Arias returned the gesture—a bit more deeply of course, as Bala *was* the Ardeigryph Sire after all—but Larin only rolled her eyes and continued on her way. It would've been considered quite blasphemous under normal circumstances, but Arias knew exactly what Bala was up to. And judging by Larin's unenthused reaction, she did as well.

"Have you thought about the proposal?" Bala asked. The way he shortened his long strides to match theirs somehow made him look even more sheepish than he already did.

Larin pinned her ears and increased her pace. Arias chuckled.

"Come on! You'd be perfect for it. You're a creature of action, Larin. Gryphs would follow you if you'd just take charge."

"You're doing fine, Bala," Arias assured. "Everyone knows you're the leader around here."

"But I'm *not.* Only in title, Arias. You're always the keythong with the plan. And me? I'm a coward. There! I'm not afraid to say it. I was just a convenient stand-in after our old Sire was killed, and even then, I'm not entirely sure exactly when I volunteered for the role. I almost sat out in the battle against Shadowbane, remember that? And I can never make up my mind. When you were off journeying in the north, Arias, we were all here trying to sort out our lives. And do you know who was at the forefront of that effort? Larin! She's amazing at getting things done, she just needs the title to go with it and she'd be set! You two could rule together, even, it would be perfect! After all, Arias," he said, lowering his long neck so he could look him directly in the eye, "Half of our ideas as a flock are actually *your* ideas. I'm sure you've noticed that by now."

Arias wiggled his stump of tail, amused. Larin didn't glance back.

"Larin doesn't want to be leader of the flock, Bala. Neither do I. She's happy guarding and hunting and having no one to get after except for herself, and maybe the other Sentinels. And I'm happy just being in the background and helping out when I'm needed. No more than that. We'll be here if you need us, though."

Bala sputtered, exasperated. "Everyone only listens to me because they know they'll have to answer to one of you two if they don't!"

Arias wrapped a wing around Bala's neck, pulling him in close. "You're doing fine, Bala. When did you get so worried, anyway? Sandrift eyrie is thriving, and we'll be here to help if you need us. Right Larin?"

Larin gave a reassuring chirp, still pressing ahead.

"See, Bala? How does that sound?"

Bala gave a defeated whimper. "You make it sound like it's infrequent that anyone summons you for advice. I came by to get you for a reason, however… There are five Gryphons waiting to speak with us at the edge of the hunting grounds at this very murm."

Arias stiffened, and Larin paused and shot them a confused glance. "The same five that asked to have a private audience with you a few days ago? You made it sound like they weren't in a hurry to be spoken with," Arias said.

"Their attitude didn't take long to change, I'm afraid…"

"Alright," Arias said. "Let's see what this is about."

***

Bala somehow made his tall bulk look small as he crept along a path that seemed undecided on whether it wanted to be shoreline or forest. The tall blades of the thick tufts of grass that grew in the sand waved in the wind, and Arias found it oddly hypnotic as he trudged along after Bala, his eyelids threatening to droop without his strict vigilance. Larin clicked at him with a note of worry, but he straightened up and forced an alertness into himself before Bala could peer over his shoulder at him. Lately, he'd been so tired…

but he didn't want the others to see it. Not when they already had so much else going on. Not when Bala was depending on him. Arias was afraid that whatever was holding the flock together was fragile, and that it would come apart at the merest prod. He wouldn't allow himself to be the thing that broke it.

Things like this—seeing what these Gryphons wanted to speak about—were just the beginning when it came to the issues that were pressing in on the eyrie. For instance, no one knew what lay in wait for them if they ever were able to reconnect with their flockmates on the island. Most of them had been Strigigryph, so staying put on the isle had at least meant a chance at survival… although no one knew for how long. Their short, broad wings had been a death sentence for many of them on the way across from the mainland, and Arias had lacked the heart to try to convince them to brave the ocean again.

Aside from that, there was the fact that no one had seen any signs of Arias's cubhood friend Brynne. The same was true of Tybrake, the Ardeigryph keythong who'd quickly become a close friend to both of them and many others as well. They'd been split up shortly before Arias's return trip to Sandrift, and he'd firmly and perhaps naively expected to find them waiting for him at the eyrie. Instead, everyone had been shocked to see him arrive alone. No signs of his friends had arose since.

Old troubles also stayed close, ensuring they

would never be quickly forgotten. Hilda and her fractious followers in the rogue Pale flock were still out there somewhere… at least, most likely they were. Internally, squabbles broke out in the flock here and there, and Bala was ill-equipped at dealing with them. Arias and Larin honestly weren't much better, but the three of them together produced better results than any one of them alone. Enough Gryphs respected them each individually that together, they could usually calm things down enough to return to peace.

Arias was aware that many Gryphs that had been in their twilight years had lost their lives either in the battle at Arborochre, on the long journey to this new land, or during the extended amount of time it took to settle down here at Sandrift. The lack of senior wisdom was palpable in the flock, and, with Bala being a conflict-avoidant pushover, Larin having trouble communicating with large groups, and Arias having little experience with his own kind in general, the eyrie had been subjected to some rough early development. In truth, none of them were honestly old enough to be Sire or Matriarch of anything, and yet… here they were.

Arias had initially been fairly good at distancing himself from the weight of the issues hanging over the flock, but as they piled on, other things began to sneak into his mind. He couldn't stop replaying the death of his Kirin friend, Ly-ra, and he couldn't silence the thought that it was his fault. If he didn't tear himself from the thought, others crowded in to join it: that perhaps the events that had forced everyone to leave the mainland were also his fault, and that, from the very beginning, the value of his own life was questionable. Arias frowned and shook himself from crest to tail stump, emptying his internal chatter and focusing on keeping up with Bala's long stride instead.

The beach grass gave way to a shorter, more plentiful field of rolling green grass, and Arias made out the shape of a small group of Gryphons sitting against a backdrop of trees. They called out and bowed respectfully as he, Larin, and Bala drew near, but Arias couldn't help but notice that they didn't drop their gaze despite the submissive gesture. Only the two youngsters among them, younger even than Arias himself, averted their eyes when he looked at them long enough. The remaining keythong, midnight in color, and two older, tawny hens regarded him with calm confidence. The keythong had a particularly steady, bold gaze… not at all combative, but certainly determined.

"Thank you for coming to meet with us," the keythong said, his pitch-black feathers gleaming in the sunlight as he straightened. "We'll be brief. We don't want to waste your time."

Bala nodded. "You have our ears, go on."

The keythong took them all in with his gaze as he said,

"Flock life… isn't for everyone. It has certainly benefitted us and helped us to survive in the turbulent times that befell us, and we don't want to be viewed as at all ungrateful. It's a good feeling to know that when everything is falling apart, Gryph-kind is able to come together to achieve great things beyond anything any of us individually could've dreamed of. Still, things are beginning to calm down, and… well, we're hoping to go our own way now. With your blessing, we're hoping to establish ourselves in the forests southeast of here. We've already gone on enough scouting missions to know of any prominent dangers that may lurk there, and it seems fairly safe. There are sure to be others who will wish to join us, but we're even willing to limit our numbers if that plays into your decision at all. We won't cause Sandrift any trouble with our existence, and with how plentiful prey has been, we don't see how this could cause any issues—"

"You want to leave the flock?" Arias interrupted, shocked. "You want to be *Primals?*"

"Well… yes," one of the tawny hens replied, clearly surprised by the reaction. "That's what we were before we joined up with this larger group. We were lucky to have been rather peaceful with our neighboring flocks, but we decided we wouldn't run when Arborochre forced their way in and started to wreak havoc. When the uprising finally happened, we were more than happy to throw our weight behind it. Now that things have calmed down, we'd like to go back to the way things were for us. A small group will always be home to us." The two younger Gryphons nodded as she said it, still avoiding anyone's gaze.

Bala frowned. "Is there something that

someone has said or done that has led you to this decision?"

"Sky's sake, no! Things just… get a little loud," the other tawny hen replied.

"And a little crowded," the keythong added. "It's nice to be able to grab a piece of preymeat off the pile and not wonder whether the Gryphon standing next to you was eyeing the same chunk." The two youngsters muttered their agreement, their eyes still firmly affixed to the scenery around them.

"It's dangerous out there," Arias said, worried. He felt a note of panic beginning to rise in him once again, that this was indeed the beginning of the end for the flock. He wasn't good enough to keep it together, none of them were. His senses seemed to heighten in response to the intangible threat, so much so that he could scarcely understand the words the keythong said in response. He blinked hard and shook his head to try to force himself to refocus, and, noticing the change in his demeanor, the black keythong tilted his head at him, frowning. Bala took a few steps forward and opened his wings pleadingly.

"The safety of this group is the only reason we've made it this far. Is there anything that can be done to change your minds? I don't know if I'd feel right letting you leave when we still don't even fully understand the dangers this new land presents," he proffered.

Despite his intentions, the response wasn't the

one the Primal-hopefuls had been expecting. A tense ripple ran through the small assembly, and the two younger Gryphons seemed to try even harder to look at anything besides the trio standing before them. The black keythong's tail gave a pensive twitch. "Well," he said, "all that sounds like it'll be our problem, then. I mean, I don't think we'll be the last to want to leave the flock. I don't mean that in a bad way, it's just that some of us preferred things the way they were before, when we weren't part of a giant group. Why is that so bad? If anything happens to us, it isn't your fault. It's ours."

"Hmm." Larin brushed her wing against Arias's and nodded to him, and the feeling that had overtaken him vanished like smoke as he wheeled to look at her in disbelief.

"We can't just let them head out there, Larin! It's too dangerous."

"I... suppose that I have agree with Larin," Bala said reluctantly. "We're no better than Shadowbane if we try to keep Gryphs here against their will. And we have more than enough hunting territory to support them. Besides... look at them. They'll sneak off on their own regardless, I'm willing to bet."

None in the other group replied to his last comment, but their relief was palpable as they all hurried into another bow. "If that was indeed permission granted, then I'm grateful. We all are. Thank you," one of the tawny hens said.

Arias tried not to let his disappointment show as he said, "We'll have to establish some base rules for you guys. How far you'll range, and what marking you'll use on trees to establish your passing. We'll need to announce the presence of this new group to the others in the flock, to prevent any accidental clashes." He didn't really want to add that last bit, as he didn't want others latching onto the idea that leaving the group was safe, but it was for the best that everyone knew.

The rest of the small group before him leaned down into an even deeper bow, and Arias dipped his head and turned to leave, feeling sick. He'd hoped everyone would be able to be content here. Hadn't they already lost too many? He didn't see how chasing after some sort of pointless wanderlust was worth the risk of losing your life, or especially not the lives of those who were optimistic enough to follow after you. He started as a wing fell gently across his back, and found Larin's piercing brown eyes looking at him with concern.

"Thanks, but I'm fine," he said. "Just… tired. I'm going to go rest for a bit, and then I'll catch up with you later tonight for the hunt, if that's alright."

Larin carefully refolded her wing with a look that seemed to say that she didn't quite believe him. She'd become increasingly worried about him, and she wasn't the only one. With every afternoon he spent fighting the urge to nod off instead of hunting or helping out around the eyrie, the murmurs and the sidelong glances at him grew. His temperament, normally friendly and a bit reserved, had depreciated despite his best attempts, and not a day went by that someone didn't ask if he was alright, if he was *really alright*. He always nodded and gave a reassuring chuff, and said whatever it took to get them to go along on their way.

Larin's expression hadn't changed, but she gave him another tap with her wing before trotting ahead toward the eyrie, throwing a last glance over her shoulder before lengthening her stride and hurrying off. Arias secretly hoped that forcing himself to join her on a hunt would help him to shake off the malaise he'd fallen into. He'd previously tried casting for wrigglers, but had ended up falling asleep in his tide pool, and more embarrassingly, he'd awoken to wrigglers nibbling at his toes and a couple of amused Ardeigryph trying to hold back crows of laughter as they'd watched. He'd also tried going out with others to scout for Brynne and Tybrake, but in a group he couldn't keep up, and alone he could barely focus enough to discern tracks, let alone to tell what creature had made them. He felt woefully deficient.

It didn't help that most Gryphs practically forbade Arias to lift even so much as a claw to help out, understanding that the journey to and from Dantzik had been long, hard, and necessary for him. He admitted that being able to just relax had been nice… for a while. Now it was mostly just annoying.

Arias reached Sandrift eyrie some time after

Larin and, as always, he was amazed by the absolute beauty of the heart of the flock. Sandrift stretched from the beach all the way up into an old growth section of a grand forest, with dens dug in between the mighty hardwoods and conifers. From what Arias had heard, the eyrie had come together intuitively, with almost every bit of it being agreed upon unanimously… well, except for one little bit. Against Arias's wishes, the flock had given him one of the largest dens. He shared it with Larin and their Ardeigryph friend Lue, but it still felt too empty to Arias, only serving as a reminder that Tybrake and Brynne weren't there to take up some of the space.

Arias veered away from the dens and pushed deeper into the forest, away from the crowds of Gryphs who were no doubt waiting to trill greetings to him and ask how he was doing. He trotted past the communal preymeat that had been piled up on the hard, clay packed earth just beyond the dens, whistling back a greeting to those who acknowledged him on his way past, but keeping up a brisk pace that would deter them from trying to start any conversations.

Holding an esteemed position in the flock due circumstances – sometimes beyond his control – of which he continually found himself part of, Arias often found himself treated with deference by the others. Exaggerated shows of acknowledgment were common among most Gryphs, ranging from courteous nods to encompassing bows, and while he often found the actions to be unnecessary, he had to admit to himself that it was nice to be acknowledged so highly by others.

The favored paths of patrols and hunting parties were already beginning to wear in, and the tamped earth felt comfortable under Arias's feet as he made his way into the quieter section of the forest. A scurrying from above caused him to freeze, but looking up, he made out the form of an Ardeigryph just settling into the thick branches above. *A sentry just beginning patrol,* Arias realized, raising his crest to the young keythong. He received a brisk nod in response, and then the sentry went back to surveying the surrounding area, and Arias couldn't help but to think to himself that he looked just a bit comical up there on account of his sheer size and long limbs. The old growths easily supported his weight, however, and he was clearly determined to do his job well.

Arias studied the sentry for just a while longer before moving on. He'd had been impressed by the adaptability of his Ardeigryph counterparts, and envied their even-tempered demeanors. They were incredibly slow to anger and thus served as great peacekeepers, and while unsettled by change just like any other Gryph, they had wasted no time in fitting themselves into their new lives here. A few were even beginning to take an interest in becoming keen hunters despite their primarily piscivorous diets, while others were starting to tag along on guard patrols. The one Arias had just passed was evidently seasoned enough that he was trusted to have his own area to guard.

Arias pressed on just a bit further, away from

the sentry, but in an area that would be still under his watch. Then he found a cozy spot against the gnarled roots of a tree, pulled his wings in extra tight, and turned to rest his head along his back, his beak nestled just underneath his wings. He tried to wrap his tail around himself, but the nub that remained of it was too short to do so. Funny, how he'd been missing it for so long, yet always seemed to forget. With a long yawn, he faded into sleep.

***

Thwap.

The sudden sound jolted Arias awake, and he was met by an apologetic Seale.

"I didn't know you were asleep, sorry. I thought you were just resting here," the Ardeigryph keythong said.

Arias peered down at the long, narrow wriggler that lay just in front of him, its silvery scales seeming too bright against the brownish ground. Seale settled back on his haunches and leaned down, his sleek feathers fluttering in the slight breeze. Seale had been close with Tybrake, and was one of the most dedicated in the flock when it came to taking trips out to scout for his missing friend. The keythong was just a bit more mature than Arias, though he wasn't sure of his exact age, and he possessed a particularly amicable personality. Seale gave the wriggler a doubtful nudge.

"Larin told me that you mentioned wanting a wriggler, and I've had a good day of casting, so…

I figured I'd share. The others told me they'd seen you come this way. Unless you'd prefer to have some preymeat, of course. I'm not too good at catching anything like that, but I bet one of the Gryphons—"

"No, this is great, thank you." Arias stood up and stretched, shaking out his plumage. He felt just as tired as he had when he'd lain down to sleep, and he was dismayed to find that he still had to will his eyelids to stay parted. "I was just taking a little nap. This looks like a good one; I appreciate it. I'll eat it in a little bit."

Seale picked absently at a few feathers on his chest, taking far too long to lay them carefully into place. He cleared his throat and looked about. "It feels like it's going to be a bit colder these next few nights. I always sleep better when it's a little cooler out. Maybe you will, too?"

Arias looked up at Seale. "Maybe," he answered.

Seale shuffled on his long legs and then, seeming to notice that he was fidgeting, straightened back up. "You know," he said carefully, "if there's anything you ever need, you can just ask, right?"

Arias glanced up again. He wished it was as simple as asking another Gryph, that an action so simple could fix everything. He only became aware of how long he'd been staring when Seale frowned and leaned in a bit closer.

"Arias," he said softly, "I can fly over to the island to check on the Strigigryph and Nanchu if you're worried. I know it's been a worry of yours ever since we left them. It was the best option we had at the time. It would be no problem at all, I can take a few of the others with me; I know many that would be more than willing. I know you don't want us to; that's the only thing that's stopped us. But we would be fine. We know how to read the wind and waves. I tend to fly out a lot further than the others when I go casting, anyway, and the open ocean doesn't bother me at all."

"No!" Arias replied immediately. "You can't go out there. I know you say it doesn't bother you, but casting off the coast and being out in the middle of the ocean are two different things. We were lucky on our way over here. Who knows where that sea serpent could be lurking, and no one can predict everything. A bad storm could start up, or some sort of strange predator, or anything, really. I don't want to endanger you or anyone else. I'm trying to find a safer way across, I just need more time. Same with finding Brynne and Tybrake. I know they're out there and I hate that I'm not with them right now. But whenever I try to join those search parties lately, I just slow everyone down."

"Arias…"

"It is what it is, Seale."

The big Ardeigryph was quiet for a long murm. "Why don't we go looking together sometime? If you feel up to it. Then you won't have to worry about the pacing," he finally said in his low rumble of a voice.

Arias looked up at Seale again. His eyes were crystal clear, blue like the water he always flew over. Earnest.

"I'd like that," Arias said finally. "Thanks."

A look of excitement spread across Seale's face. "Well, alright then! Come find me when you're ready to go. Maybe we can bring Larin with us. She's an amazing tracker. And I bet that Lue would be happy to join. That poor hen has been torn up about Tybrake missing, more than the rest of us."

"I know he'll turn up, Seale. They both will. It's just hard not knowing. Hey… thank you for stopping by. And for the wriggler, too."

"Of course!" Seale spread his massive wings as he leaped to his feet. "And you let me know if you need anything, alright? And try not to worry about Tybrake… he's a tough one. You're right, he'll turn up. They both will." With that, he gave another staunch nod, and then he trumped off through the forest, headed back toward Sandrift. Arias listened to the sound of his friend's retreating pawfalls as he tried to take comfort in the words that had been spoken. And then he let out a long, slow sigh, allowing the exhaustion to creep back in. He had no idea how he'd survive going on an entire tracking mission without wanting to lie down and sleep with every other step, but he'd worry about it later.

After a murm of convincing himself to eat, Arias devoured the wriggler. He had to resist the urge to throw it back up, and then he sat until he was sure he wouldn't. He hated wasting food, even more so if someone else had gone through the trouble of procuring it for him, but eating was almost abhorrent to him these days. He looked up, noticed that the sun would be heading on its way down before long, and decided he'd better go find Larin. With a final stretch and yawn, he ambled back the way he'd originally come, toward Sandrift.

CHAPTER TWO

Arias found Larin lying on her back at the edge of Sandrift eyrie, sunning herself. Tufts of fur were caught in her claws—a few stray strands even clung to her beak—indicating that she and her Sentinels must have had an intense sparring match while he'd been sleeping. A devious inclination to startle her lanced through Arias, and despite his own fatigue, he found himself stooping down to gather himself into a pounce. After a quick murm of deliberation, he launched himself onto her, and the hen shot upright with a savage hiss. Her crest and ears snapped upward as she recognized him, and she flung herself playfully back at him. He tried in vain to pull himself from her grasp, but, whereas she used to be an equal match for him, he quickly found that she could overpower him these days. Luckily, she only punished him with a modest amount of pinching before letting him drag himself free of her claws, and he flopped down next to her, panting to catch his breath. She gave a pleased smirk, her eyes sparkling.

"Still worth it," he said, tensing as she made as if to grab him again. Instead, she spread a wing and ignored him, turning her attention to beginning the lengthy process of preening her glossy feathers. Arias allowed himself to relax. The mellow gusts of air that stirred around them smelled warm and green. It felt nice.

"Larin," he said after a long murm. The gryphoness turned to look at him when he didn't continue speaking, her intense brown eyes searching his. She gave the slightest tilt of her head.

I'm listening.

"I don't want to alarm anyone," he started, then paused again. There really didn't seem to be a better way to put it, so he went on. "I think there's… something wrong with me. Something serious. I don't think it's going to get better, and I don't know what'll happen if I keep waiting for whatever it is to fix itself. Nothing I've tried has helped. I'm hoping that maybe I can try to make it to Hlaena or at least to see To-shin. Maybe they'll know what's causing this. Will you come with me? I don't trust myself to make the trip alone."

Larin frowned, concerned, and nuzzled into him. She was as warm as the sunshine, and Arias found himself leaning back, embracing the rare sense of calm that seemed only to truly fall on him when he was with her. A sudden burst of distant shrieking shattered the moment, the sharp cries echoing across the eyrie, and Arias and Larin both sprang to their feet. They took off toward the disturbance, and it was only once they got closer that they realized the cries sounded jubilant. They'd hardly made it to the dens before they were surrounded by Gryphs, some running, others flying, all milling about and jostling one another in excitement. Most of them spilled away like a wave when they noticed Arias and Larin, their eyes expectant. Confused, Arias looked ahead and suddenly realized that one of the dens was occupied by a smudge of orange.

"Brynne!" Arias roared, rushing to tear across the clay-earth toward her. Larin was at his heels, her own excitement nearly driving her to overtake him. Brynne laughed in sheer joy as she stretched her amber wings wide to take them in, and in their zeal they bowled her completely over. Those watching the reunion gave clucks of endearment at the sight, then scrambled to part as a single Ardeigryph hen darted through the assembly to stand before the trio.

"Lue!" Brynne exclaimed, jumping up and running forward to cross necks with the diminutive Ardeigryph hen. Lue seemed so overcome at seeing Brynne again that she was speechless. She spun and bounded in a wide circle of exhilaration, her crest raised high.

"You're alright!" Lue finally managed to exclaim. She scanned the area around Brynne, her crest slowly falling. "Where's Tybrake?" she asked, faltering.

Arias froze in the silence that hung behind the question. Brynne's bill dropped open as if to speak, but she didn't, and Lue reeled back as if the coming answer had somehow physically struck her. Before she could find her words again, a new voice spoke up.

"You mean he's not here?"

The newcomer's voice was low and husky, different enough that the entire flock snapped their heads toward it in surprise, their hackles raised. They all peered past Brynne and into the depths of the den from which the gritty voice had originated, but Brynne simply threw a casual glance over her shoulder. "It's alright, Roarick," she said. "Come on out."

Something large moved within the darkness, coming forward enough that two gold eyes ringed in crimson could just be made out. After analyzing the crowd beyond, Brynne's companion hesitantly revealed himself. Arias tilted his head as he tried to make sense of what he was looking at. The creature was obviously a Gryph of some sort, though he had no crest. Instead, he sported a brilliant ruff of cream colored feathers around his neck, and the plumage along his back and wings were so deeply bronze that they almost seemed reflective. The rest of him was an unremarkable sandy color, but the truly impressive thing about him was his size. He made even the big Ardeigryph keythongs that were gathered around appear average, and it was clear to see that he certainly possessed a good amount of muscle. Arias spied a nasty scar that spanned all the way from his neck to his foreleg. It was recent enough that it was still healing by the look of the raw flesh.

Roarick took a single step back into the shadows of the den, but Brynne hurried to usher him back out. "They aren't going to hurt you. Stop being so anxious, you're making me jittery." She raised her voice louder. "This is Roarick, everyone. He's a Barbagryph. I guess there are more of them around, but you wouldn't know it. They're apparently all as reclusive as he is. He's shy, if you can't tell that already."

Roarick ducked his head in a short, awkward bob. "Hello," he said, his voice so low and quiet that Arias had to half-guess at what he'd said.

Arias remembered how the first time he'd ever seen an Ardeigryph, he'd caught himself gawking as he took in the details of a creature he'd never seen before. He recognized the familiar feeling of his own gaping now, and he hurried to dart forward introduce himself instead. "My name is Arias, it's nice to meet you. This is Lue, and Larin, and… well, that's the rest of Sandrift flock. I'm afraid my introductions end there, however. You'll have to go through them all individually if you want to know all of their names."

This elicited a soft chuckle from the stranger, and Arias was glad he seemed a bit more at ease. Arias looked from Brynne to Roarick and back again, then added, "It looks like you've already know our friend Brynne." The magnificent cape of feathers around Roarick's neck rose as he nodded fervently.

"Yes! She helped me out of quite a situation. I'd imagined that had she not come along when she had, within a few more days I would've been sent to the great Yawning itself. Brynne healed me with some foul plant… I don't remember which, but it was unpleasant."

"Blackroot!" Brynne exclaimed, snapping her wings in and out with emphasis. "I remembered you helped me with it when I was just a cub, Arias. Roarick nearly lost his leg trying to contest some half-eaten carcass against an ursos, and it was the only thing I could remember that could've helped him. And it did! But enough about that." Her expression darkened. "I thought for sure that Tybrake would be here. We need to get out there and look for him! It's been way too long for him not to have returned by now. Halada's sake, I would've been back ages ago had I not run into *him*. Er, no offense," she added, to which Roarick blinked.

"I'd hoped you two were together…" Lue's gaze fell as she said the words, and Arias felt something sharp twinge inside him at the heartbreak in her voice.

"The flock has been looking for him since before I returned," Arias said. "No one ever stopped looking for you two; search parties leave every day to canvas the territory, even now."

"The territory?" Brynne said, almost sounding indignant. "We went far beyond the territory on that journey to Dantzik, Arias. He could be literally anywhere between Dantzik and the path we took to get there. Please tell me you've led searches at least along that route?"

Arias looked down at his talons. He felt minuscule, like the reminder of his own inaction had sucked the wind out of him. Larin moved closer to him, defensive, and Brynne frowned. "Is there something I don't know?" she asked.

Arias thinned his eyes. "Others have searched along the routes I've described to them." He shot Brynne a meaningful glance as he eyed Roarick, but Brynne was quick to say, "It's fine. He can be trusted."

"Alright then," Arias said. "I'll tell you everything. Come on."

***

Sunset fell in glinting streaks across Sandrift, filtering through the treetops in hazy gold lines. Most of the Gryphs who were gathered at the communal preymeat had already eaten, but not Brynne. She set into the offerings with gusto, consuming three longears, a quarter of a peryton, and a tusker hind leg. After she was done scrupulously stripping all the flesh away from the hind leg, she pushed the bone toward Roarick. The Barbagryph dove forward with eagerness to snatch it up, then meekly made his way toward the outside fringes of the group.

"Roarick," Brynne said in a pleading tone.

He dropped the leg bone, looking startled.

Brynne gave a dramatic sigh, and Roarick shuffled with discomfort and started to mutter something, but Brynne cut in and said, "No one cares what you eat, Roarick. We didn't all gather here to watch you, I promise."

Except that evidently, that wasn't true. Brynne's words had only served to pique the interest of anyone close enough to hear her, and the circle surrounding the newcomer imperceptibly leaned closer as they studied his every action. Roarick sent another nervous glance around before picking the bone up again. He balanced it precariously in his bill for a moment, then flipped it back into his gullet in one swift motion. In a two swallows, it was gone. Sounds of amazement immediately filled the air, and he cringed back, startled.

"How did you not choke on that?" A wide-eyed Gryphon hen asked, her voice almost accusatory. "Bones don't have any give the same way that meat does."

"Does it actually taste good?" An Ardeigryph keythong cut in before Roarick could answer, shoving the wriggler he'd been about to eat aside.

"It's really only worth it if they still have the marrow in them," Roarick instructed quietly, his feathers smoothing as he finally relaxed. "I can explain what good ones look like, if you'd like."

"Guys!" Brynne shouted, stamping her foot. "That's all fine and well, but we have more pressing matters to attend to. Her eyes shot over to Arias. "Like Tybrake."

"I'm thinking that you'd be the best Gryphon to take an expedition to search for him further out," Arias said. "You probably know the way we took better than I do. You've always been a better navigator than I have."

"I wouldn't be opposed to that," Brynne replied, "but you don't want to come along? He's your friend, too, and... Well, I guess I'm surprised that you're not already running yourself ragged searching for him."

Arias looked across to Roarick, then the rest of the waiting Gryphs. Brynne waved her tail, waiting.

"I can't."

Brynne's eyes to traveled over him carefully. "Why not?"

Arias shook his head. "I just can't. I physically can't. It's not easy to explain, but I can try. I guess I'll have to go all the way back to my arrival in Dantzik to begin."

***

The night air was deceptively chilly. Arias waited with Roarick, Brynne, and two of Larin's Sentinels. Having had their tongues ripped out in a twisted, forced ritual in Arborochre, the Sentinels had found other, less verbal ways to communicate with one another. They and held a tight, almost impenetrable fellowship with one

31

another, with Larin as their lead. The black gryphoness came loping through the brush and gave a brisk, certain nod, indicating the earlier reports of hunting parties during the day had been correct; there was indeed an entire herd of peryton browsing in the northern brushlands. The hunt could proceed as planned.

Larin took point as Arias and the others leaped skyward, and Arias tried his best to make it seem that taking off didn't take everything in him to achieve. Brynne had been understanding, but he could tell that she hadn't really quite believed him when he'd explained how he'd felt lately. He *wanted* to go back to the way things had been before, however, and so he'd joined this hunt as he'd originally planned. There was always the chance that maybe focusing on his more predatory nature could drive out whatever had been ailing him... or so he told himself

Arias was grateful when the group banked hard to land. They would travel the rest of the way on claw, as it was best to keep a buffer between them and their prey so as not to alert the peryton to their presence too soon. Arias stuck close to Brynne—and to Roarick, by default, as he never seemed to stray far from her—and he was reminded of their cubhood hunts. He remembered clumsily following along after her as he listened to her incredible boasts, trying his best to imitate a real hunter. Those days seemed very long ago now.

After what felt like an eternity of walking, Larin halted and nodded to her Sentinels, and the three of them pressed forward at a slow creep. They'd sneak past the main herd and spread out into the woods beyond, where they would act as the last strike against prey that managed to escape the initial attack. Brynne and Roarick would perform as the main pursuit team, with Roarick playing more of an observer role. A scavenger, he didn't do much hunting. When he did, he'd explained, he went solo, but he was interested in seeing how other Gryphs worked as a team to bring down prey. Arias would take up the role of flusher, running toward the herd obviously enough to cause them to panic and sprint, hopefully before noticing Brynne and Roarick were coming at them from the sides. With his very visible white coat, Arias had always been an excellent flusher; prey could see him from a long way off, and he didn't have to try hard to get them to run blindly.

Arias tried to reach for excitement, to feel the thrill of the hunt, but just the thought of the impending chase mentally drained him before he'd even started. Long murms passed as he watched the forms of his flockmates move ahead of him through the darkness, the sounds of the night unbroken by their silent passing. Arias had already lost sight of Larin and the other Sentinels, but when Brynne and Roarick froze and didn't move further, Arias knew he had his cue. Taking in a deep breath of air, he urged himself into a run.

Arias felt every breath that entered and left his lungs, and it took every scrap of his concentration to force his legs to keep churning out the sprint he leaned into. Every gasp seemed a little shorter than the last, until shadows started to flicker at the edges of his vision. Naia's seashell pendant felt cumbersome around his neck, rising and falling against his feathers in time to his rough gait. He could hear the sounds of scattering prey in front of him, but instead of the incredible drive that typically would've flooded his senses in such a chase, only a sense of duty to his fellow Gryphs kept him going. He saw a blur and a flash of color, and he was suddenly behind a young peryton buck, its tail flashing in warning to the others of its kind. Arias couldn't imagine expending the energy required to leap to capture the creature, so he focused on staying on its trail instead, hoping either Brynne or Roarick would see it and make the final burst to take it out. Neither of them noticed fast enough. Arias could feel his speed tapering off, but he willed himself to keep the buck within sight. He growled as he dug in, struggling to lengthen his stride, and then...

Conk.

Arias sprawled out, shaking his head to try to clear the pain that blossomed between his ears. It took a moment for the low-hanging tree limb he'd struck to stop vibrating. He groaned in equal parts annoyance and pain, a feeling that quickly changed to embarrassment as Brynne and Roarick ended their chase and doubled back and check on him instead.

"Are you alright?" Brynne asked. "Halada's tail, did you run into that branch? How did you not see that? It's huge!"

Arias scowled and squeezed his eyes shut, and when he opened them again, he saw that Larin was dashing back toward them alone. She gave a sharp, urgent cry, and motioned for them to follow her before vanishing into the brush again. Brynne and Roarick both shot one another concerned glances. Arias shook his head to scatter the remnants of his pain, and Brynne shifted a peculiar gaze on him.

"Maybe… maybe you should stay here while we check it out," she said.

"Larin's out there, and you expect me *not* to go?" Arias replied, indignant. "I'll bring up the rear if it makes you feel any better, but I'm seeing what this about." He managed to push past her and she didn't try to stop him, though it was apparent that he wasn't bringing up the rear by choice. Even at a trot, Brynne and Roarick soon left him behind, though Brynne was clearly trying to keep her urgent gait tempered enough to keep him within sight. Arias growled to himself, his frustration growing. Even if it felt like he was putting more effort into his speed, it didn't translate into actual results.

A mass of Gryphs appeared in the distance, their forms broken up by the woody trunks of trees. They were eerily still under the weak moonlight, tense and unmoving save for their bristling fur and ruffled plumage. It took Arias moving in much closer to realize why.

There, surrounded on all sides by a Sandrift hunting party of angry, hissing Gryphs, was a Gryphon hen he'd hoped to never have to lay eyes on ever again. Even with the distance, however, her flaxen coat was unmistakable.

It was Hilda.

CHAPTER THREE

Arias approached the group guarding Hilda with caution. Larin and the others skirted around them, confirming that it really was who they thought it was. The unfortunate reality was quick to sink in.

One Ardeigryph hen, sporting a menagerie of both new and old wounds, was bristling so furiously that she almost appeared to be standing on her toes. She took her eyes away from Hilda only long enough to glance at Arias and say,

"Someone's already been sent to notify Bala. I caught this *tuca* skulking through those trees over there, probably hoping for us to make another kill that she can steal." She growled. "Not this time. I dragged her out here myself, and I would've done more if not for... well. I don't think she's going to be raiding anyone again anytime soon."

Arias studied Hilda upon hearing the words, noting that the hen's eyes flitted with uncharacteristic nervousness as they took in the bodies pressed in around her. She snarled at him when she caught him staring, and although she was trying her best to hide it, he could tell that something was seriously wrong with one of her wings. Her short, dull summer coat wasn't doing a good job of hiding her protruding hips and ribs, and although she sounded fierce, Arias guessed that more of it than she would have liked to admit was posturing.

"I wouldn't have let myself be caught by the likes of you if I was worried about what you might do to me," Hilda spat.

"If you're looking for something to worry about, I'd be happy to give you a reason," the Ardeigryph hen replied, taking a bold step forward. "It would be my pleasure."

Arias gently nudged the Ardeigryph hen back with his wing, but he didn't tell her to stand down. "Don't do anything foolish. Why are you here, Hilda? I thought I made it clear the last time we met… this land is large enough that our flocks should never meet again, and yet here you are."

"She and her followers have been attacking our hunting parties," the Ardeigryph hen growled. "One of her keythongs gave me these scars not even three suns ago when I tried to stop him from stealing a longear I'd killed."

"I didn't order any of that," Hilda hissed, her ears flattening. "Trust that I had no desire to see any of you ever again. However, there is nowhere to go in this land. The Pale went for days without food, and sometimes almost as long without water. There is *nothing* out there. Your flock seems to have settled on the most hospitable land to Gryphon-kind here. We returned to this area believing that this territory was vast enough that we could claim part of it while staying apart from your group, but it didn't take long for some of the bolder members of the Pale to tire of running into your hunting patrols, your tracks, and your marked trees. You've rightly claimed the best hunting grounds, but their eyes gleam at the prospect of hunting here instead of chasing after the odd stray tusker.

Those Gryphons now want to contest you for this land, and will do anything to achieve it. They've already turned most of the flock in their favor. I held out against a new challenger every day who wanted to be Sire or Matriarch... and after the third day in a row of fighting, one of the troublemakers, a keythong named Canik, challenged me."

Hilda paused, bristling with remembrance. "Canik fought without honor. I managed to win against him, but not before he did this to my wing. I am unable to lead without the ability to fly, and his followers immediately elected him as leader as a result."

Hilda glared at those around her, especially at the Ardeigryph, and then looked back to Arias. "The ways of our ancestors fade with each new generation, it seems. Your flock is unnatural, and you are weak, Pale one... and yet your word holds weight among others. I thought the Pale would keep to the vestiges of the old ways. Look where that landed me." She shook her head. "Just know that I would never condone the stealing of food. Halada may have turned away and forgotten me, but I have more honor than the fools who raid you."

A sudden snort rent the air, and Hilda wheeled around to face Brynne.

"Honor?" Brynne spat. "You and honor don't belong in the same sentence after what you did, Hilda."

"I did what I thought was right to protect my flock. *You* were leading us astray," Hilda retorted.

"Oh, so it's alright when you break away from the code of honor, but it's cheating when others do the same thing? If I led the Pale astray, then you did far worse than that, Hilda."

Hilda didn't reply, her eyes hard and her tail lashing. Brynne let out a small, bitter laugh in response. "Nothing to say for your past actions, then. Of course."

Arias lifted his ears, scanning the forest around them. Hilda's story was believable enough, especially considering her wing, but a little paranoia had served him well in his life. "Check the surrounding area," he instructed a few nearby Gryphs from the hunting party. "Make sure that we're truly alone."

"We are alone," Hilda snapped. Then, more dejectedly, she added, "I know when I've been beaten. I came here because I have nothing to lose… and to warn you. Canik will do whatever it takes to wrest this land from you. He's needlessly violent, and he's turning the most devout of his followers into monsters."

"I'm no skilled warrior," Arias said, "but even I can see that your numbers are far smaller than ours. I'd never look forward to a fight, but if it's what it takes to stop the raiding—"

"You aren't hearing me," Hilda said. "He'll do *anything*." She shifted her gaze to Roarick. "He's found their kind and is hoping to appeal to them for help."

"They won't help him," Roarick said quietly.

Hilda ignored his response. "Brynne, those who follow Canik wholeheartedly are lost, but there are still some who remain who would listen to you. The Pale was strong under your rule. If Canik is removed from power, those who are reasonable would be quick to accept you, and the rest would follow or be without a flock."

"You led a flock?" Roarick exclaimed incredulously, turning to Brynne. "The Pale was yours? You were a *Matriarch*?"

"It's not exactly as grand as it sounds," Brynne said, not taking her eyes off Hilda. "But none of that matters. I don't want the flock back."

"Canik is going to get innocent Gryphons killed if nothing is done. And you'll suffer casualties as well if you let him continue to go on. The raiding parties aren't going to stop. If they gain the numbers they need, I wouldn't be surprised if they start attacking your flock more openly, perhaps even picking off the odd stray sentry or hunting party."

"So challenge Canik again," Brynne said. "Only this time, don't stop at just winning. You were incredibly comfortable with challenging me and Arias, remember?" She turned to Arias, her tail lashing against the earth. "We can't forget that she tried to kill you, Arias. Halada's sake, she would've done it had she not been stopped. Why are we wasting our time speaking with her?"

"Because you know that I have nothing to lose by coming here and telling you all this," Hilda said before he could reply. "I'd challenge Canik myself if my wing healed in time, but I'm afraid that even if I did, his followers won't accept me as leader anymore. It would be merely a cycling of challengers again until his replacement comes to power. However, if you were leader and I helped to discourage anyone from actively dueling you—"

"I already said I want nothing to do with that flock," Brynne snapped. "You don't listen, do you?"

"I know that you don't want it, but you know many of these Gryphons that Canik is turning," Hilda cried. "Some of them are just yearlings.

You probably met them back in our homeland when they were just coming out of their down, and I'm sure that many of them looked up to you during your time as Matriarch. They think they're tough because they made the journey from the mainland over to here and... well, they are, but Canik is trying to turn them into killers. Their first few attacks were on unsuspecting Gryphs like her." She nodded to the Ardeigryph hen who'd first spoken to Arias when he'd arrived. "And they probably thought it was great because they had the advantage. But as soon as they run into a patrol that is ready and expecting them— the moment one of them gets their throat ripped out—it won't be lighthearted winning anymore. I don't want to wait around to find out what Canik can make them do after experiences like that harden them. They aren't bad Gryphons, but the *tuca* leading them is making them think that they are. I know you don't trust me, I understand that. But you can't tell me that you don't care at all."

Brynne growled, snapping open her wings so forcefully that a ring of dust kicked up from the forest floor. Hilda crouched instinctively, ready for an attack, but Brynne didn't move toward her. She stood there in the cloak of darkness, glaring at the other hen. Finally all she muttered was,

"Well then, tough. I hope you know none of this would've happened had you left the flock alone, Hilda. This is your fault. The gryphoness who led the Pale in the past, the one you wrested leadership away from... she isn't me anymore." She turned without waiting for a response, stalking away back toward the eyrie, and Roarick cast Hilda a last glance before following after her. Arias shared a look with Larin before asking,

"How long has your wing been that way, Hilda?"

"The lesser part of a moon... Long enough for me to know that I can't fix what's happening in the Pale myself."

Arias clucked grimly, and Hilda frowned at him.

"What?" she asked.

"Broken wings don't heal on their own," Arias said. "And you only have so long to fix them."

"Who says it's broken?"

"I grew up with Alicorns, and I definitely know what a broken wing looks like. It's been too long to fix it the easy way, and it takes magick to fix it the hard way. Claws aren't precise enough. If you leave it alone, you'll never fly again."

Hilda's eyes thinned. "Then there's nothing to be done. As I said, Halada has struck me from the sky and turned her gaze away from me. Either you may kill me here, or I will resume my exile. If you choose to do the former, know that I won't go easily, and if you choose the latter... well, I wouldn't be surprised if Canik eventually tries to end me as well, given enough time."

"Let's not think of extremes just yet," Arias

said, though he despised the idea of helping Hilda in any way. "I'd like to take some time to speak with Bala and some others before making a decision." He eyed the scarred Ardeigryph hen standing next to him. "Can you move her further into the territory and guard her while I consult with the Sire?"

The hen gave a hesitant nod. "We'll keep a close eye on her. You can be sure of that."

"Thank you. And you," he said, looking toward Hilda, "go quietly and don't make any trouble. I'll be back."

***

Bala didn't hide his shock upon hearing news of Hilda. He sat in a wide circle composed of Arias, Larin, the rest of the Sentinels, Brynne, Roarick, Lue, and a few guards who had been nearby enough to hear the calling of the meeting. Brynne had taken some cajoling to attend; Arias could tell that whether she wanted it to or not, the news Hilda had brought bothered her. Roarick was confident in assuring them that the rest of the Barbagryph would have no interest in helping the Pale, though it wasn't of much comfort considering the circumstances. After he'd finished speaking, it was up to all of them to decide on what action to take next.

Of course, there was the option of taking no side and leaving Hilda to fend for herself, although the threat the Pale provided couldn't be ignored. There was also the option to go after Canik, which was perhaps putting too much trust in the story Hilda had told them. And then there was the choice to take no chances and to kill both Hilda and Canik. While the option was popular among Brynne and some of the guards, Bala was hesitant to spill blood without being absolutely certain of all the information they'd been provided.

"There is the fact that, if her wing were healed, Hilda could do some of the work of reinstating herself as leader," Roarick proffered. "I imagine she'd be indebted to you for helping her, as she won't be faring well on her own without flight. You'd also know for certain that the story she told is true if she continues to go about trying to find a way to stop whatever this Canik is up to."

"Maybe," Arias said, "but considering how long it took you and Brynne to travel here on claw, I'm not sure anyone here has enough time to spend on escorting her to Dantzik and back. Who knows what could happen in that time?"

"Who said anything about Dantzik?" Roarick asked. "There's a Unicorn much closer who could probably help."

A silence fell, and more than a few heads cocked. Arias had heard of Alicorns, of course, but never of Unicorns. Picking up on the confusion spreading around him, Roarick added, "His name is Jance, and he isn't exactly friendly. He'll probably demand something in return for his services depending on the mood he is in, but I'm sure we could figure something out."

"Wait a murm," Brynne said, shaking her

head. "If we do anything to help Hilda out—I'm still trying to understand *why* we're thinking of helping her—then we're accepting that the Pale will be around. She already stressed that there is nowhere else they can go."

"I'm sure that we can set conditions that limit the activity and the power the Pale has if needs be," a Gryphon keythong, one of the guards, said. "It would seem that this was already done earlier for some who left the flock intending to be Primals once again."

"That's true," Bala said slowly, "but we'd have to set very stringent, careful rules. And we'd have to be swift and decisive if there are any signs of them not being followed. I don't think that bit of the decision to help her, if made, is negotiable." He let out a long, hissing breath. "I really wish I were more alright with the idea of just doing away with the lot. They've caused us enough misery as it is."

Brynne started to roll her eyes, but then, seeming to remember that Bala was Sire, averted them instead.

"Roarick," Arias said, "will you explain more about this Unicorn? Is it like an Alicorn?"

"Mmm," Roarick said. "I've heard of Alicorns, but only in stories." He glanced up, thinking. "Yes, Jance would be like that, only without the wings."

"Jance," Arias said, trying out the name.

"What sort of things does he typically ask for in return for his assistance?"

"Jance has lived in the range my kind call home for as long as anyone can remember," Roarick said. "Sometimes he'll help for free, but the things he might ask for in return are so varied, I'm not sure what to tell you. I've heard he's asked for anything as mundane as the longest primary flight feather a Barbagryph has, to a plant that grows in high altitudes to much stranger things… a regurgitated bone, for instance, or, once, I even heard he asked for one of the twin cubs that a new pair had borne."

"What?" Bala exclaimed, alarmed.

"Well, I'm not sure if they actually did it or not," Roarick said with a shrug. "It could've just been a story for all I know. But have you ever seen how much a cub can eat? I bet the parents were relieved if they were able to give one away."

Arias peered at Roarick with a bit of genuine curiosity. The Barbagryph, despite his shy and somewhat timid nature, always spoke with the same calm level tone. It almost seemed to border on the blasé.

"I'm not sure, but it's possible Jance may be able to help you as well, Arias. Provided you're willing to explore that possibility, of course." Roarick paused. "This probably sounds suspicious, but if we go to see Jance, our group will probably be better received with fewer Gryphs in the group. I can guarantee that my

Barbagryph counterparts have noticed your arrival to this land, and are perhaps still deciding whether you're a threat or not. Traveling up with a large number of your flock will probably cause some worry."

"Should we make a point to meet with them and let them know that we aren't a threat?" Arias asked.

Roarick thought for a murm before he shook his head. "No, probably not. Honestly, I'm sure they're bothered enough if the Pale or whatever the other flock is called has come to them asking for help with their squabbles with you. It is probably best to keep to yourselves until the time comes that you want to address them directly."

Arias shot Brynne a look, but she responded back with a slight tilt of her head as if to say, *I told you he's trustworthy, stop worrying.*

"How far away does Jance live?" Lue asked, pipping up for the first time.

Roarick looked up at the sun, swaying his head as he deliberated. "Oh, not far. Perhaps from sunrise to sunset walking. Much shorter flying, of course."

With Hilda's wing being broken, of course they'd have to walk. That worked out just fine for Arias, who couldn't imagine trying to fly again anytime soon. "And you could lead us to him?" he asked Roarick.

Roarick nodded.

"I'm curious to see this Unicorn," Brynne said. "It could be useful to know a creature like that. Who knows, Arias, maybe Hlaena will be interested in meeting him sometime if they truly are similar in nature. It could do her some good, being around someone like herself. And of course, I'm interested in going on this trip, if only to keep an eye on Hilda."

"So a decision has been made then?" Bala asked, looking at everyone in turn to check for disagreement. None arose, although more than a couple of Gryphs obviously weren't in favor of the plan. None spoke up, however, and Bala settled back on his haunches.

"Right, then," he said. "I'll call a meeting tonight to ensure that everyone remains abreast of these new developments. I dislike both Hilda and the flock she associates with, but a potential alliance with them would set many minds at ease, if it's possible."

Arias nodded. "Then it sounds like we should be back by tomorrow if all goes well."

Bala bowed his long neck, worried. "Inlet shelter you all from any storms," he said. "It really should be me going out there. Please be careful."

"Don't worry, Bala," Brynne said, leaning back into a deep stretch, "with Larin and me both going along, everyone will be safe."

Larin stepped forward with a determined look, nodding.

"Just us five, then?" Arias asked, double checking that everyone besides him, Larin, Brynne, Roarick, and Hilda would stay behind. Lue seemed embarrassed as she looked down at the ground, but Arias reached out to brush her reassuringly with his wing tip. "Don't worry, Roarick said we'll fare better in a smaller group anyway," he said. "You'll do well to help Bala here, and to fill in anything that he may forget to include in the meeting tonight. That goes for all of you," he added, raising his voice so that everyone could hear him. Lots of nods and confirming calls followed his comment, and he caught Lue's eye one last time. "We won't ever stop looking for Tybrake, Lue. I promise."

The Ardeigryph hen looked up at him with sad eyes and gave the barest of nods, and Arias straightened up despite feeling like he could lie down, curl up, and cease to move for one thousand seasons if he had the chance to. "Let's not waste any more time," he said. "Let's collect Hilda and get this over with."

CHAPTER FOUR

"So it is done," Hilda growled after Arias and the others returned. "You've determined my fate so soon? All I ask is that if I'm to be killed, at least give me the glory of fighting to my death."

"Don't be so surprised," Arias said coolly, "although I know it may be hard for you to imagine that decisions can be made so quickly and without bloodshed among such a large group of Gryphs. I imagine that deciding such a thing in the Pale would've required days of striking down your foes and perhaps slaying an opponent or two?"

Hilda's tail lashed once, but she didn't reply. She eyed the way Roarick stood next to Brynne with a comfortable familiarity, and a flash of obvious disapproval crossed her features before she snarled,

"What's this? You're all going?"

Brynne's eyes narrowed sarcastically. "No, we all figured we'd better come to see you off. Of course we're all going. The more eyes to watch a *tuca* like you, the better."

"I'm touched that you give me so much credit," Hilda said with equal sass. Roarick's feathers ruffled in annoyance.

"You have a lot to say as an outsider in need of help," he said without looking at her. "I can understand why you all are helping this hen, but she certainly leaves much to be desired."

Arias flicked an ear at the words, regarding the Barbagraph. Roarick seemed far from outgoing or outspoken, but perhaps he wasn't as timid as he'd initially seemed. Hilda looked ready to say something in retort, but something about the way everyone around her stared at her dulled her tongue. She snorted.

"If what you say is to be believed, then it sounds like time is of the essence, white one," she said.

Arias didn't necessarily like that she had a point, but he nodded and twitched his nub of tail.

"Let's go. Lead the way, Roarick. We're right behind you."

***

The path Roarick guided Arias and the others on was a winding, hilly one, but it was far from difficult. There were no thick curtains of brambles to claw one's way through, no impassable boulders or mossy swamps, and no perils of disturbing other predators' territories. The way was mostly an uphill climb, but even that wasn't extreme… at least, not for the others. Arias panted open-mouthed as he did his best to urge his legs to keep up their ponderous trot, each step feeling as though he were traveling through thick mud instead of on the dry, hard-packed earth that was actually beneath his claws. Larin stayed close by his side. She was quiet as she kept alert for any threats. She didn't bother to hide her mistrust of Hilda, her eyes flitting over to study the flaxen hen often. Arias would have behaved similarly had he not been so consumed with trying to keep up.

Hilda, of course, didn't have any trouble keeping up the pace, even forging ahead at times as if to convey to Roarick that he was going much too slowly. The Barbagryph was, to his credit, comfortable with ignoring her. He looked back occasionally to ensure that Arias and Larin weren't falling too far behind, and spent a good amount of the time speaking with Brynne. The duo mostly kept their voices low enough that no one else could hear them, but despite the circumstances, it was clear that they were having a good time judging by the way the journey was punctuated by their oft-amused expressions and spurts of crowing laughter.

Brynne had a bounce to her step as she trailed after Roarick, eyes sparkling and tail high. Roarick looked back at her and said something that prompted another chuckle from her, and the orange hen suddenly crouched and leaped up at him, tumbling and clawing at him.

"Brynne, quit it!" the keythong giggled, struggling to dodge her well-aimed nips. "I'm not even biting you anymore! Ow! Okay, okay!" He pried her off and danced forward a few steps, chuckling and wagging his tongue at her, and she made as if to have another go at him.

Arias watched the exchange between the two, conscious of a feeling growing within himself. It grew more intense as Brynne and Roarick fell into step together, their tails playfully crossed over one another's backs. It was almost like he was annoyed that they were being so silly, or… or he wanted Roarick to be quiet and to go somewhere else, anywhere else. Arias recognized what the feeling was in a realization so abrupt that his ears shot upright.

"What?" he uttered aloud in disbelief, shocked by the absurdity of the revelation. He ignored the glances he received at his exclamation.

Was he jealous?

The possibility made Arias even more uncomfortable. Why should he be bothered by something like this, of all things? He and Brynne had been playmates as cubs, and he was logically happy that she'd met a Gryph she enjoyed spending time with as much as Roarick. The keythong was maybe a little odd, but he seemed to be friendly enough. So why did he feel the tell-tale prickle of jealousy toward their relationship? He shook his head to clear the thoughts, still disturbed that they'd entered his mind without his permission in the first place.

Brynne and Roarick eventually settled down, and without their banter, the journey was mostly quiet. The party stopped twice to rest, though Arias was quite sure that the breaks were more for his benefit than for anyone else's. It was almost worse to stop and then to start walking again, but he couldn't pretend that he didn't appreciate the breaks. After everyone slaked their thirst at a cold, clear stream, Roarick announced that it wouldn't be much further, and that they'd arrive at their destination before sunrise if they pushed a little faster. Arias was doubtful, considering how high the moon already was in the sky, but he fell in behind everyone else and tried his best to match their strides.

The group was high enough up that they were no longer climbing uphill, and instead the main difficulty lay in staying balanced on the stretches of the rocky ridgeline that offered a sheer drop on either side. While he didn't look forward to the thought, Arias was sure that he could fly if he absolutely had to. Hilda, on the other claw, would almost certainly tumble to either grave injury or death if she placed one paw in the wrong place. She soon fell behind Arias in pace, her eyes focused as she picked her way gingerly across the more treacherous parts of the landscape, and although he disliked her, Arias found himself doing his best to keep an eye on her nonetheless.

The mountain top was shrouded in a thick mist that clung to it like a shaggy pelt, obscuring the craggy landscape until everything appeared smooth and nondescript. Typically comfortable with heights, Arias felt unnaturally dwarfed by the outline of the rocky giant before him. The mysterious landform offered no detail from afar, just an amorphous behemoth of terrifying size. The path finally twisted sharply upward, edging vertically along a cliff side until the way was lost in the mists above.

"Time to go up," Roarick said with a glance back. "Obviously, this bit is much easier if you can fly, but I've walked it before as a cub countless times. Just brace against the rock if you feel unsteady. It looks worse than it actually is." He hopped up the first chunk of rock jutting out from the cliffside and chuckled. "I said that, but it was way easier when I was smaller. Feels like I take up too much space now." Regardless of his words, he confidently eased his way over to the neck bit of ledge and then the next after it, completely missing the acidic glance that Hilda shot his way. Brynne shrugged and leaped after him, not even bothering to spread her wings for balance, and Arias and Larin hurried after her. Hilda grumbled to herself, and Arias caught an uncertain expression on her face before she shimmied up after them. She kept any misgivings she had firmly to herself.

Arias wasn't sure how long they climbed the mountain, but night was almost over by the time Roarick announced they were near the top. Arias had stopped to catch his breath more than a few times, but he had done a fine job of keeping pace with Roarick and Brynne. The air was thinner up here, and he was used to that thanks to the high flying he'd occasionally done, but here it seemed oppressive somehow, like the mountain itself disapproved of the life forms scurrying up its side. Hilda gave a small cry as her claws scrabbled against loose stone, and she pushed herself against the solid rock to her side, eyes wide as she drew in deep breaths. The group stopped long enough to verify that she was alright, and then Roarick was leading them on again. No one made any comment, Arias included. He hadn't forgotten that she'd tried to kill him, whatever her reasons were. He believed helping her now was the right thing to do, but that didn't change how he felt about her.

After what felt like an eternity later, Roarick awkwardly flipped over the lip of an overhang, stepped back, and arched his back into a luxurious stretch as Brynne followed him up onto the flat mountaintop.

"Not too bad, right?" the Barbagryph noted as Arias hefted his way up, his muscles trembling in protest at the exertion it took to pull up his own body weight. Arias simply nodded in response, hoping that the sound of his own breathing wasn't as loud to the others as it sounded in his own head. Hilda made extra-sure of her footing before vaulting over the ledge, her talons digging into the hard earth as she searched for the perfect place to brace herself before making her way onto the horizontal surface. She warily eyed the forest that stretched before them, but Roarick simply ambled toward the tree line with a carefree stride. Brynne lagged behind him, and Arias listened hard to see if he could hear anything from within the cluster of old, twisted trees.

"Wait!" Hilda hissed. "We're just going to walk in?"

"Well, yeah," Roarick said, frowning. "What other way would there be to go in?"

"I assumed you knew exactly where this Unicorn was."

"Well, this is the forest he lives in. If the stories I've heard are true, then he's somewhere in here."

"Wait!" Hilda hissed again, bounding up near him. "You've never even seen the creature yourself?"

"I never needed to," Roarick said, tilting his head. "Although it would've been nice to have had the chance after that ursos attacked me."

Hilda thinned her eyes in annoyance. "You mean it's possible we made this entire journey for nothing? What if he isn't here?"

"You say that as though you had better options," Roarick said, turning to lead the way again. "I'm not the one with the broken wing here, after all. None of us are. You should practice being a little more grateful."

"Hmph!" Hilda stalked after him, her tail twitching madly, but she made no further remarks. Arias traded a look with Larin before heading after them, a ripple coursing across the nape of his neck as he detected the unmistakable feeling of being watched. The canopy was carpeted in moss that hung like long tendrils, blocking out whatever moonlight would have shone down from above. It rustled softly in each gust of wind, causing Arias to cast paranoid glances over his shoulder. But each movement turned out to be only the ghostly waving of the moss in the breeze… until it wasn't.

Arias didn't quite stifle his cry of alarm when he realized the pale outline that had eased into their processional from behind wasn't just a figment of his imagination. The others wheeled around, and Brynne and Larin snaked forward to place themselves between the stranger and everyone else, but their new addition didn't seem startled in the least. If anything, he seemed annoyed. Arias was shocked by how similar he looked to an Alicorn… almost the spitting image of Xio, but with a steel-gray mane and a much longer beard, and a horn that seemed longer and sharper, somehow.

"Why are you in my forest?" the Unicorn snapped. He whipped his head from Gryph to Gryph until he spotted Roarick. "You - Barbagryph - explain!"

Roarick's ears and tail were already apologetically low as he addressed Jance, and his bulk somehow seemed to deflate. "I brought them here, Jance. We were hoping that you could help this Gryphon; she broke her wing." He nodded meekly toward Hilda, who'd already backed away far enough that she was half-hidden in the shadow of the woods, only her eyes glinting mistrustfully from the darkness. Something about her reaction seemed right to Arias somehow. Jance swung his head to glare at her.

"I have no need of this creature," he growled. He stared at Arias and the others with little more interest, though his gaze lingered on Arias for a bit. "It has been quite some time since I've seen Gryphons, though," he mused. "Eons, at least." He nodded toward Roarick. "Fine, Barbagryph. I am pleased that you have shown me something interesting, at least. I'll help your companion as a reward. You two, move aside, and you—do you want me to help you or not? Come here."

Jance's horn briefly glowed red, and he took Hilda in his magick, yanking her forward roughly from her hiding place. He simultaneously flung Larin and Brynne aside with a snap of crimson magick, and Arias felt righteous indignation flare in his gut. He snarled at Jance, and the Unicorn's horn stopped glowing as he released Hilda and looked Arias over with a curious expression on his face.

"How is *this* possible?" he muttered quietly, more to himself than to anyone else. Hilda had already retreated back into the darkness, and although Brynne and Larin both growled in warning, Jance paid them no heed. "Explain to me, Gryphon," he said, stepping toward him. "What have you done to possess such an ability?

Is this some sort of trick?"

"That's close enough," Brynne said, lowering herself in preparation to pounce. "I think we made a mistake coming here. We're leaving."

"You're in *my* forest," Jance said without looking at her. "I think I'll decide what happens here. Answer me, Gryphon! I'm not fond of repeating myself when I speak."

Brynne's feet left the ground so quickly that all Arias heard was a scattering of leaves, and then she was airborne, talons outstretched toward Jance, hooked bill open — and then she was frozen, hanging in midair. Jance's horn was shimmering with red light, but he hadn't turned to even look at her. Brynne was obviously alive, trying to move, but her struggle barely registered as anything more than her wide, fear-stricken eyes and the twitching tips of her claws.

Roarick snarled and rushed forward, but then he was frozen as well, his legs trapped in an awkward mid-stride. Larin held steady despite her own fear and confusion, her eyes darting as she tried to make sense of the situation. Hilda made no sign of a return. Jance tilted his head slowly as he calmly regarded Arias, waiting.

Arias had a rudimentary understanding of how magick worked from his time growing up with Alicorns, and he knew how hard it was to restrain any living thing with magick, especially if it was resisting. As a cub, he'd quickly learned that if his Alicorn family didn't manage to scruff him when they went to grab him, he could give them quite a difficult time with wrangling him if he'd felt like it. The raw strength and skill this Unicorn must have to contain not just one attacking adult hen, but a much larger keythong as well—without even expressly looking at them—was a terrifying prospect.

"I'll answer your questions," Arias said, "but only if you don't hurt my friends."

Jance released Brynne and Roarick with a disdainful snort. They both gasped and choked, evidently having been unable to breathe freely while in the grip of Jance's magick. The Unicorn continued to eye Arias.

"I've never met a creature so capable of hiding themselves in the ether," he said. "And you would've had me believe you to be a simple Gryphon. It can't be possible for your kind to have advanced so much in such a short period of time." He shook his head. "What is your real reason for coming here? To take my power?"

"What?" Arias asked, genuinely confused. "What are you talking about? Of course not, how would we even be capable of that? We came for just what we said … to help Hilda. But it's clear that we shouldn't have bothered you, so we'd like to leave now."

"Nothing slips past me, Gryphon," Jance snapped, pulling his lips back from his teeth in predatory manner. "It may have been for just an instant, but you absolutely reeked of dark magick just then. I dare say I even recognized that energy, which speaks to something much more unbelievable." He stepped toward Arias again, and, this time, no one else moved. Arias stepped backward in equal measure, his fear and confusion biting at him with every word and movement Jance made.

"Such arts are forbidden. I've no idea if a creature such as yourself would be clever enough or possess the ability to perform such intricate details of the arcane, but either way, I cannot allow this to continue. You'll tell me how you did this... or who did this to you."

"I'm not lying when I say I have no idea what you're talking about," Arias said. "There was a Kirin named Mati-jai who dabbled in dark magick, but he isn't alive anymore. I can't use magick, if I could have I would have stopped you just now."

Jance straightened up, tail swishing as he evidently digested the information. Behind him, Larin crept forward quietly. Arias wished he could stop her from doing whatever she was trying to do, but he didn't dare alert Jance to anything. So long as the Unicorn was focused on him, his friends were safe.

"So the Kirin are to blame," Jance said flatly. "And you... I'm surprised you're still alive. Your body is clearly not handling your transition into the magicked world very well. Your very life force falters in the presence of the thing trapped within you. I'm not sure why this was done to you, but

I'll get my answers soon enough. For now, however… I think that we can come to a compromise, Gryphon. I can't let you leave here. It would be irresponsible of me not to take control of the power you possess."

Arias took a step back as Jance's words sunk in, but at the same time, his curiosity rose. He swallowed, trying his best not to watch Larin's slow advance forward, her ears pricked high with concentration.

"I was wondering why I'd been feeling unwell since my last encounter with Mati-jai," Arias said. "You're saying that it's the dark magick, then?"

Jance nodded.

"If I give it to you, you'll leave my friends alone?"

Jance paused. "I'll do you one better than that. I'll heal that hen's wing for you, and leave any mention of Gryphs out when I confront the Kirin about this little mistake of theirs. I at least want answers from them regarding why they didn't catch one of their own before this point. Consider that I'll be doing you a kindness, Gryphon. Because of the way this magick was separated from its host, it will continue to seek new hosts when you die… which won't be long in coming, considering your current condition. It will be like a curse to your kind, fleeing the body of its depleted victim and taking up residence in whichever creature is closest and can support it. Like a parasite, it will do anything to not slip away to its own destruction. Only I can stop this process from happening. Still, this will all be much easier for both of us if we can come to an agreement."

"I'll gladly give it to you," Arias said, "but I'm not sure how to."

"You needn't do anything," Jance said. "There's a method I can use to strip you of your arcane presence, although conditions must be… correct in order for me to do so. To be blatantly honest, the very act of ripping such a vast amount of energy from you will probably prove to be fatal, especially in your current condition." His expression darkened. "The choice, I might add, isn't yours. I'd like to give you the opportunity to do the right thing of your own free will, but I cannot allow such an unnatural travesty to continue on. It could prove to have disastrous consequences."

Just then, Jance screamed a primal, anguished roar of pain as Larin buried her hooked bill deep into his lower hind leg, tearing past the tendons and ligaments and ripping them free. As Jance stumbled forward she, Brynne, and Roarick all bolted, and Arias didn't miss his chance to sprint out of range of Jance's magick. He felt the barest touch of the Unicorn's magick as he tore through the trees, but this wasn't the terrifying grip the creature had displayed with Brynne and Roarick. It was a subtle, muted burning against his shoulder, and he ignored it as he pushed toward the edge of the forest. Eerily, Jance's voice entered his mind as he fled.

*You're foolish if you believe that this is the end,
Gryphon. Wherever you go, I'll be there. You will never
hold onto that power, and your little friend will pay for the
inconvenience she's caused me.*

The forest opened up above Arias, and he
spread his wings with a snap, rising after his
friends into the mists above.

***

Arias only achieved a marginal amount of
distance before his fatigue, forgotten during his
encounter with Jance, returned with a vengeance.
He hadn't even processed that it had left him
until it was with him again. Fright kept he and his
friends mute, their eyes and ears sharp for any
sign of Jance. The Unicorn had displayed abilities
of such terrifying magnitude… it was hard not to
wonder whether he was following them.

Arias squeezed his eyes shut as he flew; even
just holding his wings open to glide was difficult,
and, while it was clear his friends had
unanimously and wordlessly decided to rush back
to Sandrift, he knew he wouldn't make it. The
muscles in his shoulders began to tremble
dangerously, and he gave in to them, banking
hard to land on a nearby outcropping. His friends
landed after him, their unease obvious.

"Halada's tail… I didn't even know it was
possible for a creature to do what that Unicorn
did," Brynne said. "That was risky, Larin, but I'm
glad you did it. I don't trust being out in the open
like this, but…" She trailed off, scanning around
for any place remotely suitable to rest safely. The

67

rocky landscape offered no suggestions.

"I'm so sorry," Roarick said, trembling with terror. "I had no idea he could be like that. Everyone I've ever talked to said he helped them, that maybe he could be a little crotchety at most. I almost got us killed! Hilda was smart enough to escape early on, but I hope she can find a way down without her wing." He looked at Arias. "What did he mean when he mentioned dark magick? Gryphons can't use magick. Why would he think you can?"

Larin clicked her bill, still stained red with Jance's blood, sharply. It was a stark reminder that this wasn't the time to be considering such things, although they were certainly pressing matters.

"Jance shouldn't be able to follow us up here, right? He doesn't have wings to fly with," Roarick tried.

"I don't think we should presume to know anything that Unicorn is capable of," Arias said. "I've seen some extremely capable magick users, and what Jance did was beyond anything I've ever seen. I…" He paused, frowning. "I heard him in my head as we flew away. He said wherever I go, he'd find me, and that Larin would pay for what she did." Repeating the words was sobering in the worst possible way, and he ruffled his feathers against his discomfort. "I think it's going to be safest for everyone if you go on without me. Especially you, Larin. When Jance said what he did, it didn't sound like idle talk… he made it sound like a promise.”

Larin was already shaking her head, preparing to retort, but Roarick cut in tentatively. “Wait,” he said. “All of this happened because of me. I might know of a way to hide you until we can think of a better way to deal with all this. There has to be something else we can do. But the place I can take you… I don’t think even Jance knows about it. There’s an entrance, close to here.”

“Where? How do we get to it?” Brynne asked. “And what location could be so secretive that a creature that calls this mountain home and that is old as Jance wouldn’t know about it?”

“The Barbagryph homeland,” Roarick explained, “dates before most creatures here, and is only open to our kind. It’s within the mountain itself.”

“How can it be *inside* the mountain, and how are we ever going to make it inside if we aren’t Barbagryph then?” Brynne asked, skeptical.

“There are tunnels,” Roarick said. “Only a Barbagryph can find the way in. The burrows of the homeland are extensive, ancient, and treacherous if you don’t know where you’re going. If we’re very careful and very quiet, no one will know we’re there. Trust me. I knew the place inside and out… I still do. But if we’re going to go, we should do it now while we’re sure Jance isn’t on our trail.”

“I don’t like this,” Arias said. “Too many

things could go wrong. What happens if we're found out?"

"Things have already gone wrong," Brynne insisted. "We can worry about what else can go wrong when it happens."

Larin nodded and gave Arias an encouraging nudge, and Roarick took the lack of further complaints as agreement. He gestured over the edge of the ledge, spread his wings, and glided down through the mists to another outcropping below. Arias and the others followed, their wings coasting on the moist air to an area that appeared to have suffered a rockslide some time before. Roarick picked around meticulously before digging a little around a hulking boulder. The thin shale swept away easily, revealing a dark, crescent shaped abyss that yawned downward at a slant. Roarick unceremoniously stuffed his way into the gap, looking far too large to ever fit. He continued to contort and shimmy forward with effort, then paused halfway through. Arias feared that he was stuck, but then the Barbagryph breathed out and held his breath, wriggling furiously until his shoulders and hips slipped through. Arias winced when he saw the snagged fur and feathers he left behind to mark his passing.

"It's wider inside, thank the marrow," came Roarick's muffled, breathless reply. "The entrance here is the worst part… for me, at least. You're all a lot smaller than I am."

Brynne slipped in after Roarick without a

second thought, and Arias gestured for Larin to
go on ahead of him. She paused for a murm
before proceeding, and Arias stayed on her tail to
avoid thinking about the blackness that lay in wait
for him. It took him only a little more time than
the hens to squeeze his way in on account of his
slightly larger size, but it was still nowhere near
the gargantuan struggle Roarick had faced. The
Barbagryph waited until he'd heard everyone
enter after him, and then he started forward,
edging forward on his hocks until the tunnel
opened up around him enough to walk at a
crouch.

Arias closed his eyes against the absolute
darkness as he went along, starting every time he
grazed his shoulders against protruding rock. The
tunnel reminded him of Arborochre, and he tried
his best not to think about it. The sounds of
slowly dripping water, the unpredictable droplet
of cold, mineral-laden water between his ears, and
the mournful howling of wind through distant
parts of the cavernous system unnerved him, and
he was almost glad when Brynne's voice cut
through the stillness to ask,

"If it's this dark, how do you know where
you're going?"

"I can smell the right paths," Roarick
whispered back.

"How? The air all smells the same in here,"
Brynne whispered back.

"I told you, only a Barbagryph can find their

way through here. It's how we find our food, too. You can't really track bones, you know… by the time they're bones, any tracks associated with them are long gone. Keep it down, though… these tunnels are used by others sometimes. Not often, but enough."

The shuffling continued. Arias's joints were beginning to protest at the extended forced crouching, and he could only imagine how Roarick felt. After a while, Roarick paused and sniffed at the air before whispering, "Hang close to the wall here. Don't go left, whatever you do, stay to the right."

Arias and the others obliged, and Arias thought that he could somehow feel the immensity of whatever space lay off to the left of him as he passed by it. It sent a shudder down his spine to know that something was there but not knowing what, and it was somehow a relief to sense the way the tunnel closed in around him again. They didn't get far before Roarick barked a quick, "To my right again. There's room for you off to the side."

Arias blindly hurried in after Brynne, and Larin stuffed herself in after him, pressing into a spherical space that felt smaller the further in they crammed themselves. There was a small thud as Roarick sat down where they'd entered, and, before anyone could think to question what was going on, the sound of approaching pawfalls from further up the tunnel sounded.

"Ohoho! Bones within, is that Roarick?" a

feeble voice called.

"There's a voice I haven't heard in a while," Roarick called back, the worry still in his voice, but overshadowed with genuine joy.

"Oh, yes, I toyed with the idea of leaving to one of our sister flocks for warmer weather," came the voice, obviously that of an older keythong. "But Hollowcrypt will always be home. And you can't beat the flavor of fresh bones, sunbaked against the mountain during the summer." The stranger sniffed loudly and the mirth in his tone was obvious as he added, "Well, what have we here! Roarick, you scoundrel, you. Finally brought a hen around, eh? I daresay you'll cause some trouble with that." A few more sniffles sounded. "A… rather odd smelling hen, if I do say so myself."

"Rude!" Roarick said, laughing. "I dare say that if I weren't in such a good mood, I'd have to get back at you for insulting such a lovely hen as Brynne," Roarick said. There was a long silence, and when it didn't resolve, Brynne chanced an awkward,

"Pleased to meet you."

A short cackle rose up from the stranger, and the shuffling of claws indicated that he'd started to move on again, back the way he'd come. "Whoever you are, I hope you have the blessing of patience to deal with that one, he's quite a handful! It's good to hear from you, Roarick. I thought I'd smelled you, but I thought that it couldn't be true… can't remember the last time I saw you around here…yes, quite some time…" The stranger's talking devolved into quiet mutterings, shifting further down the path, and, when the sound of him scraping along the tunnel could no longer be heard, Roarick let out a long sigh.

"That was close," he said. "The keythong that came by is named Regal. He used to be one of the elders of Hollowcrypt, though he stepped down from his leadership years ago. With every year, his mind slipped a little more, and he recognized it and decided to let someone else take his place. It's clear he doesn't remember much, but he was always very nice to me, even when he was much sharper of wit. I'm glad it was him and not anyone else; anyone else probably would've been a lot more bothered by your scent."

"What's that supposed to mean?" Brynne snapped.

"Just that you guys don't smell like we do," Roarick said. "To be honest, I'm surprised Regal's nostrils pick up anything at all at his age."

"Shouldn't we keep moving?" Arias asked, looping his neck across Brynne's back so he could stretch out a little.

"Yes," Roarick said, "but I'd like to explain a bit about the upcoming part of the tunnel. It is used a little bit more than the portion we've come through so far, and so I'd rather give you an expectation of what it coming up before we hit it.

The faster we pass through this stretch, the better."

Roarick continued talking, but Arias was distracted by an intense itching against his shoulder. He couldn't reach it - not really, at least - but he could crane his neck to nip at the spot. Larin gave a hiss as he backed into her, and Brynne tried to edge forward as he leaned against her, plucking and nipping at himself.

"Arias, quit it!" Brynne growled, shoving back against him, but the spot on Arias's shoulder evolved from an itching to an intense burning, as if someone had pressed the hot coals of charred wood against his flesh. He jumped up, yelping, literally crawling across Larin and Brynne's backs in an attempt to escape the pain, and then all at once, it was gone.

I told you that wherever you went, I've be there," Jance's voice said, worming into Arias's mind once again.

And I told you that your friend would pay. There are many things that I am, Gryphon... but I promise that a liar isn't one of them.

CHAPTER FIVE

A curious sound reverberated through the tunnels, like the groaning of a large tree's roots begrudgingly losing their hold on the earth. A scattering of dust and grit showered across Arias as he sat there listening, trying to pinpoint where the sound had originated from.

"What –" Brynne started, but Roarick cut her off sharply.

"Shh! Listen…"

After a long murm, the sound came again from somewhere high above their location, and with it came the unmistakable sound of rock moving against rock.

"We have to move!" Roarick said, abandoning his post in front of Arias and the others. Arias shook his head as more of the grit drifted down, sharp and irritating against his eyes. He darted off behind Brynne and Roarick, and he could feel

Larin at his heels.

"What's that sound?" Brynne demanded, grunting as she grazed her wings in her haste to keep up with Roarick, who was suddenly moving through the tunnel with the hectic grace of a Gryph half his size.

Roarick barked a quick, "jump here!" and Arias heard the Barbagryph, and then Brynne, clear some sort of ledge before them. Arias miscalculated his own leap, managing to catch both ankles against the sudden rise in the terrain. He hissed at the sharp, unexpected pain, but didn't stop.

"It sounds like the mountain is shifting," Roarick finally replied. "I've never seen it or heard it before, but smaller tunnels have caved in before down here. We don't want to be in here if this one goes."

"It's Jance," Arias said, terrified. "He knows I'm here somehow. What if this is his doing?"

"I doubt even he could do something like this." Roarick turned another sharp corner, and there was a scraping of claws as Brynne tried her best not to crash beak-first into it. When Arias rounded the corner, there was a hazy light off in the distance. It felt like it had been eternity since he'd seen light. Small chunks of stone rained down from above, pelting down in a maelstrom of stinging blows, and Arias resisted the urge to duck his head down. The increase of speed was already starting to get to him; the air down here felt too heavy, and it seemed to take more effort to breathe. He was drawing ever closer to the distant light, however, which promised him uncertain salvation. He dug in, watching the end to the passageway eke toward him.

"The only way out of here is straight through the heart of the eyrie. If we're quick, maybe we can cut through before anyone really notices. The other tunnels should be safe… just keep your heads down and stay close."

There were no complaints to be made, just the sound of pounding feet and the glaring question of what would happen if the other Barbagryph *did* notice the strangers in their midst. With the mountain threatening to come down above them, Arias and his companions crowded out behind Roarick into the light, finding themselves within the mysterious Hollowcrypt eyrie.

***

Stalagmites rose up from the ground of Hollowcrypt, reaching toward the stalactites hanging down from above like menacing pairs of stone teeth. There were holes in the stone somewhere high above the cavern, letting in light that cut through the darkness in hazy lines. Somewhere nearby, a stream of water of considerable size was burbling, but Arias didn't have time to focus on much more. A ring of Barbagryph were watching the tunnel, and some of their expressions of alarm were rapidly changing instead to ones of shock and anger.

"You!" one of the Barbagryph yelled, but Roarick didn't give them time to add on more.

He barreled toward a smaller hen, and she
jumped aside with a yelp, giving Arias and the
others just enough space to pass through. The
other Barbagryph were already reacting, though,
and when Roarick made a dash for a larger tunnel
just ahead, a big hen—impossibly, even larger
than Roarick—dropped down from above to
block it. Barbagryph were poking their heads out
from everywhere to watch, appearing over ledges,
peeking out from behind boulders, and stalking
forward to surround them. Roarick's tail
immediately tucked between his legs as another
hen, this one about the same size as him, stepped
toward him from the crowd, her expression
serene despite her lashing tail.

"What is the meaning of this?" she asked,
looking Arias and his friends over with disdain.
She looked Arias up and down a few times, and
the slight raising of her ears indicated curiosity.
Then they flattened back against her skull, and
she turned her attention back to Roarick.

"We didn't want to disturb anyone," Roarick
said. "We were just taking a shortcut through one
of the tunnels when it started to sound unstable.
You never would've seen any of us otherwise,
honest. I'm sorry, Talia, please!"

"Don't you dare use my name," she hissed.

Roarick dropped his gaze. "Yes, Matriarch."

"You would've done well to let that tunnel
crush you alive," Talia continued. "What you've
done cannot be excused. I was a fool for not

tracking you down and ending your pitiful life when I last cast you out. And now you've brought these outsiders into our mountain? You won't leave here again, Roarick. Not with your life."

"Now wait a murm!" Brynne growled, snaking forward. Standing before Talia, she looked like an angry cub more than an adult gryphoness.

"Don't, Brynne," Roarick hurried to say. "I was the one who went to them, Matriarch, not the other way around. Please don't punish them."

"Silence!" Talia roared, snapping her wings open with a fantastic rush of wind. "I don't want to hear another word out of you, you worthless keythong."

Above, the pounding sounded again. A few rocks, larger ones this time, crumbled down from above, sending a murmur of concern through the gathered Barbagryph. Inside Arias's head, Jance's voice whispered,

I'll give you this one chance to come out, Gryphon, to make this easier for me. I'll keep my word and leave everyone else to live if you do. If you don't, I have no problem with killing everyone in that little mountain you're hiding in. I'll send you all scuttling like vermin from a rotted corpse. The choice is yours.

"Jance is the one trying to bring down the mountain!" Arias blurted, eyes scanning for an escape. "He wants me, but if you allow me to escape, he'll let everyone else live!"

"Jance?" Talia's voice displayed something other than anger for the first time… fear. Her eyes cut into Roarick's. "What did you do?" she hissed.

The sound came again, showering the area below with more shards of fallen rock. Somewhere in the cavern, a stalactite sheared free from its ancient holding, toppling to the ground in a thunderous eruption of dust and rock. Barbagryph cried out in fear and darted for the nearest exits, but Talia held firm, canvassing the high ceiling above with uncertainty.

"Please!" Arias cried. "I don't know what your quarrel with Roarick is, but I'm not making any of this up! We're all going to die if we —"

With a tremendous explosion, something high up in the ceiling gave way, exacerbating the pandemonium below. The very bowels of the earth groaned as tunnels caved in, trapping those inside and burying others alive. Larger tunnels remained stable, but were soon so full of exiting Barbagryph that they trampled one another and clogged the way, their screams of terror melting into the other sounds of anguish filling the air. Cubs were abandoned, youngsters were crying for their parents, adults were streaking past one another both on the ground and in the air, their coats seeming to blend together as they all sought safety. Talia finally turned and vanished into her frantic flock, and Arias looked to Roarick for guidance, but the keythong seemed to be rooted in horror, his crimson-ringed eyes snapping from the distant sky above to the too-full tunnels all around them.

Cracks formed along the sides of the cavern, which had been made unstable by the sudden collapse of the networks of tunnels, and the shafts of light from above became more pronounced as the crust of earth that had sheltered Hollowcrypt for centuries was blasted open, letting in the blood-red rays of a rising sun. Throngs of Barbagryph took flight, rising toward the salvation of the sky. And up above, barely visible to Arias's eyes and silhouetted like a dreadful marker of death, was the outline of a lone Unicorn.

***

Arias hardly had time to think. The ground was quaking, rumbling as sections of Hollowcrypt lost support and caved in, and fleeing Barbagryph barreled into him and the others as they sprinted past. Roarick shook himself from his stupor and yelled out.

"Hey! This way! If you follow the stream, it'll lead you out! Stop trying the tunnels! Follow me!" His voice was lost in the chaos, but a few Barbagryph listened to him and followed after him, and Brynne took up the chant as well. Larin reached out with her bill and snatched up a lost cub that was nearly trodden underpaw by a fleeing hen, and she placed it under her wings to keep it safe, nodding to Arias. Together, they took off in the direction Roarick and Brynne had headed, finding and following the underground stream as they avoided sections of falling debris. The sights and sounds of the havoc that had befallen the Barbagryph so swiftly was nerve-fraying to behold, and, above it all, Arias tried to smother the thought that he'd brought Jance here. Had he just defied Roarick and given himself over to the Unicorn, none of this would have happened.

The path forward widened, dipping and leading to a deep pool that ended where a low section of rock separated Hollowcrypt from the outside world. Dozens upon dozens of Barbagryph leaped down into the pool, swimming deftly through the dark water to the mountainside outside. Larin, pushed by the Barbagryph behind her, cast a final look at Arias before jumping down into the water with her wings closed, keeping the cub close to her. Arias froze at the sight of the depths, but the Barbagryph behind him removed the choice of whether to swim or not by shoving him over in their haste to save themselves. He screamed as he fell, then the shock of cold spring water was all around him. He frantically paddled for the light, panting and choking the entire way to the edge of the stone wall. The only way out was under, and he wasted no time in clambering beneath and paddling furiously to the shallows and then, finally, to blessed land.

Larin, Brynne, and Roarick had been lost in the turmoil, but Arias knew it wouldn't take them long to spot him with his coat color. The burning against his shoulder returned, but it was a muted annoyance, like the feeling of being stung by some irritating plant or insect. He parted through the feathers with urgency, finding an odd outline crisscrossing against his skin, the same ruddy color as old blood. An attempt to pick it off did nothing.

You can run, but your efforts are futile, Jance's voice whispered in his head.

Remembering the burning he'd felt against his shoulder when he'd first escaped Jance, Arias realized the Unicorn must have marked him this way somehow. Maybe through magick, he was being tracked… in which case, Jance was right. He'd never be able to escape.

Arias turned, working out where he'd last seen Jance from inside Hollowcrypt, and he tried to hurry in that direction, sticking to the nearest source of cover—in this case, sparse brush, stringy grasses, and stunted trees. He couldn't let things continue in this way. He didn't think his guilt would allow him to, even if he tried.

Out of breath and too tired to speak, Arias found Jance on a ridge, a satisfied look on his bearded face. The Unicorn was standing tall, with no sign of the injury Larin had inflicted onto him. He didn't attempt to do anything to Arias, just pointed with his nose behind him.

"Smart move, Gryphon. Let's go."

"Why don't you just kill me and take the magick for yourself?" Arias asked.

Jance snorted. "It's ironic that such a daft creature as you should be gifted with such power," he replied. "You know nothing of magick. Carelessly trying to take such a force could risk destroying it. If you're lucky, you may even survive the transfer to come. Come."

Arias followed, seeing no other option. Jance walked a fairly easy path away from the eyrie, but it was quite a distance before the sounds of the grief-stricken Barbagryph were no longer discernible. Arias looked over his shoulder at the site of the destruction, then back at Jance.

"You didn't have to do that," he said.

Jance laughed. "Didn't I? You didn't believe that I could, did you? Now that you know my capabilities, perhaps you'll finally stop with your foolish games."

The Unicorn kept an ear swiveled toward Arias, and any sudden noises caused the Unicorn to turn a watchful eye to him. It was interesting behavior for such a powerful creature. If Arias tried to fly away, he was clearly within reach for Jance to simply pluck from the sky with his magick. So why was he being so careful?

"It's not like I could've replied back to you," Arias said. "Even if I'd been trying to escape, you still would've done what you'd done."

"Yes, I would have, and it doesn't matter whether you were trying to escape or not. I know how creatures like you are. You would've stayed hidden until you had no choice. If a boulder fell onto one of your legs, crushing it, you wouldn't try to gnaw it off as a first choice, would you? Of course not; it would be a final decision. I just made this choice a little easier for you, that's all."

Arias didn't reply. He thought hard about the little he did know of magick. A distant memory from his cubhood touched his mind, of an Alicorn filly trying to heal a dying Gryphon in Glendale, and of Xio, the herd stallion, saving her life after she'd proved unable to do so.

"Fool!" Xio had yelled in anger after severing the filly's connection to the dying beast, *"You cannot give what you do not have to offer!"*

Arias watched Jance closely. The Unicorn was picking his way carefully along a ridge, his stride slow and his neck bowed, even stumbling a few times as he went along. Arias took his chances as he said, "You're right that I didn't know any creature was powerful enough to drive a hole into a mountain. And I believe your reason for not killing me by now and taking this power for yourself. It seems that it must have taken quite some effort for you to do what you did to that mountain, though. Whether you want to admit it or not, I think you're too tired to do whatever you need to in order to extract the magick from me."

Jance peered over his shoulder at Arias, and curiously, the corners of his lips pulled back as he let out a quiet chuckle. "You're not quite as stupid as you look. If you'd shown a little more discretion earlier, we may have avoided this entire debacle, and I may have shown you how to bond the power within you. But no; I cannot risk leaving such a reckless and imprudent creature as yourself to freedom."

Arias didn't offer any further comment. He had from here until they reached Jance's forest to think of something, and perhaps a bit longer, but he wasn't sure. What he was sure of was that Jance could kill him if forced to do so, but he also knew for certain that he wouldn't allow the callous Unicorn to take the magick—not after what he'd done. Arias glanced off to his side at the sheer drop the mountainside offered. He swallowed hard.

If I have to and I'm fast enough, he thought, *I will.*

The rising sun burned the mist off the mountain top, banishing its nightly cloak of fog, though the clouds themselves still hung low in the sky, sluggishly moving in the wind. The morning chorus was just as vibrant up here as it was down in Sandrift, and it would have been beautiful under different circumstances. Jance's forest rose up in the distance, and the long moss billowing from branch tips painted the image of a serene respite from the cold and rocky behemoths surrounding it. As they drew closer to the forest, Arias briefly wondered whether he could appeal to the Unicorn somehow, but he couldn't bring himself to do it—not from a creature who'd just hurt, trapped, and killed so many to prove a point. If anything, with the warm sun against his back, he tried to force his thoughts toward how his friends would be safe going forward, even if it was without him. He focused on that thought.

They'll be fine without me, he told himself.

There was a distant scraping sound, and Jance turned sharply to examine the direction from which it had come, but there was nothing to see. He settled an accusing gaze on Arias. "I hope your companions are smart enough to leave you to your fate," he said. "I think you know I have no issue with dispatching those who get in my way."

"I slipped away before anyone could follow after me," Arias said honestly. "I've made my choice. It appears that even attempts to harm you don't stop you for long." He was still shocked that there was no sign of Larin's earlier attack on the Unicorn. Jance didn't seem satisfied, and he waved Arias past him.

"Go on and walk ahead," he commanded, eyes narrowing. "And be quick about it."

Arias urged himself into a trot, ever aware of the tip of Jance's horn just behind him, but the extra exertion tired him out almost immediately. His pace flagged, and Jance squealed in annoyance, preparing to give him a jab of encouragement, but just then, the scraping sounded again. It was followed by the unmistakable sound of claws against stone. Jance scanned along the right side of the ridge and, seeing nothing, gave Arias a meaningful glare as he checked the other side. There, tucked in as well as she could to stay out of sight, was Brynne.

She cursed as Jance spotted her, and the Unicorn immediately tilted his horn toward her, the tip bursting to life with crimson light.

Arias growled and sprang forward, hooking his claws into Jance's hide and clamping his jaws down around the stallion's neck, and, although the Unicorn reared upward with a scream, the muscles there were as strong and as unyielding as tree roots. Jance bucked, flinging Arias free, and twisted to face Brynne. Arias scrambled back to his feet, and as he did so, Larin revealed herself by clambering up from where she'd done a much better job of hiding against the cliff side. She gave Arias only a flicker of a sign before she tossed the cub she'd been harboring to him—he miraculously caught it by the scruff of its neck— and then she rushed toward the Unicorn. It was a feint, however, and a good one at that; as Jance focused on her, a high whistling sang out from above, and Arias hardly tracked the lightning-fast movement of Roarick plummeting from the clouds above.

Wings tucked to his sides, the Barbagryph dove directly at Jance, extending his talons at the last moment to rip him from the ridge. Jance tried to anticipate the attack by dropping down on his forequarters, but it didn't save him from the sheer force Roarick put into dragging him from his footing. Roarick stumbled in midair, his talons desperately extended to keep hold of Jance's hide, and both Barbagryph and Unicorn vanished over the ridgeline. Brynne immediately flew over the edge after them, and Larin prepared to follow but turned to look at Arias first, her brown eyes fierce.

"Don't get hurt on my account," Arias pleaded. "If I don't come back, you can't come after me. None of you can. And by Halada, don't go after Jance. The flock needs you."

Larin held his gaze for a long murm, seeming to debate crossing the space over to him. Instead, she leaped after Brynne, Roarick, and Jance… leaving Arias alone on the mountainside with the Barbagryph cub.

CHAPTER SIX

Arias glided toward the only place he could
think to go, angling toward the Kirin temple.
Jance had already mentioned wanting to question
them, and they deserved to know he was coming.
That, and they were the only creatures even
remotely nearby who were possibly capable of
dealing with a Unicorn.

Jance's voice hadn't entered Arias's mind since
he'd left the mountain behind, and a part of him
wished to believe that meant the creature had
been killed, but he knew better than to be so
optimistic. The stallion hadn't reached his age by
being easy to slay, either by the perils of the
mountain or by anything else.

Arias was frustrated that he'd allowed his
friends to place themselves between him and
danger yet again. It was clear that they'd do
whatever they believed to be right, even if that
meant ignoring him. He couldn't fault them for
that; he would've done the same thing for them if

he could have. Unfortunately, Jance was after him and him alone, for reasons that didn't entirely make sense to him. Arias just hoped that his friends had managed to stay safe.

Arias found a rising air thermal as he departed the mountain, and he spiraled up on it as high as he could before setting out. The land below passed by swiftly, helped by wind at his tail that pushed him along. If conditions kept up—and with an exact knowledge of where the Kirin territory was—it wouldn't take him too long to reach the temple. He felt fine for now, but he remained cautious and didn't try to flap his wings to gain any additional altitude. Just as his fatigue had vanished after his initial conflict with Jance, it had done so again when he'd left the mountain, and he wondered if his body responded to his proximity to the Unicorn, but that didn't seem to make sense. The entire time Jance had been prodding him along the ridgeline back to the forest, he'd hardly been able to maintain a trot, so it couldn't be that. At this very murm, however, he felt as if he could fly up to the sun and back. He was afraid that if he did anything other than coast along as he'd been doing, the fickle burst of energy would depart from him.

As it turned out, it didn't matter whether Arias tried to conserve his energy or not. As the visage of the mountain grew smaller and smaller, and finally vanished from view behind him, so too did his disloyal fragment of stamina. Just holding his wings steady was taxing enough, and then he had a none-too-happy cub dangling from his bill to deal with. The little creature had started whining and hadn't stopped for most of the flight so far, and he honestly wasn't sure what to do with it. If he left it anywhere, he was almost certainly consigning it to death, but he could barely take care of himself. What was he supposed to do with a cub?

Arias tried to ignore both the mewling of the cub and the haunting implications of what had happened at the mountain eyrie he'd left behind. He wondered what Roarick had done to turn a whole flock against him... did he want to know? If the Barbagryph wasn't trustworthy, he wouldn't have continued trying to help them, would he? Arias wasn't sure if he should be worried about leaving the keythong behind with his friends, but they were both capable hens. He especially trusted Larin's judgment... she and Brynne would look out for one another, and for Roarick, too. The way the other Barbagryph had treated him had been concerning, but Arias wanted to believe that the keythong really was entirely on their side, especially with the lengths he'd evidently gone to trying to help them.

The canopy of the trees below Arias gradually stretched upward to meet him, and he drifted in a wide arc as he flew, searching for more air thermals to exploit. Finding none, and lacking the energy to seek out more, he picked out a clearing within the forest below and landed atop the dense litter, ears high as he listened. The typical sounds of nature resumed, and, deeming the area to be safe, he placed the whimpering cub on the ground and stared at it in consternation. The instant the cub touched the earth, it stopped crying and instead opened its mouth expectantly, lowering its head just enough to stare at him with round, needy eyes.

"What?" he asked, prompting it to press a little closer to him and open its mouth again. A glance at the bright pink of its gullet answered his question, and he sighed, squeezing his eyes shut.

Why? He was barely surviving by himself. Why did he have to get left with a cub of all things? Wasn't there already enough death to his name? He didn't know anything about caring for cubs.

"I'm sorry if you're hungry," he said, "but there isn't much I can do about that right now. We'll be there before too long, come on." He picked the cub up and placed it onto his back, covering it over with his wings as he walked on, but the tiny creature began to cry out even more loudly, its tiny claws digging into his hide. Arias flicked his wings open, indignant. He prepared to give the cub a talking to about how it would invite every predator within range over to them with its scream, but the absurdity of trying to reason with a cub of its age dawned on him before he could. He sighed.

Its, he thought, realizing he wasn't even sure if the cub was male or female. He picked at it, nosed it over, and finally flipped it over, deducing that it was a little hen. Was he allowed to give her a name? He decided that he'd have to call her something, even if she probably didn't understand anything he said. Could he give her a Gryphon name even though she was a

Barbagryph? The only three Barbagryph names he'd heard of were Roarick, Regal and Talia, and, well… He looked the cub over, taking in the ruddy color of her down, her huge, crimson-ringed eyes, and the little dark spots that mottled her chest and hindquarters. No truly distinguishable traits, at least not ones that he didn't figure other Barbagryph cubs had. Was he wrong to name her? What if her parents were found, and wanted a different name? He reasoned that he couldn't very well call her nothing.

"I'll call you Kail for now," he said, scooping her up and placing her on his back again. She started to whimper again, and he turned to look at her. "I can't very well go looking for food if you're going to carry on like that. I'll try—we should be far away enough from Jance that I can do that, at least—but you've got to be quiet. Please. Do you understand at all?"

Kail stared at him with bright, unblinking eyes. She stopped whining.

"Thank Halada," Arias said, taking a deep breath. He took in the type of forest around them. All the trees had needles instead of broad leaves, and he recognized some of the plants tusker liked to live around. "I suppose I should feed you bones," he said idly, scanning the lower part of tree trunks and the ground for any signs that prey liked to leave behind. "Or maybe you're too young for bones, and should only have meat?" The ground was relatively untrodden, and there wasn't any scarring on the wood of the trees. Arias knew just how empty the land had been when he and his companions had originally traveled it, but this was a new area, so it was at least worth taking a look. Besides, Kail probably wouldn't fuss about needing good meat… if he could find carrion that had bone with any amount of marrow in them at all, it would probably be enough.

Having not found anything in his immediate area, Arias shifted his approach and decided to look for water instead. He tried to keep to the most direct course that would lead him to the Kirin stronghold, but when he started to see lush vegetation and he found a gully, he followed it down. A drink of water would probably do both of them well, even if he couldn't find anything for the little one to eat.

The ground was moist against Arias's paws, and the grasses growing in the gully were high enough to brush against his belly. His ears flicked nervously as he went along and listened for any disturbing sounds; he kept glancing around to keep a good lookout for any danger. The sun was bright enough that he couldn't see very far, and he found himself feeling more and more like he wanted to check the area and then leave as soon as possible. He was so busy surveying his surroundings that he almost missed the drag marks he'd been walking over, and he started to walk more quietly without thinking about it. The drag marks were fresh, and he could only hope that whatever had been dragging its kill had already left the area.

The scrapes led up and out of the gully and

into a particularly dense stand of conifers, and
Arias followed the marks with a wary step. When
he caught sight of a pile of dry earth and needles
heaped up conspicuously before him, he stopped.
Whatever had left them hadn't tried very hard to
hide the leftovers, which meant they'd probably
be returning soon. Arias hadn't even approached
the stash before he made out a shape laying
against a nearby tree, watching him.

Two small, black eyes bore into him from
above a broad snout that was already parted to
reveal yellowed teeth. The ursos sow huffed
toward him, drawing in his scent. Arias
immediately made himself as small as possible
and started to back away, trying his best not to
look directly at the massive beast.

I didn't touch your kill, he thought as he eased
backwards. *I just came across it. No need to send me
away, I'm already going on my own, see?* The ursos rose
and stalked toward him, oddly insistent, her lips
curling upward into a snarl that morphed into an
ear-splitting roar. A small movement off to her
right caught Arias's attention, and to his horror,
he realized that she had her own cub scampering
after her. As far as she was concerned, Arias had
already made his intent clear. She exploded
forward, the spittle flying from her lips as she
charged, and Arias's mind raced. He couldn't fly
or outmaneuver her here, and none of the trees
had lower limbs he could climb even if he had the
strength to make his way up them. Time ran out
on his options before he could make a decision.

Too slow to dodge, the sow bore down upon

Arias, and he did the only thing he could think to do, which was to make himself look as intimidating as possible. He threw his wings out and hissed, arching his back, but the sow hardly paid him heed. Without breaking her charge, she reared up, and her true size was terrifying to behold. Her forepaw shot out toward him, and Arias just caught the glint of the long, curved claws shining in the sunlight before they contacted his body. The mighty clout sent stars through his vision, containing enough force to lift him airborne. He landed hard in the detritus, bits of moss and earth showering over him, and when his vision stabilized, it showed an enraged ursos running toward him to complete her mauling.

The strength to rise did not come.

An uncertain cry cut through the air, and the sow skittered to a stop, turning to survey the source of the sound. Kail had been knocked free from Arias's back during the attack and, undaunted, was now confidently romping toward the ursos cub to investigate the similarly-sized creature. The cub was much less curious, and backed away with haste, a plaintive call for its mother on its tongue. The sow put on a burst of speed as she rushed to protect her offspring, her attention shifting to Kail.

Something flickered to life within Arias, and suddenly he was on all fours, sprinting toward the ursos with purpose. Vitality the like of which he hadn't felt in long days flooding through his limbs, seeping through him like blessed rain on parched earth. He leaped onto the sow's back and locked his talons around her wide shoulders, savagely digging his beak into her thick, meaty neck. He wrenched his head to and fro as he tore past the dense coat and into the living flesh beyond, and the sow gave a trumpet of pain, twisting around to snap at him. He leaped out of range and dashed to outpace her, sliding himself in between her and Kail, his back arched high as he roared at her, crest standing on end like a crown of spikes above his head. The sow, undaunted, barreled toward him with a furious bellow, and Arias snarled and stood his ground. When he threw his head back and took a deep breath, however, it wasn't a roar that issued forth… it was *fire*.

***

The ursos sow's thunderous bellow transformed into a squeak of fear, and she stumbled sideways to avoid the swathe of flame. She fled without a glance backward, calling desperately for her cub to follow after her. Arias watched them go, his eyes wide with shock. How had he done that? As he stood there trying to understand, Kail wandered over to him, undaunted, and resumed her earlier display of asking for food, evidently oblivious to how close to death she'd been. Arias walked over to the ursos's stash of food in a stupor, unearthed what was left of a peryton carcass, tore a chunk of flesh from it, and absently stuffed it into Kail's waiting mouth.

Had he always been able to do what he'd just done? No… no, of course not. But, could he do it again?

Arias faced away from Kail and took a deep

99

breath, intent pm creating the fire again, but all he managed to do was to scream into the now-empty forest. He frowned, trying to detect if anything felt different. He felt… normal. The revelation dawned upon him all at once. He felt the way he'd been before he'd started feeling fatigued. He jolted back as something tugged at his toes, and Kail made an unhappy cheeping sound before opening her mouth again.

Right, Arias thought, tearing a few more pieces free for her. The cub wasn't picky at all; skin, meat, and bone marrow all went down without complaint. When she was finished, she stretched both nubby wings, yawned, and curled up where she was on the ground.

"I don't think so," Arias said, picking her up and placing her onto his back. She gave a weak squeak of protest but didn't resist, curling up on his back instead, and he realized that flying while she slept probably wasn't the greatest of ideas. If she fell, he couldn't guarantee he'd be fast enough to catch her. For the first time in ages, he actually felt as if he'd like to eat the food before him, but he was too paranoid to spend more time here. He couldn't afford to spend time eating with Jance potentially on his trail, and if his prior experiences were of any merit, he knew his time of feeling normal wouldn't last long. He'd survived this long with hardly eating, and he'd have to just go a little longer.

"We're going to try something a little different," Arias said. "You probably won't like it, though."

Kail chirped back at him without opening her eyes, and he took her by her scruff and found a suitable opening in the canopy. He ran toward it, opening his wings and flapping, gaining just a little bit of height before opening his mouth and dropping her. She gave an unhappy squeal of surprise as he caught her in his talons, and he made sure he had a good grip on her before he ascended higher, up through the treetops and into the sky beyond, flapping hard for his destination.

***

Kail didn't seem to mind her sleeping arrangements, and had promptly fallen asleep. Her body small and warm and fragile against Arias's claws. The sun slanted low before finally vanishing from the sky, and he was lucky enough to find another air thermal to utilize before his fatigue could catch up with him. He'd been dreading crossing the perilous thunder plains that the Aquila used as their nesting grounds on his first trip through this area, but he hadn't yet spotted the massive thunderhead that had heralded their presence before. As the dry shrub land below passed by uneventfully, he realized that they must have raised their chicks and moved on. In the silence, he stifled a yawn. The air was so warm… he forced his eyes open and stretched his beak wide in another yawn again, almost wishing for Kail's whining to keep him awake. It had been so long since he'd slept, since he'd *really* slept, and now it was all he could think of.

Arias double checked his positioning and then closed his eyes for a few murms, relishing the fuzzy feeling of allowing his mind and body to

drift. He creaked his eyelids open to check that
the distant horizon was still as it had been before,
and then he closed them again. The sounds of the
night chorus couldn't reach him up here, and the
only noise was the whistling of the air through his
pinions. The breeze ruffled through his plumage,
and he found himself sighing, sinking into the
forbidden comfort of rest.

So quiet… so warm…

So…

***

Arias jumped to consciousness. He was in the
dry grassland just beyond the thunder plains, face
down, wings still outstretched, surrounded by a
scattering of his own fur and plumage. The sun
seemed to have skipped setting, and was now
approaching its zenith in the sky once again. How
Arias had endured his impromptu landing while
managing to remain asleep was a mystery, but
when he moved to get to his feet, he realized that
his body was much less forgiving of his rapid
descent. Pain lanced through the myriad of cuts
and grazes crisscrossing his hide, and he winced
as a now-familiar pain in his shoulder sang out,
growing to overshadow the ache in his side where
the ursos had clawed him. He forced himself to
his feet, mentally frantic despite his sluggish body,
aware that the burning only could mean that
Jance was near. His panic grew into a frenzy.

Both his beak and his claws were empty.

"Kail!" he yelled, trying to see down through
the tall, waving blades of grass for any sign of the

cub. What if he'd dropped her? He swiveled his ears to listen, but the rustling of the plants revealed no secrets. "Kail!" he called again, tracing the flattened outline where he'd crashed for any sign of the little Barbagryph. He steeled himself against the inferno that seemed to be engulfing his shoulder, willing himself to focus. There was no answer, and then the tiniest of movements caught his eye. He turned sharply, and was just able to make out the shape of an uncertain Kail studying him from a safe distance away. She perked up when he noticed her, and he heaved a sigh of relief that she appeared no worse for wear.

"Come on," he said, hurrying to pick her up. "Let's go. Sorry, I didn't mean to drop you... I've never had that happen before." He cast a look around, worried that he couldn't see anything beyond the grass. It undulated like waves wherever the wind touched it, the perfect cover for both predator and prey. The last thing Arias wanted to do was to figure out whether they were truly alone or not.

Arias glanced up at the sky to get his bearings, and then took off as fast as he could. He was aware of his ponderous pace, but the brisk trot was the best he could manage. He clenched against the pain that jolted from his shoulder to his battered side with every step, his eyes trained on the forest ahead. It approached painstakingly slowly, the tips of grass brushing his belly teasingly as he went, as if not wanted to divulge the secrets of the Kirin within too soon. There was no sign of Jance. Indeed, as he finally entered the forest, the insignia on his shoulder ceased to inflict its maddening pain. He didn't dare slow down, however, and he clucked in warning when Kail leaped down from his back, her attention caught by the swift flight of a Fae. The winged creature hid under a nearby leaf, and Kail pounced onto it, her eyes alight with mischief. The Fae spun in a wide ring around her, then flew behind her, vanishing into the dense undergrowth.

Kail chittered in annoyance at her uncooperative prey before turning to rejoin Arias. She stopped in mid-stride, however, her pose unnaturally still. Arias felt a visceral chill run down his spine when he glimpsed the thinnest shimmer of red magick outlining her tiny body, and then he heard Jance's voice in his head.

I told you that I always keep my word, Gryphon, the Unicorn said. *I tried being civil with you. Why don't we try something else this time?*

***

A shape melded out from between the trees, so lithe that she scarcely disturbed the leaves at her feet. Larin bounded across the forest floor, staying well out of range of the Unicorn's magick, but being bold enough to show that she wasn't hiding. Jance gave an annoyed snort when he saw her, but mostly ignored her.

"You can follow me all you want, but I won't be falling for your little distractions again, hen. Your kind are far more irritating than I anticipated." Jance dropped Kail and watched her dart in a vain attempt to reach Arias before he snatched her back up with his magick again. The cub hissed as Jance examined her with a bored expression. "It didn't have to be this way, I hope you realize," he said. "But I see that you're all just smart enough to want to make this difficult."

Jance used his magick to stretch out one of Kail's wings, then held out one of the small pin feathers along its edge. With a ripping motion, he plucked it free, then grabbed another and did the same. The cub shrieked in agony, and Arias snarled, launching himself forward without hesitation, but his movements felt painstakingly slow and ineffective. He heard Larin growl in warning from somewhere behind him, but even as he felt the vile touch of Jance's magick, he knew he had to stop him. He opened his mouth, praying that he could once again summon the flames as he had before.

Nothing happened.

Arias felt himself jolt to a stop, caught in Jance's magick, and the stallion actually barked a laugh. He looked as though he were about to speak again, but in that instant, a flaxen blur ripped up and away from the nearby underbrush, affixing itself to the Unicorn's face and neck.

Hilda was a caterwauling whirlwind of beak and claws, gouging and tearing with merciless accuracy. She aimed the wicked point of her beak for eyes and marked her target, and Jance shrieked out a deafening roar of pain. He reared and twisted, lashing out with his hooves, his horn flaring crimson as he blindly snatched for her with his magick, but Hilda had already sprung free and vanished into the forest with the grace of a wriggler tossed back into the sea.

Freed from Jance's grasp, Kail scampered onto Arias's back, her small body pressed against his as she whimpered. Arias backed toward Larin, the canopy too low to allow flight even if he could muster the ability, and he gestured for her to follow after him, as she didn't know the way to the Kirin temple. Jance had gone ominously still, the places where his eyes had been now a tattered, bloody mess. Arias and Larin didn't stop to ponder the situation as they crept as quietly as they could, leaving him behind. They were nearing what felt like safety when a single, high-pitched cry cut through the air. Larin skidded to a stop, her eyes haunted, and the sharpest lance of guilt stabbed through Arias. Hilda hadn't been with them… he hadn't even thought of her as they'd escaped. Not until now.

"No!" He hissed, desperate. "We can't!"

Larin looked back toward where they'd heard the scream. She gestured for him to go ahead without her, and Arias shook his head, exasperated.

"Larin, there's nothing we can do. We need to go!"

She gave him a tense, pleading look, and then her eyes softened. She nudged him gently, as if to assure him that she'd be okay, and without waiting for a response, she dropped into a low crouch. As silent and as sure of herself as a shadow, she moved away from him. Away from safety.

Arias was nowhere near as quiet at stalking as Larin was, and he likely never would be. If he just gave himself over to the Unicorn, his friends would be safe, but they wouldn't ever let him do that. So long as he existed, they'd be in danger. He growled quietly in desperation.

If he went back, he'd honestly probably just get himself caught again… or worse, all three of them.

Coward, his mind whispered to itself.

He turned toward the Kirin temple, pressing toward it with everything he had left in him.

CHAPTER SEVEN

The forest passed by in a hazy blur, the green and brown all blending into lines of nondescript color. Kail held to Arias's back as tightly as she could with her small talons, and it was only the shelter of his wings that kept her from jostling free as he stumbled his way through the forest. The insignia against his shoulder blazed with vengeful pain, but he used the torment to propel himself forward. Slowing and stopping were not actions he understood, his heart slamming in his chest, his lungs throwing air back out just as quickly as he could draw it in. His senses spun with exhaustion, and sheer force of will was the only driving force keeping him on his feet. He had no idea how long he had before the fatigue came for him, there was no time to waste, Larin could be—

"Halt, beast!"

Arias blinked at the sight of the young Kirin buckling before him, his eyes shimmering gold with the threat of summoning a flame whip. The Kirin's eyes flicked back to a dark hazel when he realized what terrible shape he was in. He frowned.

"You," he said, "I know you. You're that Gryphon. Arias, the one that was raised by Alicorns. What's happened to you?"

"There's no time," Arias panted, his hocks trembling with the threat of collapse. "Jance… there's a Unicorn after me."

The buck's eyes widened at the words. "Then we need to go," he said. When Arias didn't move, he crossed the distance to him and gave him a meaningful push with his spike horns, but Arias could hardly feel the sharp tips. He was aware, only dimly, that the insignia against his shoulder was blazing with pain, and that Kail was still pressed against his back, trembling. The Kirin was speaking to him, but words no longer made sense. He watched the buck turn and begin to run, seemingly leaving him behind.

He allowed his eyes to slide shut, and then he was no more.

***

"It doesn't matter how he feels, give him more! We need answers," an impatient female voice said.

"Hush, Lurik-ma," another female voice said. "I know exactly how much mana is in this potion, and I'll give it as I see fit. If you aren't willing to let me do what I've studied my entire life, then you can go watch the fawns."

An irritated grumble followed, but no further retort. After a bit, an older male said,

"Here he is, look! Arias, can you hear me?"

Arias creaked an eye open. It took a while for the image of two eyes of two different colors—brown and green, set into the same face beneath a set of twisting horns—solidified beneath a set of twisting horns into the familiar form of To-shin, one of the Kirin elders.

"I was afraid you wouldn't come around," To-shin said, "both because Lurik-ma just gave you far too much of that tonic, and I'm not sure what did this to you. Can you speak?"

Arias slowly pushed himself upright and peeled his other eye open. He felt better than he had in a while, but not by much. He was surrounded by a number of Kirin, the closest of which were To-shin and two older does. Beyond them were a large number of odd containers filled with mysterious liquids and objects. Judging by the direction their voices had come from, the friendlier-sounding of the two does was off to his right, standing primly on sharp, cloven hooves. She had dark eyes and a coat so sun-bleached that it almost could have matched his own in color. Her thin horns angled back over her head in a graceful arc, and were so long that they nearly touched her back.

The other doe was stately in demeanor, and

her amber eyes seemed to judge him without her speaking. She boasted a set of horns that grew outward and were adorned by small bits that sparkled in the dim lighting, clinking softly when they touched. Arias tore his gaze away from them and gave To-shin a slow nod.

"You spoke to young Wy-lie of a Unicorn. Explain yourself!" Lurik-ma demanded. The other doe opened her mouth to speak, but Lurik-ma shot her a look. "These could be matters of life and death, Gali-da. There's no time for your feel-good pandering."

"We won't have any answers if he dies," the other said calmly. She peered into each of Arias's eyes with a concerned frown, but didn't interrupt further.

"A Unicorn named Jance is hunting me," Arias said, the words sounding thick, like his tongue had forgotten how to do its job. "He's been claiming that I have dark magick that he wants. I thought he was crazy, until I *did* use magick. It was fire, To-shin, and I don't know how. I couldn't do it again when I tried to. Jance seems to think all of this is somehow your fault. The Kirins', I mean."

He stiffened, recalling what had happened before he'd woken up here. "Larin is still out there! And Hilda. Have any of you seen a black hen around?" He spread his wings, noting another absence, and glanced around frantically. "Kail!" he cried, searching amongst the legs and backs of the gathered Kirin. They didn't reply, however, their expressions grim. Even To-shin dropped his gaze, his muzzle pulled into a thin, hard line.

"So our failure finally stretches beyond our kind," he said quietly. "If what you say is true, Arias, then Jance isn't entirely wrong. We let Mati-jai go on with his exploration of the dark arts far too long; we all knew what he was up to, but none of us stepped forward to stop him. Perhaps we weren't ready to admit that the buck who'd been friend and teacher to so many for so long was no longer quite as innocuous as we'd thought." There were a few murmurs, but mostly sidelong glances away from To-shin at the words. He sighed.

"None of that matters now. The cub you arrived with is safe, Arias. I can't speak for the others you've mentioned, and I'm sorry, but we must focus on the here and now." To-shin started to pace, his hooves clicking against the polished surface of the ground. "According to your own account, Arias, you were one of the last creatures to see Mati-jai alive. You said your mother found you at the site of the Crowning Point after killing Mati-jai, and you were later told that he'd killed Aaga, the Phoenix. From your description of events, it can only be determined that he took the Phoenix's power before his death, and in order for you to have such an specific ability as that of fire—and indeed, I do not believe that Gryphons have ever displayed an affinity to magick in any capacity—then it can only have come from Mati-jai.

"The flame whip is a traditional weapon, passed down through time as one of a Kirin's first magickal achievements. It isn't a core element of our kind by any means, not like fire is to the Phoenix. I mention this because I believe that Mati-jai's own essence died with him… but perhaps the one he stole from Aaga searched out another being. In the wake of its imminent destruction, it chose between Hlaena - a creature powerful enough and astute enough to reject its presence - and Arias, who evidently is complex enough to support it, but not efficiently by any means."

Gali-da perked up. "I was one of the few entrusted to archive the contents of Mati-jai's study after his death," she said. "Under oath, I'll never use nor teach any of the information I saw there, but I feel I must say that Mati-jai's notes mentioned that the exchange he wished to perform had failed on non-magicked creatures."

She turned to Arias, her eyes bright with discovery despite the content of her message. "It's likely that your poor condition is a result of your own body's disharmony with the state it has suddenly found itself in. Speaking purely by assumption, it's one thing for a creature already capable of using magick to take on essence, and quite another for a creature who was born without the ability to. If you truly were able to use fire—a true feat in itself, I might add—you likely depleted whatever mana stores you did have. It's one of the quickest ways magicked creatures can accidentally meet their demise, and it would explain why my tonic was the one to bring you back to consciousness."

Arias blinked. The explanations were slightly above him, but he understood the most important bits. "It doesn't matter how this happened, though. It won't stop Jance from coming here," he said. "He's already in your forest. He mentioned needing specific conditions to take this magick from me, and I'm not sure what he plans to do to you all when he gets here, but he seems to expect you to help him do it. He wouldn't try to gain entry to this place by force though, would he? Not with all of you here?"

The Kirin shifted, disturbed, and Gali-da broke the silence by saying,

"Our kind study magick and nature purely for the knowledge contained within such pursuits. Many Kirin are skilled and even quite powerful, few would deny that. And a flame whip is a formidable weapon against any number of dangerous creatures, just as a proper illusion can fool even an intelligent beast, but… Unicorns are different. The same way an Alicorn is drawn to healing, Unicorns are drawn instead to power. Jance has spent years mastering the intricacies of magick alone, and it's hard to say what he is and isn't capable of. I do not believe he'd tread without caution here, but I also don't doubt that he would attempt to force his way if he wanted something enough. To do as Jance wishes with you, he would likely require a large mana pool from another source, like the Crowning Point you used to revive your mother. If Jance were to try to take the essence from you without this added support, the cost would be much too high, even for him."

"I think that's enough postulating for now," To-shin said, "We have a Unicorn out there. We should find some who are willing to keep watch outside, and inform everyone else. No pupils are to be beyond the walls of this temple without their master. We don't know what will happen when Jance arrives… any who wish to flee should have the choice to do so. Those who remain should be sent to the lower levels of the temple; there are paths that will lead them far from here if need be. We'll need to gather as many of us as are willing to take a stand against Jance as well. This is a case where we should expect the worst, I think. The forces willing to face that Unicorn may dictate whether he is daring enough to try to trespass here or not. Count me among that number."

Lurik-ma attuned a look of disbelief as she watched Kirin hurry away to carry out To-shin's suggestions. "Have we lost our minds? We can't forget that casting the Gryphon out is an option. Jance will undoubtedly blame us for allowing Mati-jai to progress as far as he did with his research, but if we allow Jance to take what he wants from here and say the right things, he'll probably go back to his forest and leave us in peace. I for one don't want to see what punishment a Unicorn sees fit for allowing one of our own to dabble in the dark arts enough to result in this. Think about it. If we give him Arias, the next time we see that stallion here—*if* we see him here—will probably be generations from now, if at all."

To-shin narrowed his eyes at Lurik-ma. "It's an option, whether I agree with it or not. However, we cannot forget that dark magick has a way of changing its host. It can infect the very soul of its user… We all saw how Mati-jai changed in his final days, becoming a far cry from the innovative buck some of us grew up alongside. I feel his life and death should be a testament to the decision we make now. Allowing Jance to take whatever he wants, especially from us, would set a dangerous precedent. Do you really want to see what might happen to a Unicorn who has taken on dark essence?"

Lurik-ma glowered back at him. "That's fine and well, but it sounds like your plan is to sit here and reason with the Unicorn until he breaks into here and slaughters us all, the Gryphon included. That, and you just gave orders without consulting the council first."

"Don't be ridiculous," To-shin said. "I didn't order anyone to do anything, I merely voiced what I think should happen. If you have better ideas, I'm sure everyone would love to hear them. That goes for if *anyone* has any ideas. With that in mind, we don't have time for this kind of discussion."

Gali-da lifted her head high, her gaze determined. "I have an idea," she said. "But it may not work, and I have to be promised immunity from punishment for practicing what I'm about to propose."

The remaining Kirin leaned in imperceptibly, as if she were about to utter the secret to life itself. No one said anything to the latter part of her statement, but she took a deep breath anyway. "Jance is alone, while we are many. If we could try the part of the spell Mati-jai used that takes the essence away from a creature, while a group of our more practiced teachers simultaneously stabilizes Arias with their own mana, we may be able to separate the essence from him while also keeping him alive. It sounds like if the tainted essence is starved of a host for long enough, it will be destroyed, and those we choose should be skilled enough to avoid the threat of it inhabiting them, I think."

"No way," a grizzled buck said at once. "Count me out. Experimental processes almost never end well, you have no idea what the outcome of something like that would be. I hate to say it, but the best answer isn't necessarily the most ethical one."

"That's enough," To-shin said. "This situation is dire, but we cannot pretend that Arias isn't sitting directly in our midst. Have you no decorum?"

"Decorum isn't going to keep that Unicorn from coming in here and taking what he wants," the buck shot back. "It sounds like your minds are already made up. I'm taking my students and leaving through the lower tunnels." He shot To-shin a glare. "Your unwarranted fondness for this creature will be the end of us, To-shin. You've become rather obtuse in your old age… but I criticize you more out of respect for the great scholar you once were."

The buck didn't wait for a response before turning and leaving the assembly. A few others went with him, and To-shin watched them go, an unreadable look in his eyes. "If anyone believes similarly, you are, of course, free to leave," he said. "No one will hold it against you." He glanced at Gali-da. "Was most of the text in Mati-jai's study destroyed, or is a fair bit in the archive?" he asked.

Gali-da almost looked guilty as she answered, "Most of it was archived."

"Then go get it. We may need it."

"*What?*" Lurik-ma cried. "Now, not only are we openly practicing the work of a colleague accused of dark magick, but we're brushing up on any suggestions he may have left in notes beforehand? We haven't voted on any of this within the council, and you are severely out of line, To-shin. The others are only considering this idiocy due to your rank. Who knows what we may accidentally unleash if we just carelessly go about —"

"Then give me a better answer besides giving that Unicorn what he wants!" To-shin snapped. "If this doesn't work, our options become very distasteful indeed, Lurik-ma. We can flee, but we'll always have to wonder whether we're being hunted by Jance 'just because.' You heard the stories of what Mati-jai did with his dark magick, by the Everspring, you were there for part of it! Imagine a creature ten times more focused wielding that same power. No place will be safe from his touch. If you propose to simply give Arias up, then you are proposing something just as dangerous as what I am. If this spell doesn't work…" he trailed off, his eyes finding Arias's. The silence that followed was heavy with implication.

"If this doesn't work, then I give you my word that I will not stand in the way of whatever the council believes is best."

***

To-shin and the others organized themselves quickly. Arias was escorted from the underground chamber he'd been in all the way up to a space up on the main floor of the temple. He didn't have to do much, as he was practically carried bodily by the magick of those with him in their haste. The polished, jewel-encrusted floors and high ceiling heralded the council space the Kirin used for important gatherings, but instead of assembling to debate, they scurried about clearing out everything they could. That done, a young doe gently guided Arias to a spot near the center of the space. She gave him a reassuring nod, though it somehow seemed as if it were more for herself than for him. She and a dozen other Kirin of varying ages arranged themselves around him, and they started to walk, their heads and tails nearly touching, the rhythmic stamping of their hooves against the hard ground like a chant. To-shin, Gali-da, Lurik-ma, and three other elders placed themselves at the outside of the ring, standing just beyond their younger peers. To-shin nodded to Arias.

"It'll be alright," he called, his voice steady. "This is a modified version, but this is going to work. Ready?"

To-shin's eyes flicked to gold. The other elders followed his lead, conjuring and using their flame whips to lash the ground around them. They wielded the weapons with frightening accuracy, scorching intricate glyphs of soot where they touched the polished surface. To-shin looked over the work of the others and gave a nod. "Alright, that looks good. Let's begin."

With a flourish, the elders joined their glyphs together, and with a sound like breaking ice, the room burst to life with a blinding array of colors. Arias squinted against the intensity of the piercing ribbons of light, and the Kirin walking the circle before him started to trot, their eyes bleeding to gold one by one. Arias felt a terrible tugging sensation that seemed to grip his very soul, and panic washed over him like a torrential rainfall. He stood, wings open, seeking an escape, and he bristled as he saw a substance pooling off the Kirin surrounding him, shimmering and fluid, like an ephemeral predator circling him. The Kirin broke into a sudden gallop, gripping mouthfuls of the mane of the creature ahead of them to keep the circle unbroken, their hooves clattering and slipping on the slick floor. The elders started to chant, their voices rising as the aura around Arias grew, and it swelled in size until it seemed to fill the whole space. Then the chanting abruptly stopped, and the elder's magick collapsed in on him.

Arias gasped, shaking. It felt as if he were trapped in a giant pair of claws, and they were squeezing him tighter and tighter, seeking to crush the very life from his bones. The terrifying feeling of something being dragged, bit by bit, from his very core, and of it resisting as mightily as it could, threatened to tear him asunder. The magickal tempest was so relentless in its onslaught that he couldn't even cry out, and his body was trapped in a blinding arc of pain. He didn't know what the power within him held on to, but it *held*. One of the Kirin in the circle surrounding him dropped to the ground with a thud, their sides rising and falling with exertion, and the others hastened to close the circle, tightening it so as not to trample their companion. Arias panted, his eyes dazzled by light, his vision tinged by darkness. Lurik-ma's voice suddenly rose over the tempest, ringing out triumphantly as she yelled,

"Now! I'll be the one! Let me be championed by the burden of this power!"

"No!" To-shin's voice yelled, sounding distant to Arias's ears. "Lurik-ma, don't!"

There was nothing Arias could do. The power was seeping from him unwillingly, and, with it, his very life force. Somewhere deep within him, he knew that this fight to stay conscious was the very battle for his life. He slipped to the cold ground, the air seeming to tremble and blur. Even

if succumbing would be for the best... what of
Larin? What of Brynne and Tybrake, and his
friends back on the island? Who would look after
Kail? Even Hilda—his enemy—had tried to help
him, and he owed her still.

The touch of Lurik-ma's magick upon Arias
was subtle, but distinct alongside the combined
forces of her colleagues. It probed maliciously,
seeking to pry the last of the power's grasp from
him, but he resisted with everything he had. *He
didn't want to die.*

He rallied against the forces opposing him,
and a power flickered to life within him, surging
through him like an inferno. He cast off the
forces assaulting him like a brilliant sunrise
burning off the mists of night, and a torrent of
violent flame exploded to life in a crescent
around him, throwing the Kirin around him off
their hooves.

And then Arias was suddenly someplace else.

***

To-shin managed to shield the Kirin closest to
him from the blast of heat, and he could only
hope that the other elders had done the same for
the rest. The area was ruined, the scorched runes
smeared into obscurity, chunks of wall seared and
blackened, and the floor crumpled and buckled in
places. The Kirin that had fallen was being
attended to by their peers—still alive, blessedly—
and he spared a bit of his magick to send a gentle
breeze across the room, clearing out the residual
heat. Arias was a pale heap at the center of the
room, his eyes open, staring into nothingness,

and a sharp look around revealed that Lurik-ma was nowhere to be found. The elder doe had risked the entire spell with her own greed, vying to take the power for herself. He cursed softly. All of this, for nothing!

There was an exclamation of fear, followed by the panicked hoof beats of running Kirin, and To-shin closed his eyes, blocking out the ruined chamber. He didn't need to know what it was when he saw the amalgamation of crimson energy in the ether, rapidly approaching his location. Arias's own presence in the ether was hardly registerable as a weak violet, drifting absently over the location where he knew the Gryphon's body lay. To-shin opened his eyes and breathed a heavy sigh that carried the weight of his failure.

Jance had arrived.

***

It wasn't the first time that Arias had found himself someplace dark. There was no light and no sound, but somehow, the sound of a brassy neigh carried to him. It sounded so familiar that Arias turned about, and then *he* was there.

Standing tall, his silken mane curling down around his piercing blue eyes, Xio looked down at him with all the fatherly love Arias had known in his cubhood. Seeing the Alicorn herd Sire, Arias nearly screamed for joy. He wanted to run to the stallion and cross necks with him, but... Xio seemed to be everywhere and nowhere all at once. The stallion's eyes softened when he saw Arias's response, and he whickered softly to him.

123

"It's been a while since I've seen you, Arias. How you've grown! And yet… I sense that something is awry. What troubles you, little one?"

Arias's ears dropped as he remembered everything that had happened. He frowned as he looked at Xio, knowing that the stallion couldn't really be there. "So," he said slowly, "Jance came."

***

A flood of Kirin departed the temple, some leaping away on great clouds of steam, others hurrying to retreat to the lower levels. To-shin held firm as the Unicorn approached, each step unhurried as he drew near. At the touch of the stallion's magick, the temple's illusionary entrances shuddered and dissipated, leaving most of the entrances open to the forest itself. Jance seemed somehow disappointed as he entered into the same space as To-shin, peering about at the scorch marks in the earth with disapproval. To-shin wasn't surprised to find himself nearly alone as he faced the creature. Gali-da stood off to one side, and surprisingly, Lurik-ma to the other. Everyone else had possessed the good sense to flee. Jance didn't bother to speak, just casually reached out to grab Arias in his magick. Gali-da intercepted him with her own, equally as staunch and silent, and Jance sighed.

"I see," the stallion muttered in a deep growl. "Of course you'd like to do this the hard way. I'll find more than enough of your kind hiding about to use for my purposes; your interference is little more than a minor inconvenience." Jance closed his eyes, his horn pulsing with crimson light.

124

"Your oldest have hardly lived half my lifespan. Allow me to teach you all a lesson on what true magick looks like. It'll be the last lesson you ever learn, I'm afraid." With an ominous groaning sound, the forest around him began to wilt and brown, and To-shin gritted his teeth, pressing in close to Lurik-ma and Gali-da. *So it begins*, he thought.

***

"Wherever I go, bad things happen, Xio. It doesn't matter if I try to help. What am I supposed to do? I just want my friends to be safe... I just wanted to have a normal life."

Xio stood serenely before Arias, his long tail swishing in a breeze that didn't seem to be there. "Sometimes things truly are our fault," he nickered softly. "And sometimes the lessons learned therein are truly terrible. I can see that you blame yourself for much, Arias, but tell me: Had you never left Glendale to search out your own kind, would everything that ended up happening still have happened?"

"Shadowbane wouldn't have had the knowledge of blackroot," Arias said. "He still would've existed, but I gave him that knowledge. I didn't know what he'd do with it."

"Ah," Xio said. "You still blame yourself."

"Of course I do!" Arias cried. "It was my fault. You'd still be alive if I hadn't done it... many creatures would be."

"You can't be certain of that," Xio replied.

125

"You can't know what events the flow of time would have brought, Arias. Who can say that Shadowbane wouldn't have found another way to defeat Naugi, or that he wouldn't have committed any number of other atrocities?"

"I can say that to myself all I want," Arias said. "But I know that it's lying."

"Is it?" Xio asked. "Or is it the truth? You can hold yourself solely responsible for everything that has happened to everyone around you since your birth, but that alone doesn't make it true. In doing so, you strip yourself of the glory of your own accomplishments." He frowned, his voice taking on a more serious tone. "We don't have much time, Arias. You have a decision to make."

***

That morning, To-shin had risen and taken his pupils to the arena for their training. They'd talked far more than they should have, and they desperately needed training in forming their fire whips, but, well… some days were simply like that. Besides, he rather liked hearing what was going on in their lives, even the mundane, insignificant parts. Oh, to be young again! To-shin was advanced in his years, but he had a bit of time ahead of him yet. He'd been favoring his right hip, true, especially on chilly mornings, but he wasn't at the point of taking herbal medicines to dull the pain like some of the truly old elders did. Bing-ye had retired from even teaching a couple of years ago, opting to focus on his studies instead. Now *that* was a truly old buck!

To-shin dimly recalled hoping to find some

sweet cane to chew after lessons while he revised some scrolls that needed updating, but blast his memory, he'd forgotten to grab some from the garden. Now he stood facing a Unicorn old enough to make him feel like a fawn, and he wondered how he'd found himself in such a situation. He could have just run away like the others, perhaps began a new life elsewhere, even. Both arthritic hip and sweet cane seemed like distant, fanciful issues in lieu of the current situation.

To-shin knew that he was no match for a creature like Jance, and Gali-da and Lurik-ma were no better. The price of not trying, however, was too great. He didn't blame the others for running and hiding, for fear could drive any creature to such measures. As he watched Jance draw upon the forest around him, he didn't know exactly what the stallion was doing, but common sense told him he didn't want him to finish whatever it was. Out of the corner of his eye, he saw Gali-da leap skyward on a massive whorl of clouds, and To-shin rushed forward to test Jance with the lick of his flame whip, hoping to distract the creature.

Jance didn't even bother to move to sidestep the attack. With a tilt of his head, he severed To-shin's magickal tether to his own flame, then threw the elder backward as easily as if he weighed nothing. To-shin managed to catch himself on a puff of steam before he hit the ground, and as he righted himself, he heard an odd sound come from Jance. No, he realized, it was only odd due to context. Jance was *chuckling*.

The stallion eyed him, his horn still glowing crimson as he regarded him as a predator might regard an easy kill.

Too frightened to be infuriated, To-shin hoped that he'd distracted the Unicorn long enough to allow his comrades time to connive. Indeed, Gali-da landed on light hooves and touched her nose to the earth, imbuing two trees nearby Jance with her own mana. Taking hold of their roots, she bid them to carry out her will, and they breeched the earth with a thunderous scattering of dirt. Jance tried to slice them in twain before leaping away, but the fibrous bits of root trailed after him with rabid intensity, wrapping around his hooves and coiling upward like a multitudinous serpent.

Seeing Gali-da's success, Lurik-ma surged forward and used her magick to condense the water vapor from the air, cooling them until a shining maelstrom of glacial quills surrounded her, as deadly-sharp as the teeth of any beast. She loosed them at Jance with such speed that they screamed through the air and, not wanting to take any chances, To-shin hurried to add to the attack. He strained to lift two sections of the temple wall itself, grunting as he sent them overhead, sailing toward the hapless Unicorn. The two chunks struck with such force that the ground quaked around them, sending up a plume of dust that obscured everything at the site of the attack.

The forest that Jance had been drawing upon paused in its wilting, a few tentative branches even achieving a pallor of their former green. To-

shin craned his neck, squinting, and Gali-da had
frozen where she now stood, while Lurik-ma had
ventured to wind walk a few steps upward, her
ears pricked high as she watched the spot where
the Unicorn had just been. To-shin started as a
voice reached to him through the ether.

*So weak. You claim yourselves to be teachers and
scholars of the arcane, but you are unworthy of such titles.
I will personally dispatch each of you myself, so that upon
your death you may witness the true majesty of a master of
his craft. You've wasted my time. Now… Observe!*

A tiny movement could be seen within the
cloud of dust. Jance shouldered the sections of
the temple that rested upon him, peeling his way
out from the rubble as easily as if he'd been
settled upon by a scattering of leaves. To-shin
couldn't swallow past the sinking feeling that
encompassed him at the sight. He hoped that the
rest of the Kirin had escaped.

It's alright to be afraid, he told himself, gritting
his teeth as he steeled himself. *It's alright so long as
you're brave until the very end.*

CHAPTER EIGHT

"I played a part in everything that happened leading up to this point," Arias said. "Of course you'd see the best in me, Xio. You raised me. But I can't deny that everywhere I go, destruction seems to follow. I have no reason to believe that it won't continue to happen. I never wanted to admit it, but maybe it's better for everyone if I stop fighting. They keep following me to their own detriment."

"You believe that things would have turned out differently with certainty, but I can tell you with just as much conviction that every leader has such thoughts," Xio said.

"I'm not a leader," Arias said, "and that's part of my point. If I were truly meant to be a leader, I would've done a better job of taking care of everyone around me."

"So you believe that I was a bad leader," Xio said, cocking his head, "and Brynne as well.

Similarly for anyone else you know who have made difficult decisions that affected others. I should have done away with myself had I survived my encounter with Naugi, since I'd clearly failed so spectacularly."

"I didn't say that!" Arias said, feeling a prickle of irritation at Xio. The stallion turned to him with a mischievous look in his eye.

"You did, just not in those exact words. Imagine if everyone who ever had a failing of some type gave up, Arias. Do you believe that those who follow you truly would rather you didn't exist?"

Arias sighed. "No, I don't. But it won't matter, Xio. My body isn't equipped to deal with magick. It's killing me." He paused. "Maybe I'm already dead."

"You aren't quite yet passed from the world of the living, Arias, but you have a decision to make, and quickly. The essence of any magicked creature cannot exist where it is treated as an intruder. If you do not align yourself into an acceptance of it, it will be rejected by your very being. So long as you believe yourself to be unworthy, you will never wield the power that has been bestowed upon you. The essence you now possess was borne of Aaga, the Phoenix, and it will not allow for weakness. It now exists in you merely as a means to its own survival, and it will remain a part of you for as long as it can, even to your demise."

"So how am I supposed to try to learn more about it?" Arias asked. "You said it yourself, Xio. I don't have time."

"You're looking at it the wrong way," Xio replied, pawing at the formless ground. "I regret not teaching you more of magick while I lived, and yet I had no idea this would've been possible. The energy in the body flows like a river, Arias, and if anything stops its flow, its host weakens. *You* are your own barrier. By blocking the vital flow of energy that would allow you to have a symbiotic relationship with this essence, you now instead have a parasitic one. Starved of mana, that essence will take whatever resources it can from you to attempt to bridge the gap, literally eating you alive in a sense. The fact that I'm able to appear to you like this makes me fear that you are already at that point."

"I don't know how to do any of what you just told me," Arias said, exasperated. "I don't have anyone to teach me. I couldn't even figure out how to fly until someone taught me, how am I supposed to learn this without being shown?"

Xio lowered his head, and his eyes were kind as he met Arias's gaze. "This is a lesson that I know you are capable of learning, Arias. The fact you already used magick once shows that you are capable. You need only to take that lesson to heart, little one."

"Even if I figure this out, To-shin told me that whoever possesses this essence will likely become corrupted by it. They tried to take it from me so

that they could contain it, and… I don't know.
I'm not sure if it worked or not. If I try this, I
don't want to end up like Mati-jai did."

"Any other magicked creature would likely be
corrupted by that essence, yes, as it was taken
through dark means. But you are a clean slate,
Arias; you have no prior connection to the ether
through which you can be tainted. An Alicorn has
an affinity and an understanding of the art of
healing. To kill, especially to kill wantonly, is
against our very nature, but our ancestors forbid
it for a much greater reason; an Alicorn that loses
their way ultimately pays the price of losing touch
with their abilities… and eventually dies. The cost
is so high that most will not risk slaying another.
It takes a very special set of circumstances to
allow us to remain whole in the face of taking a
life."

Xio frowned, his ears turning as if he could
hear something in the distance. He peered into
the formless nothingness, and then faced Arias
again. "Most creatures who are born magicked
have a rite of rules such as the ones I've
mentioned which they must live by. You can
either view what has happened to you as an
unfortunate accident," he continued, "or you can
see it as what it is; a very, very rare blessing. The
choice is up to you."

A long murm passed before the stallion added,
"I hope you know that I won't judge you,
whatever you decide. I'll always love you, Arias.
Your life has not been an easy one, even from its
very beginning, and if you wish to rest, you may.

You can remain with me for a time, if you wish."

Arias looked around at the blackness surrounding them. "I… don't understand," he said slowly, and surprisingly, Xio whickered happily.

"The rest of the herd has moved on, but I chose to stay here. I'm waiting for someone. The ether isn't the same as the world you knew me in, Arias. It isn't something I can explain to you. I'm little more than a memory here. Even so, I'm not alone. Soon enough, I'll move on as well, but while I wait… it can be a truly wonderful place." He closed his eyes, his mane billowing out in long, silvery locks that curled in a breeze that Arias couldn't feel. A beam of light pierced the darkness, sweeping toward them, and Arias squinted. When he opened his eyes fully again, they were standing on a vast, rolling meadow, a cloudless sky beaming down from above. He glanced around in awe and confusion, and Xio reached out as if to touch him, though he had no substance. "It's rare indeed that I have had the chance to see you again," Xio said. "Don't focus on what you think for now. Remember how you felt when you used your magick instead. And remember, Arias… Yes, sometimes bad things happen, and sometimes it is our fault. That doesn't mean that we should ever stop trying, though."

Xio gave Arias one last, fond glance, and then he turned away. He didn't walk or move away, but Arias could somehow sense him becoming more distant, slowly melding into the nothingness of which the rest of the world around him seemed to be made. He cried out for the stallion, but in the same murm that Xio was there, he was gone.

***

Jance moved forward with a speed not befitting a mortal creature. Instinct—blasted instinct of all things—grasped To-shin's mind as he saw the white blur headed directly for him. He countered with the weapon that automatically came to him without thinking, the same one he'd been wielding since fawnhood, the same one that Jance had easily turned aside once already. It was no surprise when the Unicorn deflected the flame whip, redirecting it as easily as if it were a mere seed fluff directed his way by the wind. The roaring flame abruptly fizzled out as Jance severed To-shin's magickal connection to it, and To-shin drove his cloven hooves into the ground as he faced his adversary, forcing his mind to torque into focus. "Alright then," he growled, his gaze hard. "Let's see how much magick you've really studied, you filthy hermit."

The earth, Quang-za, also referred to as the Everspring, was the source of Kirin-kind's power. Fallow and drained by Jance's magick, To-shin felt he could hear the very heartbeat of the dying land as he poured his own magick into it, urging it to awake and do his bidding. He felt resistance at first, and then through the sheer force of his will, the soil suddenly shuddered and complied, losing its solidity.

A grunt of surprise escaped Jance as he sank up to his hocks in the liquefied terrain, and in the same murm, To-shin wrenched it back into being solid. Lurik-ma wasted no time. She drew in a deep breath and when she breathed back out, it was in a glacial gust so frigid that it left the fur on her own face stiff with frost. Jance gave a small, pathetic cry as Lurik-ma's frost met with his living flesh. The elder doe didn't stop until the Unicorn was bound in a solid glaze, and then she stood, panting, to behold her handiwork. Gali-da darted over on a huge puff of steam, reaching with her magick to bind the statuesque Unicorn further, but before she could, she suddenly froze in midair, a crimson aura surrounding her body.

As To-shin flexed to move forward, the ground around Jance exploded upward, showering them with chunks of earth, and, when the dust cleared, Jance stood triumphantly before them. "Insolent beasts!" he bellowed, Gali-da held in his grasp as surely as a longear caught in the claws of some terrible predator. "I've had enough of this foal's play. It's time that I took what I came here for."

To-shin didn't have a plan. He tried to clear the distance between himself and the Unicorn to do anything to help Gali-da, but he wasn't fast enough. He knew he wouldn't be. Before his very eyes, red bands of magick crossed Gali-da's body, conglomerating at its center.

She hardly screamed before her eyes went lifeless, her form disintegrating into a fine red mist. Jance leveled his horn toward To-shin. "You're next. I'll wither you back into the ashes you were made from, you wyrmling!"

Fear cloaked every other sense To-shin had. Jance's movements were suddenly so fast! Lurik-ma coalesced moisture from the air and dashed upward and away to safety, leaping high on clouds of steam, but it seemed that To-shin had hardly started the motion of wind walking before the Unicorn was upon him. Jance's magick gripped him in an iron grasp, and To-shin choked as he felt the very vitality being drained from his bones, a million small bits of him being ripped away at once. He felt cold, so far from everything he knew and loved, dead, but not dead enough to experience the peace of rejoining the Everspring. Jance knew he could kill him, but he was clearly prepared to take his time with achieving his goal.

The strength to resist left To-shin. The darkness at the corners of his vision grew, coating everything in the same shade of midnight. He gave a final, demented cry of agony, and, just as he was going limp, just as he finally released his hold on existence, a thin bolt of something silvery struck Jance, sweeping his legs out from beneath him. To-shin dropped to the ground, shaking, trying to gasp in the air of the living, but he lacked the strength for even that. He floundered uselessly, aware that he was slipping further away from life, and then there was a piercing pain in his chest. The wound was so sharp and sudden that it dragged his faculties back into clarity, and he convulsed back into being. He frowned, blinking rapidly, the figure before him coming into focus.

The Alicorn pulled her horn from To-shin's

chest, and her maroon eyes, filled with compassion, steeled as they shifted to glare at Jance. With her ivory wings spread wide, she reared up and screamed in challenge.

Jance regained his hooves, his surprise as unhidden as his disdain. "Forbidden daughter," he spat, "this battle is not your own. Would you forsake the vow of your kind not to kill?"

"Any battle involving that Gryphon is mine," Hlaena hissed. "I'll give you this one chance to stand down, ancient one. But if you decline… I'll do everything in my power to send your wretched form from this world."

***

Arias!

Arias was alone, and yet he recognized that voice. He strained to reach for it, and yet he also knew he couldn't use the typical senses of sight and scent to search it out. He reached deeper, probing inward and tentatively touching abilities still unknown to him. The voice came again, almost ethereal in the way it seemed to come from nowhere and yet everywhere at once.

Arias, dearest little one… this is my fault. I never told you that I forgave you, Arias, and I'm sorry for adding to the weight you were already carrying. I never explained the truth of how I found you at the Crowning Point, but you deserve to know.

Arias blocked out the distractions of his own thoughts, of the odd not-world he occupied, and concentrated on the source of the voice. He felt he could detect the thinnest trail of another being, and he quested toward it, not physically moving anywhere, but feeling it draw nearer. And then there she was, standing like a radiant sunburst in the ether.

"Hlaena!" Arias tried to exclaim, but no sound issued forth. The gold manifestation shimmered, but didn't give any acknowledgment of him. He scrambled, frantic, to try to figure out how to get to her, but the darkness offered no answers.

When I found you in the lake at Dantzik, you were nearly dead. I knew the only way you'd gotten there was if you'd sacrificed yourself to save me. Trying to save you should have killed me; you were far beyond what any Alicorn should have been capable of healing. But I had the potent mana of the Crowning Point flowing through me, and through using it, I was able to bring you back. I didn't know I'd given Mati-jai's stolen essence a place to flee to, but I don't care. I'd do anything to help you now, but I can't. I hope you know what happened to Xio and the others was a tragedy, but it wasn't because of you. They made their choice, Arias, the same way you have to make yours now. Your flock needs you. I need you.

Her voice became more distant, more sorrowful, and in barely a whisper, her voice drifted over one last time.

You always did the best you could, but I failed you. You're a phenomenal creature, Arias, and I wish for nothing more than for you to believe that you deserve to live a happy life...

Arias's mind flooded with the truth. He'd

never questioned Hlaena as to what had happened prior to him waking in the destroyed Minotaur village in Dantzik. Hlaena had been honest about finding what was left of Ly-ra's corpse, of her battle with Mati-jai, of how she'd used magick to heal him, but the latter wasn't unusual in itself. In the time he'd lived among the Alicorns, he'd seen them use their ability to heal countless times. The details of how he'd come to awaken and recover in Dantzik hadn't been important to him; he'd just been excited that Hlaena was alive, and that he'd be able to return to his friends in the flock. It had taken him a very long time to recover, true, but he'd also never before suffered such injuries as he had in Dantzik, and he'd originally attributed the way his health plateaued, before beginning to decline, to that.

At hearing Hlaena's words, however, everything made sense, even his sudden, almost violent fear of water. Above it all she, like Xio, had mentioned the one thing that he'd been unable to grasp on his own for so long. The thing that seemed to have eluded him since his very birth, perhaps starting with the fact that his own parents hadn't wanted him.

Like a stifling oppression, the seed of unworthiness within him had grown unchecked into a monstrous beast. How many had died at his claws? How many had followed him to oblivion, had believed he was something he was not? He realized that the only time he'd been capable of using his magick—the only time he'd felt *normal*—was when he was acting to protect those he loved. Never had he been able to rally enough to come to his own aid, a testament to his own worthlessness. He gasped, choking, slipping away. The despair was an all-encompassing echo, welling up in his soul like the death-ritual of some wild thing. The only thing that kept it back was a single, simple thought:

He hadn't known.

He hadn't known what Shadowbane would do with the knowledge of blackroot. He hadn't known there was a sea serpent lying in wait beneath the sea he and the others had crossed, or that the Strigigryph would be at such a disadvantage on that flight. He hadn't known what Mati-jai had turned out to be capable of. He'd come to Jance for help, not knowing that the Unicorn wouldn't give a second thought to killing so many just to get what he wanted. In a sense, whether he was directly or indirectly related to the atrocities he'd been privy to was irrelevant. He'd unfairly burdened himself with guilt that stemmed not from his own actions, but from the evils of others.

Like the thinnest ray of light, the revelation dawned upon Arias like a rising sun. He stretched toward it with everything he had within him, and he felt a clarity and a peace flood through him in a burst, like an over-full river cresting its bank. Every feather, every bone, and every hair seemed to buzz with energy. He gasped again, and this time his lungs filled with air.

If I die today, he thought, *I'll die doing what I*

believe is right. I'll protect those I love until my last breath.

And as if in response to his own conviction, deep in the back of his mind, Arias swore he heard Xio's voice whisper two last words.

Well done.

***

Arias's eyes snapped open. He was lying on the floor of the Kirin temple, but, strangely, the outer illusionary entrances were gone, leaving most of the chamber open to a dying forest beyond. To-shin was barely visible off to one side, his stance bowed as if merely standing took great effort, and then there was Hlaena. The Alicorn stood taller than he'd ever seen her, her hooves planted defiantly into the parched soil as she faced Jance, but, when Arias stirred, he saw her flick a single ear in his direction. Jance immediately drove forward, his mane streaming out behind him in an ashen wave, and, incredibly, Hlaena surged forward to meet him. The two reared up, teeth bared, and their horns met with a mighty crack, the crimson and maroon of their magick nearly indistinguishable as they struggled against one another.

Arias took in the sight of Jance, drinking in the visage of the creature who'd tried to take everything from him. The stallion's lips pulled back wolfishly as he pressed into Hlaena, the Unicorn too engulfed in his duel with Hlaena to notice Arias getting to his feet. The mare grunted as she took a few steps back, the muscles in her hindquarters taut as Jance drove her backwards. The Unicorn was trembling with his effort to strain forward, the forest around him seeming to give a collective sigh as the last of its life seeped away and invigorated him instead. Arias could just see the vestiges of victory beginning to glitter in Jance's hateful eyes, and in that murm, a singular goal gripped him.

A wave of acknowledgment flowed through the ether toward Arias, and he felt energy roil up from his belly, crackling through him like lightning. With a ferocious cry, he threw himself forward, and strength imbued him as it never had before. He just saw the look of shock cross Jance's features as he scrambled to push Hlaena away from him, thrusting his own body backwards to do so. The stallion wheeled around to face Arias just as he took a final leap toward him, talons splayed and wings open. He could feel the touch of Jance's magick upon him, but he didn't slow; instead he reached almost instinctually within himself for the reserve of energy that he somehow knew he'd find there. It rose up at his command, straining to be free, and when he opened his bill, a shimmering swath of flame issued forth in a fantastic rush.

Arias closed his eyes against the bright cascade, sensing more than hearing Jance's retreat. When he opened his eyes, the Unicorn was backing away, panting, his ears pressed to his skull as his eyes flicked from Hlaena to him. To-shin had even gathered himself enough to take a few steps forward, his golden eyes determined. Jance viewed them with disgust, then fixed his disdainful gaze on Hlaena.

"What have you to do with such a wretched creature?" he asked. "You risk your very life to dabble in affairs of which you know nothing!"

"I don't expect a miserable being like you to know anything about love," Hlaena replied. "But I'd sacrifice myself as many times as it took, to protect him from you."

Jance scowled, still looming darkly, his horn shimmering with a weak crimson light. And then, to Arias's surprise, he turned and dashed away. To-shin let out a long sigh, slumping to the ground, and Arias ran to Hlaena, embracing her with his wings. She nuzzled into his shoulder, her warm breath ruffling his feathers.

"I should never have kept so much from you," she said, pulling back guiltily. "Perhaps I could have helped you sooner had I known. I'm so sorry Arias. I realized something was amiss, and I came as quickly as I could." She paused. "Not soon enough, by the looks of you. You look like you haven't eaten in moons, little one."

"Had you come any later, I wouldn't still be here," To-shin said from where he'd slumped down, his head bowed as if his horns weighed too much. "I've never come so close to my own mortality before. To say thank you isn't enough, but I don't know what other words to offer. I can postulate who you are, though I know we've never formally met." He said the words with an inflection of reverence despite the absolute fatigue he exuded. "However, I'm sorry about the circumstances through which I know of you and through which we've met. I apologize on behalf of my kind for our failings. Mati-jai was a force who should have been stopped long before he made so much trouble."

Hlaena eyed To-shin, seeming equally curious about him as he was of her. "I have heard a little of Kirin through the stories Arias told me in Dantzik," Hlaena said. "I'd usually help you more, but… I'd like to save my strength, just in case. Will you be alright as you are?"

"Ah," To-shin said, "you've done more than enough. I'll be just fine. I don't expect Jance to return, considering Arias's new relationship with his essence. It'll be much harder for him to be parted from it now that he's accepted it, and, judging by his appearance in the ether, he's done just that. I imagine that using the method Mati-jai did is the only way it could be taken from him now, and if Jance knew how to do that, he certainly would have done it by now. Still, I worry… his thirst for power will be more firmly within him now. If a Unicorn ever tried to study dark magick, much less succeeded, we'd be in far deeper trouble than we just were."

Arias didn't want to think about that. He'd just begun to dare to sink into the first sense of relief he'd felt in a long time, but it ended before it could truly begin. He went rigid with urgency, and he ignored the questioning glances To-shin and Hlaena cast toward him; instead he turned and ran through the forest. He couldn't even form words with which to explain to them, which was just as well, because he didn't have time to waste on trying. The only thing that filled his mind was thought for one creature.

Larin.

***

It wasn't hard to find Larin. The ground had been torn up in great chunks all around the location where she lay, as if Jance had done everything he could to capture her in his magick. There were chunks of fur and feathers all around her, too, but they weren't black. They were flaxen in color, and scattered all around, as if they'd been caught up in a great whirlwind. What was left of Hilda lay a distance away, but Arias couldn't look at her. He couldn't tear his eyes from Larin, who was lying at an awkward angle, her eyes half-open, staring into nothingness. Blood and foam coated her chest, and she lay very still indeed.

Arias ran over to her on legs that threatened to betray him. He wrapped himself around her limp body, clinging uselessly to her, and a monstrous sound tore from him, painting the dead forest with the cry of the lost. He hadn't stopped her when he'd had the chance. Had she not tried to protect him, she –

Arias froze as he felt the tiniest movement. A slow, rattling breath eked from the mass of feathers beneath him, and he peeled back, thinking with desperation of a way to help her, to take away her suffering. There was none. He dug his face into the feathers at the base of her neck, his eyes squeezed shut, wishing that there was something, anything he could do. As if in answer, a silent, gentle tug of magick guided him aside, and Hlaena nuzzled his cheek with her muzzle. She pulled back, looking into his pink eyes with her maroon ones, and said into his mind,

There is never enough time to say and do the things we wish to. With what words I can spare, know how proud you've made me, Arias. This gift I gladly give unto you… Do not despair, little one, for it was freely given.

In a fluid movement, Hlaena swept through the forest like a rush of wind, angling her horn downward and impaling Larin just below her ribcage. The gryphoness was so far gone that she hardly registered the wound, and for an instant, Hlaena held her stance. Then she sagged, like a mighty tree toppling in a storm, and her mane darkened from silver to midnight in a single murm. She fell sideways, her horn gleaming crimson as it pulled free from Larin's flesh, and by the time she'd met the earth, the light had gone from her eyes.

Arias's breath caught in his throat at the sight before him, and it was as if all the oxygen had left the world, leaving him to choke and pant on the nothingness that instead filled its place. He was dimly aware of the sound of approaching hooves, but his mind seemed just as frozen as the rest of him. He couldn't make sense of anything besides the terrible, terrible weight that sank into him, and in that instant, time stopped for him. He would always question whether it ever truly started again.

***

Hlaena stepped out onto the lush, rolling

grassland, the wind playing in her mane. Immediately, she knew where she was… but she felt only peace. She unfurled her wings and closed her eyes, savoring the inviting landscape, her ears turning as she heard a familiar sound off in the distance. She scanned the horizon, making out a pale form streaking high above the meadow, and when she heard the brassy cry again, her heart soared.

"Xio!" Hlaena cried, already urging herself into a gallop, a high-pitched neigh of excitement leaving her as she kicked free of the earth, flapping her wings to rise to meet him. Xio banked toward her, his blue eyes sparkling brightly as they met hers. Together they angled away from the meadow, reveling in their freedom, rising side by side into the endless firmament above.

Neither of them looked back.

CHAPTER NINE

Arias was aware of To-shin next to him, speaking, but the words just… didn't matter. They were just a random conglomeration of background noise, like the wind or the rain or the wind rustling through the leafless trees overhead. The image of Hlaena and Larin laying on the ground before him burned into him like a fetid curse. Each breath Larin drew next to him was slow and ponderous, as if it took all the strength she had to draw it, and Arias's mind was full of the sound, of the knowledge that although Hlaena had saved her, she was suffering. To-shin reached out and touched him, and sudden the sensation caused him to jump, whipping his head toward the Kirin. Whatever the elder saw in his eyes caused him to take a step back, but he seemed to know what he was thinking, because he started to shake his head. Arias had already given himself over to the singular purpose, however.

Jance had to die.

Arias turned away from To-shin and whatever rational argument he was attempting to share with him. He ignored the elder buck's late attempt to restrain him with his magick, and he tore through the forest, back to the last place he had seen Jance. He easily found the Unicorn's hurried set of hoof prints, and the fur bristled along his back as he honed in on the direction they led to. He growled as he took off, the mana in his veins seeming to urge him forward, his claws tearing the earth with such force that clods of peat and soil were sent airborne by his passing.

At the first sign of real resistance, the Unicorn had taken the coward's path. Arias knew well the terrifying feeling of being predated upon. He remembered the way it had wormed into his gut when a group of Primal keythongs had tried to kill and eat him and Brynne as cubs, the way it had hung over him when he was under Shadowbane's watch in Arborochre, and the fear of not knowing whether an encounter with an ursos would be his last. He'd felt it when Jance had tracked him down, but now he'd broken past the captive horror. He let his fury consume him, and in it, he hoped that the stallion would be faced with the same unyielding terror he'd unleashed upon himself and countless others.

In the stillness of the forest, Arias felt that he'd well and truly become a feral beast. He panted, tongue lolling as he sprinted, never losing sight of Jance's trail, treading hoof marks underfoot with swift sets of claw and talon prints. He wished fervently to rob the Unicorn of his peace as he'd robbed him, and his eyes furtively roved for a hole in the canopy above. When he found one, he burst up above the treetops in a few mighty wingbeats, seeking to quicken his pursuit.

The forest slowly came to life again the further from the Kirin temple Arias flew, and the cool night air rustled through his plumage like an old friend joining him for a hunt. He hardly registered the majesty of his first flight without the fatigue that had afflicted him for so long. Instead, he fixated on darker thoughts; on how a creature like Jance didn't deserve to live in such a world. He flew on for a bit longer before touching down in the forest below, seeking Jance's spoor. He didn't quite understand his new abilities yet, but he closed his eyes and attempted to search the ether anyway, and his frustration only grew when doing so yielded no new information.

It took Arias quite a while to pick up the hoof prints again, and when he did, they were of a lighter, more confusing nature. Jance must have figured out that he was being followed, Arias realized. The insignia on his shoulder was still there of course, but the pain it had brought when Jance was tracking him was absent, leaving him to wonder how the beast had sensed him. *Maybe I have a presence in the ether now as well,* he thought. *Maybe Jance could see him coming... good.*

Jance's hoof prints had turned sharply to vanish into a soft peat bog, but it wasn't hard to find where the stallion had picked his way across to the other side. It was clear that Jance wasn't used to being pursued, and his feeble attempt at throwing Arias off his trail also confirmed something else… that the Unicorn was capable of feeling fear just like any other creature.

Arias shrieked into the night, and the cry was so bestial, the night chorus hushed. Jance had hidden his tracks again, and Arias closed his eyes to try once more to find the Unicorn using his new abilities. He focused on how it had felt when he'd tried to communicate with Hlaena through the ether, and in his mind's eye, the smallest blur of emerald flared to life. Arias concentrated on the new entity, but it revealed no further information. He opened his eyes and continued on again, but when he checked the ether again just a few murms later, the emerald blur was much more subdued than it had been before. It gave no sign of movement.

Operating on intuition, Arias backtracked to the location he'd been in before, noticing that the emerald haze in the ether returned to its former vibrancy when he did so. Understanding crept into him. He slowly cast his gaze in the direction where he'd seen the greenish haze in the ether, and he was rewarded with the barest outline of a pale mass standing between two trees. Arias reached into the ether, reaching for the way it had felt when he'd tried to speak to Hlaena again, and this time, he connected with something. He narrowed his eyes as he stalked toward the trees, and growled a single sentence into the mind of the being he'd reached out to.

The green haze in the ether finally moved as Jance stepped out from his hiding place, the branches above him swaying eerily in the scant breeze. The Unicorn looked haggard, as he had when he'd tried to herd Arias back to his forest on the mountain, but his contempt was as vibrant as ever. He pinned his ears as he regarded Arias. He didn't speak, instead standing expectantly in the darkness. Arias crept forward, the mana within him raging as if begging to be let free again, and the stallion kept a wary eye on him, his horn lowered.

"You were so eager not more than few sunrises ago," Arias growled. "Where is your bloodlust now, stallion?"

"I should have killed you when I had the chance, Gryphon! I shouldn't have wasted all that time dallying with those infernal Kirin. And I didn't expect to run into that foolish Alicorn. Had you –"

Arias rushed at Jance with a roar, but the Unicorn lurched sideways with surprising dexterity. In a mere murm he pushed himself into a gallop, disappearing into the forest ahead with a thudding of hooves. Arias started after him, but the Unicorn set about to using his magick to hinder him. A dead snag snapped and toppled into Arias's path, and after leaping over around it, he stumbled over jagged branches that were yanked toward him to block his pursuit. Even without the random attacks, Arias realized he'd never catch a creature like Jance on claw. The Unicorn was streamlined for running long distances, far longer and faster than Arias was built for. He had rarely run farther or harder than it took to take down prey. He decided to turn the chase to his favor in the only way he could think of to do so, and he took to the sky again, ignoring the way the tightly-woven canopy tore at him as he crested above it.

"Stop running and fight me!" he shouted down to Jance, gaining on him quickly from above.

You're useless to me now, Jance said to him through the ether, his voice seeming distant, quiet. *It should be enough that you get to keep your life, you ungrateful whelp!*

Arias caught glimpses of Jance as he fled at a gallop, and when he spotted a sizeable hole in the treetops, he flapped hard to descend upon the Unicorn. Taking prey from the air was dangerous, but Arias pushed such warnings aside as he splayed his talons and streamed toward Jance, tucking his wings in close to his body. Jance's horn sparked to life with crimson light when he saw him, and Arias felt his right wing suddenly jerk open into a full flare. A shock of pain went through his shoulder as his wing braked against the full weight and force of his speed, and he was wrenched off balance. Jance managed to keep his hold on the wing, preventing Arias from closing it, and before Arias could do anything, the ground rose up to meet him.

A bright flash of light accompanied the jarring pain of Arias's crash. He gasped for air, and mercifully found that the breaths he tried to breathe went in and out freely. He heard Jance's retreating hoof beats, and the sound filled him with fury. He lurched to his feet, ignoring the protests his body gave in response. His right wing sang out sharply when he extended it, but it wasn't broken; it would have to be enough. He grimaced, forcing himself to run, the sound of Jance's escape faint but still reaching his ears, and he threw himself skyward again.

Arias blasted a hole through the canopy with his flame, closing his eyes as he burst through the charred bits of wood and out into the open air above. Each wing beat was like driving splinters through the base of his right shoulder, but he forced himself past acknowledging it, relentlessly gaining on Jance's position. It didn't take long. Jance had tried to deviate through thicker forest this time, but Arias stayed far above his reach. The Unicorn slowed as Arias matched, and then surpassed his location, flying ahead of him until there was a decent buffer between them.

Drawing in a deep breath, Arias tapped into using his mana. He concentrated on the ground below, but nothing happened. Jance changed position, trying to keep space between them, and Arias followed him from above, trying to focus on the rapidly-moving terrain far down below him. He hissed in frustration, feeling a twisted sense of desperation as he held his breath, urging the mana within him to flow differently than it had before, in ways he'd yet to try but felt capable of doing. A small puff of violet flame rose and died on the forest floor, and he banked hard and turned, holding the image of that one spot in his mind as he closed his eyes.

With a roar, a wall of fire exploded to life, cutting off Jance's path of escape. The stallion screamed in shock, skidding to a stop before his trajectory could deliver him to the heat of the flame. He turned toward the unburned forest, his only escape route, but from above, it wasn't hard for Arias to close the gap. Arias breathed a stream of flame down, painting the dry forest with a jagged ring of flame until the Unicorn was completely encircled. The fire smoked and crackled, growing on its plentiful diet of dry twigs and brush until it soared high into the sky, bringing a new light up alongside the stars and the moon. Arias watched Jance change direction over and over again, trying to test his way past the heat, but the fire had grown too rapidly. Slowly, Jance retreated to the center of his shrinking prison, and Arias landed opposite of him. Fatigue rose in him, but he resisted it, meeting the Unicorn's gaze.

"Clever, for such a daft beast," Jance said, long tail swishing.

"Insult me all you want, but I'm not the one trapped here." Arias shook his head. "No more running. It's time to face what you've done."

"Hardly," Jance said. "All of this could have been avoided had you just given me what I'd wanted. Your kind will never accept you as you are. *Especially* not as you are now." He backed away too far, and the flames licked at his hocks. He squealed, jumping forward, and while the vestiges of panic touched his eyes, the expression bled away just as quickly, leaving something else much more cunning in its place.

"I see that you've just learned what happens when you use too much of your mana too rapidly, Gryphon. Magick is a dangerous thing to play with, deadly even, without knowing your own limitations. Perhaps you can still have a normal life among your kind... with the right training. Most beasts are terrified of fire, you know. Imagine how they'd react if they knew what you were capable of? What you need is a good teacher... someone who can teach you to control your new gift."

Arias was quiet as he regarded Jance. Sometimes when prey was caught, and it knew it couldn't escape, it chose to fight instead. Tusker and peryton fought with what they had; teeth, hooves, and antlers. Although Jance wasn't doing exactly the same thing, the effect was the same. The stallion didn't wear the same harried expression of a downed beast, but he'd still do anything he could to live, and Arias knew, among other things, how dangerous it was to give a creature like Jance time to think. All things considered, he was glad he'd allowed the Unicorn time to speak. It was apparent to him now why Jance hadn't retaliated with any of his much more threatening abilities. It was the same reason that he hadn't more forcibly tried to take Arias back to his forest earlier when they'd been on the mountain. Arias laughed, but it was a mirthless sound, alien even to his own ears. A hard sound. He frowned.

"You were so sure that you'd succeed that you've exhausted all of your mana, haven't you? It's why you decided to run instead of face To-shin, Hlaena, and myself. And I'm afraid that your offer doesn't appeal to me. The lives of those you killed is worth far more than anything you could teach me." He took a step toward Jance, cautious at first, and then another, and the Unicorn pressed back, dancing forward again as the heat of the fire scorched at his hide. He skirted the edges of the rapidly-shrinking bit of unburned forest he had access to, horn beginning to glow faintly.

"My life brought me here, and I feel I didn't have much of a choice. But you had so many chances to not have things end this way, Jance. You were probably hoping that no one would follow you, that you could retreat to recover somewhere in peace and then do as you saw fit later. Justice of any sort is far beyond me, but I do know one thing... For what you did to those Barbagryph, to the Kirin, to my friends—for the choice you made my own mother make—I can't allow you to live. Suffering will never end, I know that. But no one will ever suffer because of you again."

Arias rallied himself and opened his beak, sending a blast of violet flame at Jance. The stallion reflexively threw himself away from it, and in the murm it took Arias to cross the space between them, the stallion reared up, lashing out with his hooves. Arias dodged him with ease, and the Unicorn wielded his horn against him, slashing down with it in a glittering downward arc. But the move was clumsy, the last defense of a creature who'd probably never properly fought for his life before, and Arias again easily evaded the blow. Arias made as if to leap sideways in a quick feint, and Jance automatically turned to defend against the imaginary threat, horn poised to joust again. Instead, Arias flung himself up and onto the Unicorn's back, his claws hooking into hide, and the point of his bill found the soft, fleshy underside of Jance's neck. Arias bit deep and wrenched his head sideways, and the stallion screamed, the sound cutting into a hollow gurgle as he staggered sideways to the ground. His life blood left him as he convulsed, his centuries of life draining to an end, and at last he fell still, his eyes lying open as they looked blankly up into the fire-scorched night sky.

Arias stood in the ring of fire, trying to use his talons to wipe Jance's blood from his bill. He felt no joy at having killed the stallion. Instead, perhaps more chillingly, it had simply felt… *necessary*. He looked up at the moon above, watching the purple tongues of flame flicker and dance, alone with his discomfort.

Even after everything that had happened, nothing seemed to be fixed. He still felt very cold and very, very still inside. Broken.

That was it, he thought. *He felt broken.*

***

159

Arias stared at the wall. The individual grains in the earthen structure stood out, scattered and nonsensical. He could shift his focus to another stretch of the wall in the Kirin kingdom, and then take long murms differentiating the specks in that section of wall next. He did so now, slowly moving his eyes across the rough surface, content to continue doing so, until an annoyed keening sounded at his feet. Arias flattened his ears at the sound, dropping his eyes from their granular search to peer down at the source of the ruckus. He already knew what it was before his eyes found her. Kail sat at his feet, her mouth held open expectantly, a defiant glint in her crimson-ringed eyes. The cub had frequently tried to engage him, wrestling his tail, batting at his eyelids, crying incessantly… and Arias truly did care, somewhere deep inside himself. Not enough to act, usually, but he did. Today seemed different, though. Perhaps his shame tugged at him harder than usual.

Kail deserved better.

Arias glanced over at Larin, who was resting quietly on a plush heap of dried grasses. She hadn't woken since her encounter with Jance, though her rest was encouraged by the water tinged with herbs that the Kirin administered her. The herbs had to be harvested far beyond the boundaries of the forest that had been affected by Jance's magick. The wing Arias had injured in his pursuit of Jance had been securely bound by the Kirin, though he refused any of the medicines they offered him.

Arias had caused quite a stir when he'd returned from his hunt for Jance. The Kirin had balked at the sight of him, with his feathers streaked with blood and a feral glint in his eye. Some had even lashed out at him with their flame whips to send him away; To-shin alone had allowed him here, assuring the others that it was fine, that he would see to it that Arias behaved. Arias had been reminded of how he, Brynne, and Tybrake had been treated when they'd initially come to the Kirin kingdom, each of them viewed as base, mindless carnivores. Maybe the Kirin had been right all along.

Arias squinted, breathing in the stale air of these deeper chambers, wondering how many days had gone by. How long had it truly been? It was impossible to know. There was no sunlight down here, just the dim light from the single sphere of magickal light the Kirin kept here. He wondered when Larin would wake up. *If she wakes up*, his mind reminded him. The thought awoke a dull sense of panic within his numb mind, and he quickly refocused on the strange source of light instead, allowing his thoughts to drift away from anything substantial. They seemed to gravitate toward the worst possibilities, and he could feel the acidic thought waiting for him to acknowledge it, that not only might Larin not wake up, but that equally bad things had already transpired. After all...

She was gone.

Arias blinked hard to try to clear the thought from his head, and, as it had many times before, the thought scuttled to the back of his skull like a cowed opponent after being snapped at. But he knew that it would be back. Had his mind always been so cruel? He knew he couldn't run from the misery, that it was a part of him, inescapable and real. The best he could do was to distract himself in meaningless ways, and he'd found that the wall was the best for that. He settled down, feathers ruffled, and allowed himself to sink into the mindless task of connecting the little specks on the wall. He would have been successful at distracting himself, but Kail started to whine again. He pinned his ears, looking down at her. If he ignored her for long enough, the Kirin would take her to find something to eat and something to do. But today, something caused him to continue staring at her. Was it really his own guilt?

Encouraged by the kernel of attention, Kail settled down to wrestle with one of Arias's talons, and he breathed out softly, wishing it were somehow easier to care. The little hen deserved so much more than life had given her; so much more than *he* could give her. The sound of advancing hooves distracted him, and he glanced up to watch To-shin and one of his younger pupils approach, the latter carrying a dished piece of wood. It held a liquid that sparkled when it was carefully placed onto the ground, and To-shin used the tip of one of his horns to slide it a little closer to Arias.

"You should drink something, Arias," he said. "It's been far too long since you've had even water."

Arias didn't move. To-shin used his magick to carefully unwrap his wing, and he pulled at it gently to unfurl it. Before it could reach its fully-splayed position, the familiar spike of pain Arias had felt the last time he'd tried to open it returned, and he winced and snapped at To-shin, pulling the wing shut again. To-shin didn't attempt to dodge him, seeming unbothered by the reaction. He knew he wouldn't hurt him.

"You really should drink," To-shin urged again, but Arias didn't reply. He instead shifted his eyes to find another section of the wall to stare at, but Kail wandered over to To-shin, crying to him instead.

"Yes, alright," To-shin said, picking her up with his magick and placing her on his back. "We'll go out to see if we can find you something to eat again, how about that? It's rather fascinating… I feel that nothing I've read on your kind has accurately depicted just how much you eat at this stage." He paused, looking over to Arias, and then back to the little buckling who'd accompanied him to the chamber. "Wy-lie," he said slowly, "would you mind taking her for a bit, please?"

Wy-lie nodded and, eager to comply, hurried to pick the cub up with his more unpracticed touch of magick. He clumsily levitated Kail over his back, dropping her onto his shoulders with enough ineptitude that she scrabbled with her claws to steady herself. He didn't seem to feel it through his thick mane, however, and busied himself with trying to get the cub to sit still. To-shin slid the liquid aside, tilting his head and frowning as he regarded Arias.

"Arias," he said sternly, "I know that to say you've had a bad time is a severe understatement. I won't begin to try to find words to tell you how sorry I am, but either way, you can't continue on like this forever. Larin will need something solid to eat soon enough, and I don't think that scavenged scraps are going to be enough. We're already having plenty of trouble finding enough for this little one to eat, let alone a full grown gryphoness. And you… you haven't had anything since you got here. We Kirin will never be hunters, and it's hard enough finding someone willing to pick over a dead carcass in the first place. Everyone has an important job to do after what Jance did to this place… I need you to help out a little, if you can."

Arias nodded absently. He got to his feet and turned toward the entryway, but To-shin stepped into his path.

"Wait. There's something else. There wasn't time to tell you when you first arrived, with the way everything was pushed aside due to certain unsavory events transpiring. Listen… there's an Ardeigryph that took up residence in our forest some time ago. He hasn't caused any trouble, but we'd hoped to try to identify him. So far, he's remained on the edge of the river, nearby where young Ly-ra's tree was planted. He's terribly elusive and quite defensive, and in light of keeping the peace, we've left him alone. I seem to recall you were traveling with a big male keythong similar to him when you first entered our territory, but I figured the chances of them being the same individual were slim. You're not missing anyone in your flock, are you?"

Arias lifted his eyes to meet To-shin's.

"Where?" he asked, the first words he'd spoken in days. Kail gave an excited squeak upon hearing him, scuttling from Wy-lie's back and climbing up Arias's foreleg. She burrowed under his wings, only her long tail visible from beneath her plumage, and Wy-lie half-moved as if to try to pick her back up in his magick. He paused and gave To-shin a withering look.

"Don't worry about it, Arias will take care of her," To-shin said. "Why don't you go help the others with restoring the forest? You can take the rest of the day off from any studying."

Wy-lie nodded reluctantly and departed back the way he'd come, the sound of his retreating hooves filling the silence that rose to claim the space between Gryphon and elder Kirin. To-shin was staring at Arias as if he expected something, but Arias had nothing to offer him. To-shin sat down, the movement forcing a sigh from him in his age, and he eyed Arias again, his bearded lips pulled tight into an expression akin to a grimace.

"I'll answer your questions, Arias," To-shin said, "but first, I want to tell you something. I'm not sure how this sound, but sometimes I wonder if it wouldn't be sensible for us to intentionally study dark magick, so that we can have a better grasp on what we're facing when we inevitably must face it. Perhaps we would have known how better to help you. Maybe Gali-da would still be here. But by its very nature, dark magick would lead too many down a terrible and irredeemable path."

Arias slowly turned his head peer at To-shin. He hadn't realized that any of the Kirin had died in the battle against Jance, but… it unfortunately wasn't surprising. He looked away.

"I'm sorry," he said.

A brief silence stretched and then died as To-shin said, "It does get easier. It's just hard to know that when you're in the thick of it. You don't get to be as old as I am without realizing a few things… without a fear of losing those dear to you."

Something in the tone of To-shin's voice resonated with Arias, and as he looked at him, his breath stilled. To-shin wore a hollowed-out, haunted shadow of a gaze, the kind that seemed to stare past whatever was before it. It looked the way that Arias felt. *Here*, Arias realized, *is a creature who knows what it's like.*

"I won't try to lessen your grief," To-shin said, "and you shouldn't, either. The only way to get past it is through it, but…"

His voice drifted off, and he stared up at the rocky ceiling, as if he could look beyond it and to the open sky up above. "Many of the plants that grew here are fully lost to Jance's magick," he said. "Carefully bred and selected fruits, herbs, seeds… we'll have to start over from scratch with creating them again. My beloved sweet cane was among them. How I loved chewing that stuff! Jance's foul magick even ruined the seeds we had in storage, believe it or not… we'll be fine, though. There is plenty of wild forage beyond the touch of his magick, and at my age, it all nearly tastes the same anyway."

To-shin chuckled a little at that, though his eyes were still sad. "You know, my former mate passed on five summers ago. She would have been thrilled to meet you and your friends. I should say that we were chosen to be together based on a variety of factors, but that didn't matter. I loved that doe from the moment we had our first walk through the garden together. Few knew just how much of a treasure she was—she was so quiet, I thought she might have been mute for the first little while after our introductions— but, oh my! By the Everspring, she was so witty…"

He huffed softly, a little smile playing across his muzzle. "She always shirked her duties as a teacher, so the council finally let her go off on her own as a researcher, and she stayed buried up to her hocks in all the mushrooms and seedlings and grasses she harvested. She had the loveliest voice. I wish I could hear her rattle on about flora again, just one last time. She would have been leading the charge up there, helping to propagate the forest Jance destroyed. If I'm honest, Arias, I always knew that there was a possibility she'd pass on before I did. She was quite a bit older than me. But it always seemed too far off to worry about… It sounds crass to say, but sometimes I'm glad she died before me, so she wouldn't have to feel the way I feel now."

He paused and looked at Arias, his odd-colored eyes somber. "Your mother gave you a valuable gift, Arias. She knew exactly what she was doing… trust me, she did. If you sit in here and ruminate on all the terrible things that have touched your life, they will consume you. I'd hate to see that happen to you." He nodded toward Larin. "I can tell that you care quite a bit about that gryphoness there, and while I know it doesn't look like it, she's recovering just fine. When she wakes up, the last thing she needs to do is to worry about anything other than herself. You should take care of yourself so that she can do that. The essence within you is no longer a danger, but plenty of other, less-substantial things are. It's a lonely battle, but you didn't make it this far because you're weak. Neither did I."

Arias frowned and met the buck's gaze. Everything he'd said had sounded true enough. He gave a hesitant nod.

"Good," To-shin said. "We're social creatures, Gryphons and Kirin. I hope that you know you are welcome to seek me out anytime. I've grown rather fond of you in the short time that I've known you."

Arias waited, and when To-shin didn't speak

again, he turned toward the entryway again. Now it was his turn to pause, however.

"To-shin… can I ask you something?"

The old buck flicked his ears forward.

"When Jance came for me here, it felt like I was somewhere else. Somewhere dark. I was speaking to Xio. He was an Alicorn, Hlaena's mate, and he was a father to me. I knew he wasn't alive when I saw him, but somehow it didn't feel like a dream, either."

"Ah," To-shin said. "I've only ever heard accounts of such a thing before. Some say that within the ether, the presence of those already passed can live on for a time. But I can't say for certain."

Arias closed his eyes, daring to feel the power of the mana flowing through his veins. He peered into the ether, his feathers ruffling at the sudden vibrancy of the experience. Already, the ability to experience magick this way was beginning to become something he couldn't ever remember not being able to do. It was like dipping below water to open his eyes, and seeing fleeting glimpses of a world beyond, blurred and ephemeral. To-shin's signature undulated in the ether, bright and orange, like the sun just as it began to set.

"Your signature is a color I've never seen before," To-shin said, startling Arias into opening his eyes.

"It's a deep violet color," the elder went on, "so rich that it's almost hard to see."

Arias wondered at that. "Will you teach me more?" he asked.

"Of course! I am a teacher, after all. Who am I to turn away willing pupils? But not now. There will be plenty of time for that later."

Arias nodded, feeling grateful for the elder's presence. Their exchange could hardly be considered a conversation, but he felt different somehow. Lighter.

"Thank you, To-shin," he said, and, after a moment, he dipped into a bow. When he straightened, he was surprised to find the Kirin mirroring the movement.

"No, Arias," To-shin said. "Thank you. Had you allowed Jance to take that essence, the situation would have been very dire indeed. I feel that few would have succeeded at doing the incredible feats you've achieved in your short time. Besides that, I still have plenty to learn, even at my age, and you are a good teacher whether you know it or not. Go on, now. Some fresh air will do you some good, I think. And mind that you are careful of that wing. It isn't broken, but being left alone will help it tremendously."

Arias dipped his head in acknowledgement, casting a look at Larin's sleeping form before heading out from the small space, winding his way up the intricate passageways that laced the interior of the temple. The ways through them were almost intuitive to him by now, and they became much busier the closer to the surface he got. He tried his best to be mindful of the Kirin who passed him, shrinking to the side as appropriate. He was quite aware of his status as a guest here, and not an entirely welcome one to all.

Kail popped her head up as Arias reached the main floor of the temple, her thin tail lashing with excitement as she took in the sights and sounds with wide eyes. More than a few curious Kirin stopped to gaze at her, some even pulling out sheets of bark on which to scribble furiously. A fully grown Gryph was one thing, but few could resist the fluffy curiosity of a cub. Kail obviously enjoyed all the attention, even clambering down from Arias's back to weave through the legs of some of the closer Kirin, prompting delighted exclamations and curious sniffs from those she approached. When she noticed Arias ambling toward the outdoors, however, she hurried after him, her short legs taking her many furious steps to catch up to his longer stride.

The Kirin hadn't managed to re-erect their illusionary entrance, so natural daylight spilled into the far edge of the main hall. Arias squinted against the magnificence of the sun, its brilliance magnified by the fact that there were no leafy plants around to filter its intensity. The young buck that had been with him and To-shin just murms ago saw him and walked over with an uncertain step. Arias recognized him as the same buckling he'd seen on his last visit to the Kirin temple. He was the same pupil that had led him to To-shin's chambers for the first time, though he'd grown a little since then.

"Wy-lie," Arias said, remembering the name. "It would seem that you've been helping To-shin quite a bit. I imagine you've looked after Kail as well. Thank you."

Wy-lie ducked his head, entirely unprepared for the praise. "Oh, not at all! I just do whatever master To-shin tells me, really. Hey, I just wanted to ask you… ah. Well, I understand that Gryphons typically spot their prey from above and then track it on the ground. Since you shouldn't be flying, I wouldn't mind going up and seeing if I can spot anything for you, so you at least know which direction to go in to hunt? I don't think To-shin would mind at all if I did that for you. Unless you don't want my help, of course, which is totally fine! I won't be offended at all."

Arias blinked. "That would actually be quite helpful," he said, "but doesn't it bother you what I'm planning to do after that?"

"No, not really," Wy-lie replied after a moment of thought. "It's the way of life, after all. I certainly don't want to be around to watch it, though. And honestly, if it gets me off of scavenging duty…" he shuddered. Arias gave a soft huff of amusement, then peered about at all the surrounding Kirin.

"What are you all doing to the ground here?" he asked, watching a nearby doe touch her nose to the earth, her eyes closed.

"Just giving things a little extra boost to recover faster," Wy-lie said. "No magick is eternal, and that goes for what Jance did here as well. He stripped the mana from all the plant life here, and while it will naturally return over time, we can shorten how long it takes for that to happen by introducing some mana. As you walk farther, you'll see that the vegetation near the outer reaches of his attack weren't nearly as affected, and it's already starting to grow back."

"That's good," Arias said. He wondered if he could help with what they were doing, but he had a feeling he wouldn't be able to. That, and he didn't really want to just go about wantonly trying to use his power. He'd feel terrible if he were to hurt someone.

"Alright," Wy-lie said, "I'll be off, then!"

"Wy-lie," Arias said, stopping the buckling. "To-shin mentioned there's an Ardeigryph around here. Have you seen them for yourself?"

"I've only ever heard of them," Wy-lie said. "To-shin wouldn't permit me to seek them out, though."

"I see," Arias said. "I'm going to see if I can find them, but I'll return here later. It may be quite a bit later in the day… I hunt better at night."

Wy-lie nodded. "Alright," he said, "be careful. I'll find you later." He turned away, pulling a shining rivulet of water from the gourd he wore around his torso, leaping up in a massive bound to wind walk away on giant puffs of steam. Arias watched him go, then he started to walk toward the river.

"I'll take you on your first hunt later, Kail," he said to the small cub perched upon his back. "But for now, stay close. I'll keep you safe. Let's see what we can learn about this Ardeigryph."

CHAPTER TEN

Arias struck out along the river that cut its way through Kirin territory. It was low and reedy at this time of year, though even the reeds had died and been swept away where Jance's magick had touched them. It was terrifying to think of what Jance would have been capable of if he'd been capable of doing the same thing to fauna instead of flora.

The further Arias went, the more the typical sounds of the forest that he was used to hearing returned, a chorus that started off softly and then grew louder as the day wore on. Kail occasionally jumped down to the ground to explore a particularly interesting looking patch of dirt, or to chase any number of fluttering creatures. Arias even pinned his ears in faux-anger and gave chase after her a couple of times, which spurred her into shrieking gleefully. She was laughably easy to catch, of course, and he flipped her over and pinned her with one talon until she wriggled away, having had enough. It was nice to see her

exploring and having a good time, and not to
have to worry while she did so.

Arias stopped, closing his eyes, feeling the
warm rays of sunshine as they fell across his pelt.
The fresh air made him feel as though he could
walk for ages without tiring. He was glad that
he'd gone out, and he stopped by the edge of the
water and dipped his bill in, sucking down some
of the earthy-tasting river water. As he walked on,
it was almost a pleasant surprise to realize that the
idea of finding something to eat had occurred to
him, and it actually excited him.

Kail stopped by the edge of the river and kept
placing her own tiny talons in the same spot over
and over. She called to Arias, pouncing up and
down with flee, and he ambled over to see what
had captured her attention, freezing as he
recognized the tracks imprinted in the soft earth.
The tracks were fresh, and the long, thin
impressions were distinctly Ardeigryph in nature.
He gave Kail a little nudge.

"Why don't you ride on my back for a while?"
he asked her, and she obligingly climbed up,
stretching her nubby wings and yawning as she
returned to happily examining everything they
passed by. She had a surprisingly good grasp of
most words despite the fact she didn't speak
herself, and Arias wondered how old she really
was. He didn't remember when he'd first learned
to use words himself.

Arias felt himself lean into a crouch as he
stalked along the riverbank, his head low as he

followed the tracks away from the river and part of the way through the forest. The tracks took him around a thicket, back to the river, and up through the trees again. Arias stopped, frowning.

What kind of nonsensical pattern is this? He thought. Was this Ardeigryph trying to keep someone from following his tracks? If so, what was he afraid of? Maybe this wasn't Tybrake after all. He couldn't see the big keythong behaving so oddly as to wander aimlessly. He picked the trail up again, following it a bit faster this time, looping ahead until he could see a tree, stark and pristine in its placement. He stopped at the sight of it, his breath catching in his throat as memories took hold of him.

Ly-ra's tree had grown wonderfully, sending its branches up high to cast shade over the riverbank. It was, by blessed chance, far beyond the reach of where Jance's magick had blighted the land, and a bittersweet remembrance took hold of Arias as he pictured the plucky Kirin doe who'd accompanied him to Dantzik. He didn't have the heart to sit underneath its limbs of the tree, but he spared a murm to remember Ly-ra. She'd originally been an apprentice to Mati-jai, the Kirin elder who'd turned to dark magick, but she'd been incredibly sincere, and had turned against him to help Arias instead. Her final act had saved his life, and in the short time he'd known her, he'd felt that they'd become good friends. He wished he'd had more time to spend with her.

Arias sat down, feeling the wind rustle through

his plumage. The insignia Jance had burned into his flesh was still there on his shoulder, a silent reminder that there would always be a battle to fight. Ly-ra's tree waved slightly in the same breeze, as if in quiet tribute to the thought. After a time, Arias stood and turned, intending to take up tracking again, but be became immediately aware of the pair of eyes upon him. He frozen, taking in the figure before him. The keythong was tall and imposing and had plumage that was frayed and muddied, but his features were instantly recognizable.

"Tybrake!" Arias cried, leaping forward with glee. The keythong bristled and snarled, his wings half open, and Arias slid to a stop, his heart racing. He was horrified to realize that he'd been reaching for his mana at the sight, and he stuffed the impulse away. This wasn't some rogue, attacking beast. This was his friend. Arias scrutinized the keythong again, determining that it was indeed Tybrake and not some eerily-similar lookalike. Tybrake was still bristling, his eyes mistrusting, and Arias took a single step backwards. "It's me," Arias said. "Arias. Remember? We've been looking for you for so long, Tybrake. What happened?"

Tybrake didn't move. Beneath the mud and filth that seemed to encase every bit of him, Arias spied a long, crescent shaped wound that ran from the left side of his throat all the way up to the center of his forehead. It barely missed his eye, passing just behind it, but the eye was held a perpetual squint nonetheless. It wasn't a particularly fresh wound, but it was still raw despite some healing. His ribs shone easily through his muddy coat, and his hips jutted out at a sharp angle, each bone seeming perfectly outlined. Arias knew he himself wasn't the perfect picture of health after how little he'd eaten since Dantzik, but Tybrake looked much worse than even Hilda had been. He looked like he was on the brink of starving to death.

Kail had grown utterly quiet, perhaps sensing that there was some danger present. Arias wracked his brain on the best way to proceed; he didn't know much about head injuries, except that this one looked particularly bad. It was amazing that it hadn't gone bad, especially considering how filthy Tybrake looked.

A few leaf Fae drifted lazily around the keythong before landing on his long neck. They communicated among themselves in their unintelligible language, staring at Arias with expressions that seemed out of place. Almost hostile. Kail saw their fluttering movement and craned her neck, obviously wanting to chase them, but Arias folded his wings a little more tightly around her. *Not now, Kail,* he thought.

Tybrake slowly stopped bristling, though he shook his head, seeming agitated. "You," he finally said, his voice dry and cracked. "I didn't expect to see you here. So you made it through that gale at Dantzik."

"I did," Arias said, glad to hear him speak. "Just barely. I nearly died, but some creatures called Minotaurs helped me. And as for not expecting to see me here, well, I could say the same thing for you!" Arias tried his best to sound friendly despite his caution. That, and he didn't want Tybrake to ask him more about what had happened at Dantzik. He didn't think he could bear to speak of Hlaena, even to tell the keythong the truth.

Arias glanced to the side, noting that he had the river to one side and Tybrake to the other. The river was too deep and too fast for his liking, and he didn't want to have to attempt to fly. He also didn't very much want to entertain thoughts about what would happen if he got into a conflict with the keythong, but Tybrake was acting very odd. He wanted an easy escape, just in case. He didn't have one.

"How did you get hurt?" the other keythong asked. "Was it at Dantzik? I lost you and Brynne at the wind barrier, but we recently found Brynne again. Or, rather, she found us. She's back at the eyrie. You're going to love Sandrift, Tybrake. I can't describe how great it is."

Tybrake shook his head again, pawing at his face violently, and the leaf Fae took to the air with a burst of chittering, swarming Arias. He balked as they descended upon him, some pulling at his feathers while others bared their tiny teeth to try to nip him. They reminded him far more of Pixies than Fae, and he hissed and swatted at them. Tybrake growled, and, standing at full height and with back arched, he was a terrifying sight to behold. Arias didn't have much of a tail to tuck, but he drew himself down to become as small as possible. Kail whimpered softly, and he sent her a mental apology for bringing her along with him, though he hadn't expected any of this. He could use his flame if he had to, but he really didn't want to.

"I don't know what I did, but I'm sorry," Arias apologized, hoping to offset Tybrake's sudden temper. "Are these Fae friends to you, then?"

Tybrake didn't advance, which didn't ease Arias's mind any, but at least the Fae hurried to recircle around him instead of continuing their assault. Tybrake didn't answer his question, just held his wing out to let the Fae settle down along its length, which seemed to switch their demeanor back to a happier mood.

"I'd prefer that you didn't bother them," Tybrake finally said. "Eh…and I think that you should go. I don't want to hurt you, Arias. But before you do… Can I ask you a question?"

"Of course you can," Arias said. "But I don't understand. You seem…different. If you'd just speak to me, maybe I can help."

"Maybe," Tybrake said. "But as I said, I don't want you to get hurt. Can you tell me where Lue is?"

"She's back at Sandrift. She's worried sick about you. Larin's here too… she's at the Kirin temple. She isn't doing so well right now, but To-shin, one of the elders, says she'll be fine. I have a lot to tell you, if you want to hear it. Will you come back to see the Kirin with me at least? Maybe they could do something for that wound."

"I don't think that's a good idea," Tybrake said, looking away with his one eye. "I'll be fine here, I think."

"Tybrake –" Arias started, but the Ardeigryph was backing away.

"It's safer for you if you stay away," he said. "I get angry, and I don't know why. I can't tell what will cause it, and I don't know what I'll do when it happens. And I have trouble remembering things... A few of the Kirin have come out here looking for me, but I don't want to risk attacking one of them. So I do my best to stay out of sight. They aren't very good at tracking, so it's easy enough. I can't hurt anyone out here, and that's what matters. These Fae they keep me company, and they're too fast for me to harm. They help me, too... whatever they put in this clay seems to help, at least. I wish I could understand their language." A bit of the kindness Arias knew him for returned to his gaze as he regarded the little creatures, and he slowly pulled his wing back against his body, causing the Fae to take flight in an upward flurry of green bodies.

"You know," Tybrake continued, "I saw you, and even though I knew you, it took me a murm to remember where from and your name. If I were to see you again sometime, it would probably be the same for me. It's irritating. I don't leave this area because of that... this area is good casting, when I can get my aim right. I don't trust myself to try to find my way to anywhere else, if I'm honest. But it's alright. Don't pity me Arias… I'll be fine. I've been fine for a while now, and like I said… I can't hurt anyone out here."

"You're not fine!" Arias cried. "Tybrake, I can make out every single bone in your body right now. I don't know how often you 'get your aim right', but it's clear that either it's not often enough or the casting isn't as good here as you recall. Please, let me help you."

"No," Tybrake said, shaking his head. "I can't risk it. Thank you for finding me, though. It's nice to know that you came for me, even if I end up not remembering it tomorrow. And it's good to know that Lue is safe. I hope I remember that much."

"Don't be ridiculous," Arias said, taking a step forward. "If I leave you here, it's as good as leaving you to die."

Tybrake snarled, shaking his head again. "I'm not here to argue with you," he said, feathers beginning to bristle. "I've made my choice."

Arias wavered, and Kail cringed against him, letting out another frightened whimper. Tybrake tilted his head at the sound, noticing the cub for the first time. His good eye widened in shock as he looked from the Barbagryph cub to Arias and back.

"It's probably obvious that she isn't mine," Arias said quickly. "She's… another story, I suppose."

Tybrake stared at Kail for a murm longer, and then he let out a long, slow breath. "It was good to see you Arias, but it's probably best that you don't tell Lue you found me. I'd rather she remembered me the way I used to be. I want you all to."

He turned away, and Arias's mind raced. "Wait!" he cried, and Tybrake peered at him from over his shoulder. "Will you at least let me catch you a wriggler?"

Tybrake didn't agree, but he didn't disagree, either. The big Ardeigryph had always been particularly fond of food. He sat where he was, watching Arias with an unreadable expression, and Arias edged over to the riverbank and spread his wings, angling them forward so that they cast a shadow over the swift water. He had to step a little into the shallows to do so, but that wasn't too bad because the water only came up to his forelegs.

"Watch closely," Arias murmured to Kail, lowering his head between his outstretched wings, poised to strike. "The preymeat that lives in the water are called wrigglers. They're a bit of an acquired taste, but they're as good as any other meat. Well, at least if you ask me they are."

Kail moved forward until she was hanging on to Arias's shoulders, her line of sight partially blocked by his wings. After an uneventful few murms, Arias poked his head up to see if Tybrake was still sitting where he had been. The keythong was, and so Arias returned to his task, scanning the water. He was rewarded a murm later with a flicker of silver, and Arias sprung forward with jaws open, feeling triumphant as he felt the hook of his bill close around sleek scales. He bit down hard and turned, victorious, and Kail gave a cry of excitement upon seeing the odd creature. Tybrake stood, his eyes gleaming with interest.

"That's for me?" he asked, and even the leaf Fae around him seemed impressed by the catch. Arias nodded, crossing the distance between them and placing the wriggler on the ground nearby him. He was glad that it was a sizeable wriggler; he would've felt bad had he wasted his friend's time for nothing.

"Seale taught me that casting method," Arias said, shaking away the droplets of water that clung to his forelegs and chest. "I'm sure you remember Seale."

Tybrake nodded, eyeing the wriggler. "Aye, I do. He was a good friend."

"Well, he makes doing that look way easier," Arias said. "He said something about wrigglers being attracted to shade. I bet you'd be good at casting that way, too, since your wings are way bigger than mine. And your bill isn't quite as short."

"Maybe," Tybrake said, reaching to pick the

wriggler up. "Thanks, Arias. It makes me feel better knowing that you'll be around to take care of the others."

Arias tilted his head as he regarded the Ardeigryph. He didn't want to risk angering Tybrake again by suggesting that he come with him, but maybe he could try something else. "Do you mind if I visit you again?" he asked. "I'm staying here until Larin recovers, and I'd like to talk to you while I cast here, if that's alright."

Tybrake considered. "Well," he said slowly, "that would probably be alright, I suppose. I don't stray far from here, so I'll notice if you're anywhere near here. And we should probably keep at least this much distance between us. Just in case."

Arias nodded enthusiastically. "Alright," he said, "that sounds good. I'll see you later, then." He turned and headed back the way he'd come, holding his breath with the hope that Tybrake wouldn't change his mind. The big keythong didn't, however, and Arias nearly ran back toward the Kirin temple, feeling alight with joy. He knew things weren't perfect, but that didn't matter. *Tybrake was alive!*

***

The sun was starting to slant into its descent in the sky by the time Arias made it back to the Kirin kingdom. He paused to watch the plethora of Kirin scour the blighted forest, touching their noses to the earth for indeterminate amounts of time before moving on. Their concentration seemed absolute, which was part of why Arias was so surprised when he heard a sudden voice

"That's a lot more exhausting than it looks, Gryphon. Be glad that you don't have a master to put you to such tasks."

Arias spun around to find Lurik-ma. The doe regarded him with an indifferent expression, the trinkets that hung from her regal horns sparkling in the fading light.

"I've come to you on my own accord to say that my behavior during the dissolution spell we performed on you was… unacceptable. I risked lives due to my own selfish desires, although I do still firmly believe that I would have been the best choice among those present to take on the essence, if it came to that." She paused, as if realizing she was sliding away from an apology. "Regardless," she continued, "I was out of line, and more than a few of my respected colleagues saw a side of me I wish they hadn't. I'll shoulder the consequences of my callousness with dignity."

Arias eyed her. "Consequences?" he asked.

"Oh, yes. I've already been judged by a group of unbiased others for my actions, and my title as an elder of the council has been stripped. I could have countered it and perhaps retained my status as a result, but I declined to do so. I suppose I'm disappointed in myself for succumbing so easily to the allure of power, especially considering my prior position." She snorted. "I'll remain a teacher, which is enough. Perhaps in time I'll attempt to reclaim my title as an elder, but regardless… what's happened to me will be a worthy cautionary tale for any others who are mulling over any less-than-savory activities."

Lurik-ma regarded Arias primly as she gave a curt nod. "I heard what you did to Jance. I'd hate to say good riddance, but I don't think any of us would have had the gall to go after him the way you did. To witness a creature that had pushed himself to the height of wielding his magick was incredible in every negative sense of the word. Such awesome, horrible power… I swear I felt it when he stripped the life from this forest, and I shudder to think of what he would have been capable of with the addition of your essence. If I'm honest, when I found only myself, To-shin, and Gali-da standing against him, I was ready to consider cowardice, but in the time I could have fled, he was upon us. It's heartbreaking what happened to Gali-da. We had our differences, but she didn't deserve what happened to her. I was also told what happened to the Alicorn and to those two others Gryphons… I'm very sorry to hear it."

She turned to go then, and Arias stared after her. He didn't really want to expend the mental energy on sorting whether she was right or wrong for her intentions, and he ultimately decided that it didn't really matter. They were all just lucky to be alive still… especially when others weren't so lucky. "Lurik-ma," he said, stopping her. "I was hoping to ask you something. Do you know much about injuries?"

Lurik-ma faced him again, tilting her head. "It isn't my focus of study, but I know a bit. I could refer you to someone who knows more than me, but what would you like to know?"

"My friend has an older wound, but it's pretty bad. It runs down the entire side of his head. He doesn't act the same as I remember… and he's aware that he's different, but doesn't seem able to do anything about it. He's always been brave, but never needlessly aggressive. He is now. And he's deeply suspicious, even of me, but I think he needs my help. I'm wondering if there is anything I could do for him."

"Ah," Lurik-ma said, "so the Ardeigryph is one known by you after all. A few Kirin tried to go after him, but they couldn't pin him down. Or so I've heard. What you're speaking of isn't unheard of. The mind is a strange thing, and a spike in pugnacity isn't unusual with such injuries. We had a buckling many moons ago who endured a crippling fall when he was first learning to wind walk. He was unconscious for a few days, and when he awoke he was fearful and confused. It seemed that you could bring him food one morning, and he would have forgotten who you were by that evening. He was lucky and recovered well, however, even regaining most of his memories. Your Ardeigryph friend may change drastically over time as he recovers, although it is difficult to tell with these sorts of things. How is he overall?"

Arias pictured his friend in his mind. "Skinny and ungroomed. He looked like he should've starved to death a moon ago, though I was able to catch him a wriggler from the river to eat. I hope to bring him more food when I see him again. He at least agreed to meet with me again."

"That's good," Lurik-ma said. "Depending on his status, the world may be a frightening place for him right now. It sounds like he trusts you, at least. Try to give him every reason to continue to do so. I can task my students to find you some herbs to give him to help him to recover, if he'll eat them. Try to keep him well-fed if he can't find food on his own; he'll do much better if he has the energy with which to heal. Just don't get too optimistic… it's possible that the way he is will be the way he'll remain."

Arias nodded gratefully. "Thank you."

She gave a dismissive wave of her hoof. "It is the least I can do, after all that has happened. I'll see to it that the herbs are collected and reach you."

Lurik-ma wandered off to begin combing the desolate ground again, and Arias scanned the remaining Kirin around him for Wy-lie. While he looked, Kail clambered down from his shoulders and hit the ground at a run, calling excitedly after a group of fawns that were playing under the watchful gaze of an older buck and doe. Arias started to go after her, but after seeing the familiar reception of the group, he realized that having Kail around must not have been an uncommon occurrence. He supposed that wasn't too odd. Kail had been looked after by the Kirin for an extended period of time when she wasn't with him, after all. They had to have taken her somewhere safe, and where else made sense than with their own young?

Kail caught up to and pounced on one of the fawns, eliciting a squeak of surprise. She played with the fawn as if it were another cub, pulling at its ears and attempting to wrestle with it, while the fawn seemed largely confused by her behavior, but happy to challenge her in other feats of dexterity. The fawns mostly leaped and raced across the forest floor, and while Kail seemed more interested in chewing on her friends, the gusto with which she engaged them showed that she didn't mind the different play styles of her friends too much. They certainly seemed to be having a good time, and Arias gave a soft coo at the sight.

Steam hissed and puffed overhead, and Arias caught sight of Wy-lie drifting down over the skeletal treetops. "You've got good timing!" he called, landing in a little cloud of dust. "There's a group of peryton not too far from here. They probably won't have moved far in the time it took me to get back here. I could show you where they are if you'd like."

"I shouldn't have too much trouble finding them," Arias said. "Where did you see them?"

Wy-lie used his nose to point in the same direction as the setting sun. "Head that way until you come to where the forest hasn't died back. You'll come to a ridge—it's very hard to miss—

and the herd is grazing just beyond it. Good luck, although there are so many of them, I don't think you'll need it."

Arias nodded gratefully. "I appreciate it."

"It's not much, really. Did you learn anything about that Ardeigryph?"

"I did," Arias said. "I'm hoping to learn a little more about him when I can. He's actually a friend of mine, and he needs my help. But first things first."

***

Wy-lie's information regarding the peryton was accurate. Arias crouched in the growing shadows of twilight, watching the herd mill around, browsing on the greenery of their surroundings.

"The first rule of hunting," he whispered to Kail, who was perched atop his back, "is to be as quiet as possible. The less the prey knows you're there, the higher your chance of a successful hunt. I'll teach you all the methods I know some other time, but for now, I want you to sit here and stay hidden." He carefully scruffed the little hen and placed her onto the ground beside him, and she started to protest, causing a few peryton ears to prick up among those nearby in the herd. Arias gave her a sharp look, and she quieted.

"It's safer for you to be here, out of harm's way," he said. "You're too little for now, and hunting is dangerous. I don't want you to get hurt, but I'll let you come along on a chase when

192

you're older." The young hen seemed to find this acceptable, because she settled back, watching the wandering peryton with wide eyes and a twitching tail. Arias gestured with his beak to a group of bucks at the edge of the group. "You see the ones with the pointy things on their heads? Those are the males. They fight with their antlers. They don't have them all the time, and the ones that don't have them—the does and the fawns—tend to be smaller and easier to take."

Arias crouched low and crept forward. "Watch closely."

Kail lay flat against the ground, her ears pricked high, crimson-ringed eyes studying his every movement. Arias remained behind cover as he eased closer to the peryton, scanning for any easy targets. The large herd made enough noise to cover the sounds created by his movement through the bush, and he zeroed in on a doe and her fawn that were hanging back from the group. Arias edged a bit closer, garnering a few snuffles of alarm in his general direction. He froze, muscles taut as he waited, eyes unblinking. Most of the herd was focused on his portion of forest now, and he took in a long breath, deepening his crouch.

The tiny movement was enough to set the herd off, and they burst away on their sharp hooves, wings held ready for the first patch of open sky they saw. Fawns, of course, couldn't fly, and the one Arias had singled out was no exception. It had run only a short distance with the others before falling into a pitiful limp, and its mother circled it twice before leaping away. With very little effort, Arias seized the small creature by the neck and shook the life from it. He was glad for the food and the easy kill, although he supposed it was a little sad. He called for Kail to join him, and she came scampering through the greenery as fast as her legs could carry her.

Arias settled back, though he hadn't exerted himself enough to need to catch his breath. The idea of utilizing his flame hadn't occurred to him during the brief hunt, and he imagined the impulse would probably only arise when he truly needed it. Kail gave a piercing cry and opened her mouth, head tilted back, waiting expectantly, but Arias gently picked her up and put her back onto his back.

"I'll feed you when we get back," he said, and it slowly dawned on him that he'd have to travel through the Kirin temple with the carcass. If he'd felt a bit awkward walking through the corridors before, he could only imagine how it'd be now. *Ah well*, he thought. *May as well get it over with.*

✳✳✳

The walk back to the quarters where Larin was ended up not being as bad as Arias had feared. It was night by the time he returned, and most of the Kirin had already retired. He decided that it was fortunate that he preferred to hunt at night, and he returned to the little space he shared with Larin and Kail without incident. Kail immediately demanded to be fed, and, although she snapped down the bits of meat Arias offered her, she eventually refused until he stripped some bones of meat and cracked them open to offer her the

194

marrow within. The carcass was small enough that Arias ate most of it on his own, and then he was left with the awkward dilemma of what to do with the rest. Larin wouldn't be able to eat until she woke, and he supposed he could take the leftovers back outside to bury, but…

Arias glanced around. It was relatively cool down here, and the meat would definitely keep until morning. He'd just make sure he left early when he went to visit Tybrake. He placed what was left of the carcass into the corner of the space, and then took some of the extra grass lining Larin's bed to cover it with. He viewed his work with satisfaction, figuring that the carcass was nearly as well covered as it would have been out in the forest anyway. Then he stretched his front and hind limbs, shook out his coat, and carefully sidled in next to Larin, raising his wing so that Kail could slide underneath as he did so. With a sigh, he allowed himself to settle into a level of peace that he hadn't expected to feel ever again, and sleep claimed him.

***

Arias awoke to a cry of shock. He bolted upright, finding a horrified Kirin doe standing across from the disturbed grass pile at the corner of the space. Her eyes flashed to gold at his movement, and he froze.

"Sorry!" he blurted. "I meant to take that out of here before anyone else could find it. I just wanted to save a bit for a friend of mine instead of trying to catch something else, and I now see that I definitely should've buried it in the forest somewhere. It's from a peryton fawn… which sounds terrible, I know."

The doe's eyes slowly faded back to green. "I see," she said softly. Kail, entirely heedless of the tense nature of the situation, bounded across the quarters to play in some of the discarded grass that had been covering the carcass, using her talons to kick the thin blades up into the air. Arias gave the doe a sheepish glance.

"Usually To-shin checks on Larin," he said. "I guess I wasn't expecting anyone else. I can leave and, uhh… take that with me when I go."

"It's alright," the doe said, though clearly still a little shaken. "It just surprised me. Definitely not something I expected to find this morning." She wagged her tail in a friendly manner, using her magick to levitate a bit of grass above Kail's head, which the cub immediately leaped up to try to capture in her claws. "To-shin is resting today, so I was sent in his stead."

"Resting?" Arias asked, sitting more upright. "Is he alright?"

"Oh yes, he's quite fine. As I understand it, master To-shin is still recovering from his altercation with Jance. He walks about performing tasks as if he hasn't been ordered to several days' worth of rest, however." She rolled her eyes, and then her eyes widened. "I didn't mean that to sound disrespectful. It's just… To-shin taught me how to wind walk and wield a flame whip as a fawn. I've spent enough time with him that I know how he can be."

"Is it alright if I go to see him?" Arias asked.

"I'm sure that he'd love any distraction, but I'm inclined to ask you to leave him to solitude for now," the doe said. "Whether he agrees or not, his body truly does need the time to recover, I think. However, Lurik-ma did find me and told me to make sure I gave these to you when I came down." She used her magick to untie a series of small satchels of leaves at her neck, and when she put one of them on the ground, it fell open to reveal a number of nondescript dried items.

"It sounds like she dried them with her own flame to ensure they weren't heated too much; they retain their potency better that way," she explained. "Together, these ingredients make quite a powerful mixture. It's none of my business, but I hope you aren't planning to try to give these to your gryphoness friend. Some of these would interact quite badly with the mixture she is already being given."

Arias shook his head. "No, but thank you for bringing these to me. They're for another friend of mine, the Ardeigryph living near the river." He made an incision in the peryton meat with his beak so that he could stuff the contents of one of the satchels as completely as he could into it. He left the others where the doe had placed them for future use, hoping Tybrake wouldn't be bothered by the flavor if he tasted it.

The doe dipped her head. "I see. Forgive me for prying." She glanced at the peryton remains again before adding, "And also for waking you early."

"Not at all," Arias said. "And again, I'm sorry about all this; I won't do it again. I'll leave anything I catch outside from now on. Come on, Kail."

The little gryphoness looked at him with big eyes, circling back around to the doe and leaning affectionately against her. The doe chuckled and leaned down to nuzzle her behind the ears.

"When I'm not studying with Lurik-ma, I help watch over the fawns and take them for walks through the forest. Your cub has made friends with quite a few of the fawns. If you'd like, I can drop her off to play with the others on my way back to Lurik-ma, and bring her back here at around high-sun."

She straightened up, her ears lowering pensively. "Can I ask you another question?"

"Sure, what is it?"

"How did you end up with a cub like this? She's clearly not yours. Are Gryphs communal in watching one another's offspring?"

"Ah," Arias answered, "I'm afraid it's quite a bit less idealistic than that. When Jance was after me, he destroyed part of the mountain a flock of Barbagryph were living in. Kail appeared to have been separated from her parents, and I ended up with her. I'm not sure if her parents lived or not."

"That's terrible!" the doe said, and Kail stretched up to splay her talons against her side, head tilted at the sudden change in her voice. "Poor thing. Will you keep her, then? Or do you think there's a chance her parents are alive, and will want to return to caring for her?"

Arias stared at Kail and a somberness crept over him at the thought of never seeing her again. Of course he should look for her parents, and of course he'd return her if they were alive… right? He was silent for just a little too long, because the doe shifted awkwardly on her hooves and said,

"Sorry. Lurik-ma says I must practice having more tact in the way I speak, and I see now that it is true without a doubt. I didn't mean to cause you any upset with the question, I was just curious."

"It's alright. It's probably something I need to think about more, but I haven't. Yes, please, feel free to take Kail to play with her friends. I'll be back before long today, and I'm sure I won't have any trouble finding her if I need to."

The doe, obviously delighted, nodded enthusiastically, and Arias snatched the peryton carcass up and nodded to both of them before departing from the space with haste. He felt that he had slept too far into the morning, and his interaction with the doe had only passed more time. There were more Kirin awake than when he'd come down the night before, and he received a wide berth and exclamations of alarm from most of them when they realized what he was carrying. He kept up a brisk trot as he ascended, apologetically breaking into an ever faster gait as he reached the main floor. It was a welcome sensation when he found himself finally out in the forest again, and he almost tried to spread his wings to fly to the river, but his injured wing quickly reminded him that it wasn't a good idea. He snorted in annoyance, not changing his pace, and hurried off to see if he could find Tybrake again.

***

Tybrake wasn't hard to find. Arias paced around Ly-ra's tree for a bit, and then the keythong stalked out from the shadow of the forest, surrounded by a flurry of leaf Fae that chittered in a chiding way. Arias could see that they held tiny scoops of something viscous, and they darted toward Tybrake, spreading it over his wound despite his attempts to duck away.

Curious, Arias wondered whether Tybrake wasn't covered in filth after all, but some sort of mixture the leaf Fae had been trying to help him with. The tiny creatures him with the same air of hostility as they had the previous day, and he tried his best not to antagonize them as he approached. He pulled a loose feather free and extended it in the hope one of them would take it, but they seemed much less easily entertained than the wind Fae he'd met before. When Tybrake was near enough, he nudged the preymeat toward him.

"I went hunting last night, and it was too

200

much for just Kail and I. So I figured I'd bring some for you. One of the Kirin concocted some sort of herbal remedy that she said will help you. I don't think you should be able to taste it, though."

Tybrake sat down across from the meat. Then he looked at Arias and said, "Arias, can I ask you something?"

"Of course."

"I can trust you, right?"

Arias frowned. "Of course you can."

"Alright."

Arias paused. "Is there a reason you'd ask that?"

"I have a lot of memories of you and the others. I can't remember much beyond trying to get through that wind barrier with you and Brynne and Ly-ra. If I'm honest, I can't even recall what we talked about the last time I saw you, Arias. When I woke up alone and broken near Dantzik, I believed I'd die there. But then these leaf Fae took interest in me, and they did their best to help me, so I tried not to give up. I eventually was able to make it back here, and I decided to stay because at least I knew this area was relatively safe and had food and water, but... I don't know. My memories seem deceptive sometimes, it's hard for me to know what's real. Every now and then I figure that no one came for me because no one really cared, which is silly since I certainly didn't make it easy to find me, by doing my best to hide out."

"I wasn't lying when I said we looked for you," Arias said. "And I'm not lying when I say how happy everyone will be to know that you're alive. You're not a bad Gryph, Tybrake, I know that you're not. You said yourself that you don't want to hurt anyone, and I'm sure that we can find a way that you won't. If you wanted to come back to Sandrift, I'm sure no one will even mind your leaf Fae friends… well, not so long as they don't go around biting and pulling out feathers."

Tybrake didn't seem amused by the quip, and instead he looked up at Arias with a sad gaze. Arias sighed. "I don't know a lot about the injuries you've sustained, but I asked the Kirin who provided that medicine about it. She said there's quite a good chance that you'll recover alright. You just have to give it some time, I'm sure."

Tybrake poked the meat with his long bill, looking doubtful. "I hope you're right. To be honest, I really would like to come back with you. I just don't want to risk frightening anyone. I'm not exactly a small creature."

"Wait until you meet a fully grown Barbagryph," Arias said. "Brynne is friends with one who makes you look like a yearling." One of the leaf Fae drifted over to him to inspect him up close, looking surprisingly haughty despite its tiny size. Arias tried to ignore it as it fluttered up over his head and attempted to peer into his ears, drawing a few more of its kind to join it in its adventure. "Do you have names for the Fae?" he asked.

"Not really; it can be hard to tell them apart sometimes if I'm totally honest. But they keep me company and they always let me know when someone is around. They even manage to catch me little wrigglers sometimes. I've grown to like them a lot."

Arias shook his head as one of the leaf Fae plucked at his ear fur, and they all scurried back over to Tybrake with cries of alarm. He tensed for a reaction from his friend, but Tybrake seemed mildly amused more than anything else.

"Tybrake," Arias said carefully, "Why don't you come back to the Kirin temple with me? It's beginning to get cold at night. I don't like the idea of you being out here by yourself."

Tybrake immediately attuned a look of irritation, and Arias relented. "Alright, alright," he said, "but I have another idea. Since you have trouble remembering things, why don't you go ahead and ask me any questions about anything you may have on your mind? I'll answer them if I can, and I won't mind if you end up asking the same questions over and over again. Maybe it'll help."

For the first time since he'd seen him, Tybrake actually looked a little excited. "Alright," he said. He paused before adding, "You're every bit as good of a friend as I remember, Arias. Thank you for that. And I'm sorry in advance for any trouble I end up causing. I can't control it, I've tried."

Arias shook his head. "Don't you worry about it for even a murm," he said. "It'll be alright." He lay down then, crossing his forelegs and watching the river flash by under the light of early morning. Tybrake ate the preymeat he'd brought him, and, when he was done, he sat down as well. After a while, he asked,

"Will you tell me what happened after Dantzik?"

Arias froze. He wasn't sure if he was ready to speak of it, not just because he wasn't sure if he should tell Tybrake the truth, but because he didn't know if he was ready to revisit everything. But he'd told the keythong that he could ask him anything, and he felt that Tybrake deserved to know. He nodded.

"Yeah," he said. "I'll tell you everything."

***

Tybrake was silent for a long time after Arias finished recounting the events after Dantzik. He stared at the ground, his long neck bowed, and even the earth Fae ceased their fluttering movement. "I wish I had been there for you, Arias," he finally said. "I guess I believed that you had all figured everything out and were living happily. It made it easier for me to accept my isolation here. I'll try my best to remember what you've told me, so that I won't ask again. I can tell that it isn't something you wanted to speak of.

I'm sorry for what happened to Ly-ra and Hlaena, I truly am."

Arias nodded quietly, watching the last of the morning mist dissipate from the river. He turned to Tybrake, standing. "I'm really glad I found you, Tybrake. Talking to you makes me feel better somehow… I missed you a lot. I can probably come by again later today if you're around, but for now, I think I'll head back to the temple. I left Kail to go play with some Kirin fawns, and I should be back so that she won't be alone when she is dropped off at Larin's chamber."

Tybrake looked a little crestfallen at his sudden announcement, but he nodded. Arias held his good wing out to him. "Hey," he said brightly, "promise me you'll consider coming back with me sometime? It doesn't have to be today, but I'd worry a lot less if you did."

Tybrake hesitated. "What if something bad —"

"It won't," Arias said firmly. "I'll speak to To-shin about it first, but you don't have to worry about that."

Tybrake stretched his wing out over Arias's, dwarfing it, and then the Ardeigryph tentatively reached out to cross necks with Arias. "Alright," he said. "I will."

CHAPTER ELEVEN

Arias had fallen into a routine of sorts at the Kirin temple. In the mornings, he checked to see if there was anything that Larin needed. If the Kirin needed more herbs for her, he made note to go out later in the day to get them, and if they didn't need herbs, he sometimes joined the groups that went out to forage for their feed. He had no interest in eating the greens, of course, and the Kirin harvested much more efficiently than he did using their magick, but he tried his best to be useful to them. It was clear that they didn't need his help, and indeed, it seemed that they let him help more for his own benefit than anything. The Kirin were incredibly self-sufficient, even after the upheaval Jance had caused them.

During the day, Arias either took Kail to play with the Kirin fawns or he brought her along with him on his daily tasks. She was still much too young to seriously do anything more than play, but she was an astute observer and paid attention whenever he took her with him to hunt or gather. He introduced her to tracking, taught her the proper way to mark trees, and let her sit in on his hunts, including many that resolved quite unsuccessfully. When they weren't hunting, he showed her herbs and taught her of their uses, and she even helped him to pick some for Larin. Inevitably, her attention was always drawn away by a particularly interesting hollow in a tree or a buzzing insect, and he'd chuckle and leave her to her romping. There would be plenty of time for serious lessons later, after all.

Arias left the herbs in the quarters he shared with Larin and Kail, and they vanished and were returned as dried bundles, which he took with him when he visited Tybrake. Arias continued taking Tybrake parts of his kills and casting with him along the river. He took Kail with him a few times, and Tybrake was immediately captivated with her. Kail busied herself with trying to climb his stilt-like legs and attempting to leap up and hang from his neck, and the leaf Fae taught her very quickly that they weren't small playthings. Arias had grown at ease around his old friend again, and while Tybrake was certainly more irritable than he'd been in the past, he hadn't shown any serious indication of being physically dangerous. His explosive temper was mostly confined to growling, snapping, and bristling, and the outbursts always ended without much incident. Whenever he was with the keythong, Arias did end up repeating himself quite a bit, but he didn't mind. Besides, Tybrake seemed to have improved a little bit already, as Arias thought he was asking the same questions a little less frequently each day.

It wasn't long before Arias's wing healed enough to fly with, though the doe who came in the mornings to attend to Larin warned him not to overexert the appendage. Arias promised he wouldn't. He was planning to head out for a little test flight, but To-shin ended up disturbing his plans. The elder buck had recovered fully and gone back to teaching, but his curiosity drove him to ask Arias to display his magickal abilities for him. Arias hesitantly followed the elder buck out into the still-decimated forest, where he soon found himself under the watch of To-shin's expectant eyes.

"Go on, show me what you can do," To-shin urged, sitting down just off to Arias's side. The forest was still mostly quiet, though the sounds of the dawn chorus were beginning to creep in again. "Don't worry, there isn't much here to burn, and I'll make sure things don't get out of control. Look there," he said, pointing with his nose. "Why don't you see if you can burn that stump?"

Arias peered at the small, jagged chunk of wood that rose up just a few steps before him. He opened his beak, concentrating on the reserve of mana within him. It flowed like a fluid thing, seeming almost inquisitive in the way it reacted to his bidding, and he felt it flare as he breathed out a tendril of flame. With a steady stream, the wood may have caught completely aflame, but instead Arias's fire danced merrily across its surface for a moment before flickering out, leaving behind black char. To-shin nodded approvingly.

"Can you change the output of flame?"

Arias nodded, altering how much mana he pulled. He breathed a roaring burst of fire, and then decreased it to a tiny ember. To-shin stood, excited, and then used his magick to drag a small stone over.

"Can you pick that up?" he asked.

Arias stared at the stone, unsure of how to do such a thing. He looked at To-shin. "How?"

"Ah, that's fair," To-shin said. "It's either something you'd instinctively be able to grasp or not, and it appears that you can't. Not all creatures capable of magick can manipulate objects with it." He threw the stone away from them again. "Some things will come to you with practice, I imagine."

"I managed to start a fire a distance away from me when I caught up to Jance," Arias said. "It wasn't easy."

"Interesting," To-shin said. "You are a hybrid of sorts, Arias, something that has probably never been seen before. It will be quite a journey to see what you end up being capable of. Can you control the heat output of the flames?"

Arias shook his head. He remembered Aaga the Phoenix being able to not burn him with his fire, but he wasn't sure how he'd done it. "Not that I'm aware of," he said.

To-shin nodded again, his gaze growing serious. He looked at Arias.

"Your abilities will give you an edge over the rest of your kind," he said, "and it's uncertain how being magicked will change you in the long term. I don't think there is any way to speculate whether your lifespan, your progeny, or any other number of factors will be affected. In regard to what you are now, Arias, I won't veil my words. The path to villainy is much thinner than you may think. I suspect that your albinism has already set you apart from your kind in some respects, and I… I suppose I fear what further divide may be possible due to your new ability. I have a few good years left in me yet, and while I know that I'm not a Gryphon, I hope you know that you're always welcome here, young Arias. And I'm not just saying that because I'm interested in tracking any changes you may undergo as you discover the extent of your abilities."

He said the last bit with a smirk, and Arias gave a soft snort. When he met the elder's eyes, there was a softness to them, and it reminded him of the way Xio used to stare at him. He bowed his head.

"Thank you, To-shin. I appreciate that."

To-shin looked as if he'd been about to find another object to test, but instead he looked up as the doe who attended Larin wind walked over to them.

"I have some good news," she said, landing. "The black gryphoness is awake."

***

Arias shrieked with such joy that a number of Kirin poked their heads into the chamber he was in, concerned. He nearly crushed Larin in his zeal to embrace her, and then nearly trampled both Kail, To-shin, and the doe as he bounded up and down in fantastic leaps of joy. He pressed in close to Larin, his entire body feeling alight with jubilation, and she gave a soft, weak chirp.

"We're in the Kirin temple," he told her, nuzzling the glossy feathers at the base of her neck. "You're safe here. Kail's here, too! The cub you saved at Hollowcrypt."

Larin ruffled her feathers and closed her eyes again, and after a while the doe gently shooed him away. "She'll be up before you know it," she said, "but for now it's best if you leave her to rest. *Quietly*," she added, ushering him back into the corridor. Arias reluctantly did as she asked, but the instant he was outside again, his heart soared. He threw himself skyward, his wings taking him high above the temple and the forest, and he screamed for joy again, the wind buoying him upward as if celebrating alongside him. In that moment, he finally felt optimism for the future again.

He finally felt free.

***

Time pressed by in a blur, and soon the trees on the outer perimeter of the Kirin temple were displaying vibrant scarlet and gold leaves. The sprouting vegetation that had been carefully cultivated where Jance's magick had destroyed the existing flora seemed to pause, their tightly-wrapped budding leaves tentative in the cooling weather. The new greenery would have to endure the chill of winter before long, but the Kirin were determined that the forest would grow back just fine. Watching the leaves begin to fall, Arias found himself again worrying about Tybrake, but the other keythong had assured him that winters spent by the sea at his native Oceanside eyrie had been much cooler than anything he'd experienced so far in the forest. Tybrake still forgot things here and there, but he'd become rather adept at recalling their prior conversations. Arias had even glimpsed a return of the easygoing personality he'd come to know the Ardeigryph for.

Larin, as stubborn as ever, spent most of her time trying to escape her confinement within the Kirin temple. To-shin had tried to convince her and Arias that she should be especially careful about the cooling temperatures outside, and while Arias had believed him, Larin's opinion had included plenty of eye rolling. Arias had tried to resist telling her about Tybrake too soon, as he knew that she'd see it as a reason to go out to visit him, but it was also hard to keep anything from her. It wasn't the only secret that Arias kept… he hadn't told her about Hlaena yet. He was afraid that she'd think it was her fault. But he knew he'd eventually have to, and the knowledge of that looming murm was enough to wear him down faster than if she'd inquired herself. *It isn't fair not to tell her*, he told himself. If he were her, he'd want to know, wouldn't he? Nothing he could add to the explanation would make it any less painful, and so as they settled in to sleep a few days after she'd first awoken, Arias took a deep breath and forced himself to tell her everything. She pricked her ears upon hearing about Tybrake, but when he spoke of Hlaena, almost immediately she turned inward, and he knew that his fears had come true. She blamed herself.

It was in the way Larin averted her eyes around him, it inhabited the atypical silence that rose up between them, and it was evident in the disappearance of her fiery nature. She stopped trying to escape her confines, and she seemed to slink meekly about the corridors of the temple instead of walking them, relegating any attempt Arias made to reach her with thick silence. It tore Arias apart, and, more than a few times, he questioned whether he should have told her the truth at all. It was an uncomfortable revelation to realize that what he was experiencing now was probably what she had faced when she'd watched him wasting away back in Sandrift, and that made him feel even worse. Arias had only to look into her distant gaze to understand that she was visiting every scenario in which her actions didn't result in the deaths of Hlaena and Hilda, and when he remembered how hard it had been for him to come to terms with his own guilt, he realized that there was nothing he could do to alleviate her pain. So he left her alone, though he stayed by her side; unobtrusive, but close enough to be there if she ever needed him.

***

When the Kirin cleared Larin to go outdoors, Arias had initially gone everywhere with her, worried. She'd progressed from trekking through the forest, to sprinting down prey trails, to finally comfortably flying the borders of the Kirin kingdom without having to stop to rest, and Arias had finally calmed himself enough to stop being concerned for her every murm that he couldn't see her. She'd promised to visit Tybrake only if Arias came along as well since Arias had told her about Tybrake's somewhat unpredictable personality, but Arias hadn't counted on Tybrake seeking her out himself. She arrived one evening at sunset with Tybrake trotting along behind her, his neck hung in an apologetic curve upon seeing Arias.

"I know how it must look since I said I'd come here but always found an excuse not to… but when I looked up and thought I saw Larin flying overhead, I just had to try to track her down. I guess I only just realized that she probably out-flew me on purpose to get me to follow her here…"

Larin looked just a tad smug as she entered the temple, and Tybrake paused as he peered at the Kirin who stared at him with curious gazes from within. "It's alright," Arias said. "Come on, I'll show you where we sleep."

***

Despite Tybrake's earlier resistance, he quickly became amiable to the idea of staying the night with Arias, Larin, and Kail. The Kirin allowed the presence of another Gryph, and most seemed to recognize Tybrake as the same elusive Ardeigryph

214

from the forest. Interestingly enough, the leaf Fae that typically attended him refused to enter their temple for any reason. Inextricably tied to the forest, they zipped away from him whenever he stepped through the main threshold, but immediately rejoined his company the instant he entered into their woodland domain.

For Arias, things began to feel a bit like old times. He and his friends slept together, rose early together, hunted together, and spent their time helping the Kirin together. He told them about his ability to use magick, and showed them once they were outside, and while it initially frightened them, he showed them that he could control it. They then developed an air of curiosity in regard to it, though they remained uneasy about it.

Tybrake continued to improve, and in time he easily learned to find his way back to the quarters they shared on his own. He was more and more like the Tybrake Arias remembered, and for that he was grateful. Tybrake's wounds healed well, and he remained sighted in both eyes, although he still held the one that had been on the damaged side of his head in a perpetual squint.

Larin slipped back into her role as leader without thinking anything of it, taking point on all of the group's hunting and tracking ventures. When Arias and Tybrake woke she was often already awake, either playing quietly with Kail or sitting off on her own. When Arias eventually decided to jokingly challenge her to a spar, she'd quickly pinned him, and he'd tried with genuine effort the next time to the same result. Lying there flat on his back, he accepted that she'd fully recovered from her injuries. The spicy personality he knew and loved her for also returned in full force, and though he was glad to see it, he still found himself worrying about her.

Without much in the way of immediate worries, Arias and his friends put on desperately-needed weight, and not a murm too soon. The snow that started to drift down in flurries made them thankful for every piece of down and fat they had to cover their ribs with. Arias felt better than he had for moons. He still had murms when the past came back to torment him, but he stayed busy enough and in the company of his friends enough to ensure that the brighter bits of his days began to easily overshadow the darker ones. And then, of course, there was Kail.

Neither Arias nor Larin nor Tybrake knew a thing about cubs, so it was an interesting surprise when one day the Barbagryph hen started to speak. She'd been so quiet for most of the time that Arias had cared for her that he'd wondered a few times if she was mute; but no, her small, incoherent bits of words and phrases soon widened into a full tirade of endless questions and sentences. Indeed, Arias couldn't remember when he'd learned to speak, and he couldn't remember much from the time before he could. With Kail, it seemed that the murm she had a grasp on communication, her sassy nature blossomed.

When Kail was hungry, she was hungry *right then*. She found she had the ability to produce an ear-piercing shriek that had made Arias scruff her more than once, and she'd been in trouble multiple times for playing too rough with her fawn counterparts, though the Kirin had assured Arias and the others that it wasn't too serious. Arias had been met with a blank stare when he'd tried to explain that not every creature wanted to play by biting and with claws, and he sighed deeply after trying to find a suitable example to help her to understand. He didn't know how the Alicorns had put up with him as a cub if he was anywhere near what Kail was like. Indeed, without the help of the Kirin, Tybrake, and Larin, he wasn't sure how he'd have continued to cope.

The only creature Kail seemed to obey totally and without reason was Larin. She absorbed every bit of information the hen had taught her, and could already communicate with her using a range of clicks, whistles, and body language that Arias was still struggling to catch onto. And everything that Kail learned was subject to being double-checked with Larin first, whether it was the proper technique to preen oneself, determining whether a track belonged to a peryton or a tusker, or whether the sun stayed up longer than the moon. Perhaps only naturally, the cub had treated Arias, Larin, and Tybrake all as guardian figures, though Arias had carefully explained to her that none of them were her true parents. She'd listened, but hadn't seemed to care. Watching her zoom through the Kirin temple, stalk every living and non-living creature she could find, and pretend to fly from every small incline, Arias wondered if it really mattered. She was clearly happy, and quite unconcerned with her origins… for now, at least.

Interacting with Kail reminded Arias of how he'd eventually wanted to know more about other Gryphons despite having everything he needed to survive and be happy in Glendale with the Alicorns. If Kail ever wanted the same thing, he would make sure that she could have it… though he carefully avoided thinking of a scenario in which she ended up being given back to the care of her real parents.

Despite the little paradise Arias had temporarily slipped into enjoying with his friends, he knew that it couldn't last forever. Before a full moon had passed and come again, Larin had snapped awake to the sound of hurried hoof falls heading down their corridor. She'd nudged Arias and Tybrake awake, and they were already on their feet by the time Wy-lie poked his nose into the chamber.

"The guards sent me to wake you. Someone is here to see you. She said her name is Lue."

***

Arias sprinted to the upper level of the Kirin temple, Kail holding tight to the ruff of feathers around his neck as he went, and Larin and Tybrake were close behind him. He zipped through the main entrance with such speed that Lue actually scrambled back a few steps, pausing to stare at him with wide eyes, one talon raised. Before he could even begin to question her, however, her bill dropped open and her eyes went even wider, staring straight past him. She took a single, stiff step forward, her crest raised, and Arias followed her gaze to where Tybrake had grinded to a halt just outside the entrance. They stood there in the snow, neither speaking, both unmoving. Finally, Tybrake whispered in a barely-audible voice,

"Is it really you? Or am I dreaming again?"

Lue drifted toward Tybrake like she was afraid that, if she moved too quickly, he might disappear. When she was close enough to touch him, she buried herself into him, and Tybrake crossed his long neck over hers, pulling her closer to him. Arias leaned against Larin, and the two cooed at the sweet sight. It seemed cruel to break them from their reunion, but Arias had to know why she'd come. He figured that if anyone would have come to call for them, it would have been Brynne.

"Lue," Arias said, tentative, "Why are you here at this time of night? Is everything alright? Where's Brynne?"

Lue looked up at him, still entwined with Tybrake, and her expression darkened. "The mountain the Barbagryph had been living in caved in a few days ago. We all felt it even if we didn't see it… the dust took most of a morning just to settle. They blamed Sandrift for it, and one of their leaders asked after you. They said, 'blood has to be paid with blood.' Bala tried to reason with them, but they wouldn't hear it and attacked anyway. He was taken captive, no one has any idea where he is. Brynne is trying to find out; she rallied some Gryphs to fight back, but it soon became clear that those Barbagryph aren't standing alone. The Pale is helping them to try to take Sandrift."

"Then what are we waiting for?" Tybrake snarled. "Let's go drive them out."

Larin obviously shared the same sentiment, but Arias found himself shaking his head. "It's safer for you all here, maybe I can go and sort this out."

"No way," Tybrake growled. "I may not know what's going on entirely, but I know that I'm not just going to sit around here being safe while Bala is held captive. You can try to appeal to the attackers' better natures while we keep the flock safe."

Lue nodded in agreement. "There has to be something we can do, Arias, and we won't figure it out by sitting around here. Brynne and the others are in harm's way *now*. We already tried speaking with those other Gryphs, and look what happened. They clearly don't want to talk."

"It sounds like they let their actions speak for them," Tybrake said. "I say it's time that we do the same."

"Uhh… it's probably none of my business, but is everything alright?"

Everyone whirled around to find Wy-lie standing behind them, the buckling's two spike horns glinting in the moonlight. Lue stared with a particularly rapt intensity, having heard of but never seen a Kirin before. Wy-lie shuffled uncomfortably under their gazes.

"Ah… sorry. I didn't mean to eavesdrop or anything. When you all came out here with such haste, I followed and… well." He gestured to the entrance. "It's not air tight or anything, so I maybe heard a little."

Arias found himself hesitating as he looked down at Wy-lie. If he told him the truth, he'd almost certainly tell To-shin about it, and then what? Could he really expect the Kirin to be involved in every issue that rose up among him and his flockmates? As if in affirmation of his thoughts, Wy-lie added, "I can wake my master if you'd like."

"No," Arias said. "Thank you, Wy-lie, truly. However, I'm afraid that this is something that we'll have to handle ourselves. I do have one favor to ask, however." He turned to gently grab Kail, placing her on the ground at his feet. "Is it alright if we leave Kail here for a little while?"

Kail stamped a tiny talon, indignant. "Not fair!" she cried in her shrill, tiny voice. "Why? I want to go with you."

Wy-lie looked at Arias, and something in his eyes must have communicated the seriousness of the situation, because he didn't ask any other questions. He walked over to nuzzle Kail between her ears. "I'm sure they'll be back soon. Besides, there's something I've been meaning to tell you."

Kail looked up at him with a sharp gaze, and he leaned down conspiratorially. "Zin-ha said he could easily beat you in a race."

"What! No he can't. Wake him up!" Kail shouted, indignant. "I'll beat him right now!"

Wy-lie carefully guided her back toward the entrance. "We should let him get some sleep so that he won't have any excuses when you beat him tomorrow. But for now, I bet I can get away with showing you the crystal corridor, since no one else is awake…"

Wy-lie cast a final look over his shoulder as he passed through the entryway, and Arias gave him a grateful nod. He turned to his friends, their feathers rustling in the chilly air.

"Let's go," he said, spreading his wings. One by one, they took off into the darkened sky, unsure of what they'd find when they reached Sandrift.

CHAPTER TWELVE

It had been so long since Arias had flown any considerable distance that he'd forgotten how it felt to fly high and fast, particularly in the presence of other Gryphs. Lue flew point, her long, narrow wings breaking the wind ahead of the rest of them. Under normal circumstances, the moonlit flight would have been pleasurable. The sky was clear and, while the breeze was chilly, it was at their backs, granting speed to their travel. Arias had hoped, naively perhaps, that while on their journey they could come up with some ideas regarding the situation they were heading into, but the flight had remained dead silent. He couldn't think of anything himself, so he couldn't fault his friends for their lack of communication.

As they approached Sandrift eyrie, throngs of Barbagryph took flight to close in around them, leaving the claw-marked and feather-strewn earth in a great rustling of wings. The gigantic bone-eaters made their intentions clear, snarling and swooping in close, and Arias gave a warning hiss.

"We aren't here to fight. I'm hoping to speak with Talia."

One of the Barbagryph eased in so that she was flying above Arias, her size dwarfing him. She barked a grim laugh down at him. "The time for speaking is long past. If you were hoping not to fight, you should've turned back long ago!"

The hen tucked her wings and dove into Arias, seizing him by the shoulders and driving him downward. A flurry of shrieks up above signaled that the rest of his friends had been set upon, and Arias growled, pulling at his mana. He craned his neck backwards so that he was looking directly up at the hen, took a deep breath, and spat a burst of flame into her face, eliciting a shrill howl of pain from her. She threw him away from her, her plumage alight as she cartwheeled through the air. Her agonized screaming cut off long before she hit the ground.

Arias regained his flight, righting himself and flying up to rejoin his friends. The other Barbagryph were already clearing off by the time he made it to them, and Lue gave him a particularly wide berth. He saw the fear in her eyes, and he realized he hadn't had time to explain things to her.

"Wind and waves, Arias, what was that?" she cried.

"I know it's strange, but it's alright. I'll tell you

the whole story when I can, but this is something that I can do now. Please don't be afraid."

She didn't move closer to him and he could see that she had questions, but they'd have to wait. Larin clicked, looking down, and Arias followed her gaze to see Brynne sitting in the upper limbs of a tree, waving her bright wings to capture their attention. They all dipped low to fly down to her, and when she caught sight of Tybrake, she nearly fell from her perch. Arias and the others landed at the base of the tree, and Brynne ran toward Tybrake at a full sprint, her eyes sparkling.

"I'd hoped it was you!" she cried. Tybrake responded by arching his back and hissing, and she skidded to a stop and jumped back.

"Tybrake?" she asked, confused, and he slowly settled back onto his haunches.

"I'm sorry," the big keythong rumbled, his plumage slowly settling. "You startled me… I didn't mean that. It's good to see you too, Brynne."

Brynne frowned, but as with other things, it would have to wait. She turned to Arias. "Where's Hilda?"

Arias paused, glancing at Larin. "She didn't make it."

Brynne nodded, her eyes hard. "We found where they're keeping Bala, but we're waiting for the right time to try to get him back. A lot of the flock fled the moment the fighting started, and I don't blame them."

"Where's Roarick?" Arias asked. He'd become accustomed to seeing the keythong with her.

"He's safe. We're staying at the cove near the beach, the same one we stayed in when we originally made it to this land. We should head there as well. I'd rather not sit out here in the open longer than I have to."

Arias nodded, falling into step behind her. They kept to traveling on claw, their eyes and ears alert, until they made it to the cove. It looked abandoned from afar, although the closer they got, the more easily Arias could note eyes peeking out to view their arrival. Larin's Sentinels immediately rushed to her upon seeing her, surrounding her with obvious concern, but she shook her head and gestured to the cove, clicking urgently. She sat down, and watched and listened as they started to describe recent events to her, each Gryphon taking a turn to explain.

Arias entered the cove and took a look around at the Gryphs present, and while it was a goodly amount, it was nowhere near enough to make him feel comfortable with their defenses. Only a few had seen the losing side of a battle judging by their lack of wounds, and, by the way they confidently tipped their heads toward him when they saw him, Brynne had done a good job of keeping their spirits high.

Tybrake and Lue sat near Larin as she received updates from the others, and the sight somehow made Arias worry. His eyes lingered on Larin; they'd sparred and play fought plenty in the Kirin kingdom, but she hadn't seen a real battle since Jance had injured her. He knew she'd ignore any suggestion of his not to defend their home, but the idea of her getting hurt again scared him.

Brynne gestured for Arias to follow her further into the cove, and he hurried to catch up to her. She settled down to speak, but he couldn't help but notice the heap of fur and feathers just behind her, sitting far back beneath the overhang of a ledge. A pair of crimson-ringed eyes peered out from the shadows.

"Roarick?" Arias asked.

The eyes looked away.

"He'll be alright," Brynne said. "He's just worried." She called out, and everyone in the cove drew nearer to her to hear what she had to say.

"Before the enemy has a chance to gain any more ground on this eyrie, we should strike," she started. "There's still a chance that we can drive them off this territory, and, lest anyone forget, nothing good awaits us if we lose Sandrift. We've fought to get this far, let's fight a little more to keep what we have."

A cheer rose up in agreement from those gathered, and Arias eased forward, careful in his wording.

"We cannot and should not abandon Sandrift," he said. "We also shouldn't ignore the fact that the Barbagryph would still have a viable eyrie if not for what happened with Jance. Some of you may know the story, most of you probably don't, but either way, the blame falls on many for the way this situation has turned out. I'm hoping that, if I can speak to the Matriarch of Hollowcrypt, maybe we can come to some sort of agreement that avoids bloodshed. Aside from that, the Pale has been a growing issue for quite some time now. In my opinion, they shouldn't be offered the same leniency as the Barbagryph. They've preyed upon this situation for their own benefit, and their decision to use this unrest to further their own goals more than shows their true intentions."

"The Pale and Hollowcrypt are one and the same if you ask me," an Ardeigryph hen growled. "They're trying to drive us out of here by combining their forces, so I'm dropping any enemy I can get my beak through regardless of whether they're Gryphon or Barbagryph."

A few murmured their agreement with her, and Arias took a deep breath. "Let me attempt to speak with the Matriarch first," he said. "And then drastic decisions can be made. I think they're holding me responsible for this entire mess, anyway."

"Talia isn't the sole leader," Roarick said quietly. Heads swung around to look at him, and he reflexively looked away from them.

"What do you mean?" Brynne asked.

"Hollowcrypt had three leaders. We had two Matriarchs and a Sire, but it looks like one of the Matriarchs died in the cave in, from what I've heard during your discussions. I keep hearing the names Talia and Swiften… and I can guarantee that at least one of them is out for blood, and he's going to be the more popular of the two in this battle."

"So then, the choice is easy. It's decided," a young Gryphon keythong said. "A Barbagryph himself admits that the leadership of his kind is planning to ruin us. Let's do it to them before they can have a chance to crush us!"

"Aside from that, if we allow you to go to speak to their leaders, you may just end up being caught as well, Arias," the same Ardeigryph hen from before said. "We'd be in a far worse place if that happened."

"I have to try," Arias said. "The chance to avoid further bloodshed makes it worth the risk. And…" He looked at the gathered Gryphs, and To-shin's words seemed to sound in his head.

I fear what further divide may be possible due to your new ability.

"I know it sounds like pure stupidity, but please don't worry about my safety," he said. "I don't think they'll try to capture me, even if they end up not agreeing with what I have to say."

No one spoke directly to him, but the uncertainty in the room was so thick that Arias felt as if it were almost tangible.

"Fine," Brynne finally said, "you can go attempt to smooth things out, but if that fails, we can't just leave Bala to his fate. I'm coming with you —"

"No," Arias said quickly. "I won't put anyone else in danger. I'm doing this alone." He flattened his ears as Brynne opened her mouth to retort. "I'm not going to argue the point," he said.

Another silence fell over the gathering. Many glanced at him as if he'd gone mad, but no one spoke against him. Perhaps they thought themselves foolish for having followed this flock to its apparent ruin, or perhaps they wished they'd fled long ago like the others had. Maybe a few actually believed in him. He couldn't tell.

"Do what you want, Arias," Brynne said. "But if dusk falls and you still aren't back, we strike."

Arias nodded, and the meeting slowly dissolved. Some headed out to rejoin guard patrol, others settled down to discuss battle tactics, and a few brave souls prepared to do a little covert hunting. It would be a necessity eventually, although food was probably the furthest thing from anyone's minds at the moment.

Arias found himself glancing at Roarick again. The keythong met his gaze with reluctance.

"I didn't mean for any of this to happen," he murmured. "I was just trying to help."

"I know," Arias said. "You didn't do anything wrong, Roarick."

"It feels like I did. I should never have brought you to Hollowcrypt, but I couldn't think of anything else to do. I didn't know Jance would do what he did."

"None of us knew," Arias said. "You can't blame yourself for the terrible thing another creature did, Roarick. I wanted to do the same thing, but neither of us could have anticipated what happened. The fault lies with Jance." He paused. "I don't know if it was right or wrong, but I killed him, Roarick. Maybe there was another way, but… I don't regret it."

Roarick stared at him, shocked, and Arias turned away, walking toward where Brynne had started to catch up with Tybrake and Larin. "Alright, Brynne," he said. "Tell me where I can find either Talia or Swiften… whichever has Bala."

***

Arias flew low above Sandrift, heading past the den complex and into the westernmost reaches of the forest. He didn't want to draw undue attention to himself, but it didn't take long for him to hear Barbagryph cries of alarm, and within a few murms many were flying after him.

He ignored them as he flew, finding the spot
Brynne had spoken of without difficulty. The
little clearing in the forest was heavily occupied,
and Bala was the only Ardeigryph visible among
all the Barbagryph and Gryphon warriors. Arias
slanted into a descent and landed, and was
immediately surrounded. Bala looked hopeful
despite his battered appearance, and Arias
grimaced at the bite and claw wounds his body. It
was clear that he hadn't been treated kindly.

Arias didn't have to ask to see either Swiften
or Talia; an older Barbagryph keythong pushed
his way through the ranks to eye him. He was
thin and gaunt for his age, but powerful looking
nonetheless. Most of the others shuffled
backwards to give him a respectful buffer of
space, though one Gryphon keythong remained
near him. The Gryphon was a little older than
Arias, and slate gray with eyes of the same color,
his coat marred with new and old scars, some
overlapping. The old Barbagryph circled Arias
slowly, eyeing him.

"So the fool delivers himself to us on own his
accord," he said. "It's regretful that we won't be
able to hunt you down and drag you screaming to
your death. I was quite looking forward to that.
Those who died in Hollowcrypt didn't have the
luxury of a swift death, did they? Cubs alone and
without their parents, their small bodies trapped
beneath the lightless rock even now… entire
generations of knowledge swept away due to your
folly. As for the one who helped you, that
Roarick, well… at least you had the gall to show
your wretched face on your own. I imagine the

hunt to throw him to his judgment will be particularly zealous."

His expression darkened as he came to a stop, looking him up and down. "I warned Talia that letting your kind settle in along the coast was a mistake," he spat. "Of course I was right; maybe now she finally believes me. What is your name, cursed one, that I may condemn it as I, Swiften, cast your unworthy bones into the deepest crevasse I can find?"

"My name is Arias," Arias said, "and I don't wish to disrespect the tragedy that has befallen your kind, but you shouldn't blame Roarick. He was only trying to help."

"Don't blame Roarick," Swiften said mockingly. "I've heard that before. Left to me, that dumb keythong would have met his end seasons ago. Bah!" He waved a dismissive claw. "No more of this nonsense. You annoy me, Gryphon. Hollowcrypt was strong in the days of my generation, and it has been made weak by the foolish ideals of Gryphs like Talia." His eyes gleamed. "It'd be a shame if that blasted hen died in this skirmish, wouldn't it, Canik? A shame indeed… with the way those Gryphons from the Pale fight, I wouldn't be surprised to hear news that there was a bit of an accident during a particularly heated clash."

The Gryphon next to him chuckled, and Arias's eyes flashed over to him. *So this is Canik,* he thought. Arias wasn't sure what he was expecting, but Canik was a remarkably normal looking Gryphon, save for the exceptional amount of scarring he bore. He shifted his gaze back to Swiften.

"I understand your anger, and I'm inclined to say that it's justified. I can't make right what has happened, but there has to be some way to atone. Punishing Gryphs who are innocent won't fix anything."

Sneers and snorts sounded from those surrounding Arias. Swiften tilted his head, a slow frown creeping across his face. The fur along his back bristled, just a bit.

"You don't understand, do you? You're far more foolish than I believed possible. You don't have any ability to bargain here, and yet you still act as though you do. The very fact that I've allowed you to draw breath this long after showing your wretched face is a travesty in itself. No, Gryphon. Your ability to atone was lost the murm you set claw into our hallowed mountain. It was lost when you were brainless enough to show up here. It will *begin* with your death."

Arias allowed himself a brief glance at Bala. The Ardeigryph was standing still, his feathers ruffled as he hardly breathed, his eyes wide with terror. Deep down, Arias thought he could see something else in the keythong… a flash of betrayal. Bala, like Arias, had never wanted to be Sire. If it were up Bala, he would have already fled halfway across the ocean, leaving behind this battle for the chance, however slim, of finding peace elsewhere. Of all Gryphs, Bala didn't deserve to be here.

"If I give myself up," Arias tried, "and the others stand down, will you let Bala go?"

Laughter erupted around him in earnest. Swiften threw his head back, his tail lashing as he guffawed. When he finally stopped, his featured were contorted with rage.

"You still don't get it," he growled, shaking his head. "Canik, why don't we help him to understand? It's the least we can do before we send his worthless likeness to the Yawning." He flicked a claw toward Bala. "Kill him."

Arias didn't think. He just reacted, throwing himself forward, and talons immediately pierced his flesh as those surrounding him launched forward to grab him, dragging him backward, holding him down with their weight. Bala skittered backwards with a pathetic cry, and Canik easily caught him and took him down, taking his neck into his jaws. Canik's grey eyes found Arias's, and there was a disgusting satisfaction in them as he started to bite down, the muscles in his cheeks bunching as he prepared to do the terrible deed.

Arias opened his beak, exhaling a tongue of flame so hot that it licked across the distance between him and the other keythong with a crackling roar. Not stopping to breathe, Arias turned and scattered the Barbagryph holding him, hearing gasps and screams of agony as the flame met with its targets, setting plumage aflame. The victims rolled and fled, setting undergrowth aflame as they went, and, watching them, Swiften lost his composure. He stood rooted to the spot, transformed by fear, and when Arias laid eyes on him, he shook his head in mute horror. The Barbagryph elder finally backed away, but Arias cleared the space between them in a great pounce, knocking the keythong to the forest floor.

Swiften started to plead, but the only answer he received was Arias opening his beak and taking a deep breath. Whatever begging Swiften may have proffered never materialized into words, instead being taken away by a blast of flame that left a charred skeleton in its wake. Arias panted as he waited in the burning clearing, surrounded by the sounds of screaming and fleeing, but no one came to challenge him. Bala was silent where he stood, tail tucked, his eyes haunted. Arias turned to him.

"I'm sorry things ended up this way," he told him. "I know you never wanted to stay Sire, and I'm also sorry I never took you seriously when you tried to tell me so. I wish I had listened before any of this happened." Despite the cool weather, the fires were spreading, and it took Arias a bit of effort to dampen the flames before they could spread further. Bala watched them sputter out, his mouth falling open as his shock grew.

"This is something I can do now," Arias said. "I know that it's terrifying to you, but I hope that you can believe that I'm still the same Gryphon I was before." He took a step toward Bala, and the keythong imperceptibly leaned back. He paused. "Head to the coast, Bala," he told him. "You'll be safe there." And then he turned and flew back the way he'd come, not waiting for a response.

***

Arias found that most of the Pale and the Barbagryph had deserted Sandrift. He made his way back to the cove, noticing that while he hadn't used a great amount of his mana, he did notice the absence in his reserves. It left him feeling tired, and, by the time he made it back to the sea cove, he found that more than just the enemy had vanished. Upon seeing the fire, many of the Sandrift Gryphs had fled as well. Arias's friends were there, of course, but they looked troubled. There was a look on their faces, a wary expression of discontent, and Arias realized that it was aimed entirely at him.

"They were going to kill Bala," he said, feeling cornered. "I'm not some monster, but I wasn't going to let them do that." Even as he spoke, however, Jance's words swirled in his head:

Your kind will never accept you as you are. Especially not as you are now.

"So that was you," Roarick said quietly. "The Unicorn was right. You are different."

"Lue told us what she saw you do," Brynne said, "but it was a little hard to believe until I saw the fire starting to spread in the forest. Halada's sake, Arias… if you can do that, then this is the safest place in the land."

237

Tybrake nodded in agreement. "No one will dare to try to take this territory again so long as you're around."

Arias felt like he was somehow on display. He didn't like it. Larin watched him with an intense stare, her expression unreadable. He especially didn't like that.

"There are limits to what I can do," he said, "and I don't want to use this power to… I don't know, to escape accountability. That's the last thing I want. I don't want the Barbagryph to feel like they're against us, either. But I don't know how to fix it." He turned to Roarick. "Swiften seemed to hold a particular dislike of you. And Talia seemed less-than-happy to see you when we were in the mountain. I want to know why."

Roarick ruffled his plumage, uncomfortable. "Talia has her own ideals, while Swiften is much more traditional. It's part of the reason Regal, the old Barbagryph keythong we ran into beneath the mountain, chose him as his successor. He wanted Talia to have some opposition to her leadership, to create a balance of sorts, and so he chose Swiften. As for why Talia doesn't like me… well, to put it simply, Matriarchs and Sires have their pick of the flock for pair bonds, and it's supposed to be a great honor to be chosen as such. Ahh…"

Brynne turned sharply. "She picked you?"

Roarick nodded meekly. "I may have done worse than simply declining: I declined through a messenger and fled the eyrie. I'm pretty sure that

Swiften sent some assassins after me as a punishment for ridiculing her, as it was obvious I was being followed for a time, but my best guess is that Talia called them off. It goes without saying that I was unwelcome in Hollowcrypt after that."

"Halada's tail!" Brynne cried. "You've got to grow a gizzard someday, Roarick! You can't run from everything forever!"

Roarick wilted, looking as if he wished he could dissipate into vapor. "I know," he muttered. "For what it's worth, her choice doesn't still stand." Brynne's only answer was a glare and a lashing tail, and Arias resisted the urge to comment on Roarick's decisions.

"Do you know where the Barbagryph may have fled to just now?" he asked.

"Hollowcrypt is the only Barbagryph stronghold in this region. There are other sister flocks, of course, but they are quite far away. I expect that most of them returned to whatever is left of Hollowcrypt."

Arias mused for a bit. "There has to be some way to try to reason with them. Whichever way, though… any attempt we make it going to have to include you, Roarick. To say that you have some explaining to do is an understatement."

The Barbagryph gave him a sheepish look, but didn't respond.

"What about the Pale?" Lue asked. "You can't be everywhere at once, Arias. What if they try to take the eyrie by themselves?"

"Unless they come up with a new leader who is just as brazen as Canik was, I don't think they will," Arias said. "He was there with Swiften, and I killed him when he tried to slay Bala. Still, it's best not to try to assume what the Pale may or may not do, I think. Regardless, without a leader, most of their members will be looking for some stability I think. If we can explain and have enough of them listen to understand that this was all a terrible mistake, there may not be a Pale left to stand against Sandrift."

"Are you proposing to offer them a chance to join this flock?" Brynne asked. "I'm not sure that's such a good idea. You know what some of those Gryphons are like."

"*Some* of them," Arias said. "But I'm sure there are plenty who are willing to assimilate into a flock with food, water, and shelter, no matter how strange they think it is on the outside."

"And if the entire idea fails?" Brynne asked.

"Then we deal with that if it happens, as well," Arias said. "If anyone has anything to add, I think we'd all love to hear it. But for now, I do have a few ideas. First, we have to let our own flockmates know that Sandrift if a safe place to return to. I promise I'll only use my abilities with discretion, especially in the presence of other Gryphs who don't know me well. I hope never to have to use it the way I just did ever again."

There was a bit of uncomfortable shifting, and then Lue said, "It's just odd to think of a Gryphon doing what you did. It seems… unnatural." She paused, ducking her head. "Sorry. I don't mean it like that."

"It's alright," Arias answered. "It is unnatural. Creatures are afraid of fire for good reason. It moves and grows like a living thing, and it destroys everything it touches. I can extinguish the flames I create, though they can still burn me. Who knows, there may even be limits to my ability to stifle them." He wriggled what was left of his tail, searching for the proper words to say. The way his friends had been listening to him had shifted. Larin's eyes had never left his, and while she was still a little uncertain, there was a sincerity in the way she gave him her attention. It was in the way everyone remained clustered around him, their ears pricked high. Listening. Things were turbulent now, but they still believed that there was a way to a better world for all of them. He believed it, too. He stood, no longer thinking about what he should say, but instead saying what felt right.

"I think Sandrift has the potential to be a prosperous eyrie for all Gryphs. Maybe even other creatures, too. But that will never happen unless we actively work to try to understand one another, and I think that without that element, there can never be harmony. It's why I want to try to help the Barbagryph at Hollowcrypt; all they know is that I brought Jance, and that

Roarick granted me access to a place that had been a safe haven for them since before a Unicorn ever lived on the mountain. And now, after I've shown them what I'm capable of, they can't even seek retribution to bring themselves some sense of justice. It must feel like they've been tossed into a dark ravine with no way up, and we're looking down at them from above.

I don't want to use my ability to control others through fear. I want to use it to protect those I love. You're my family, and if anything I can do will bring us closer to a better, more united future, I'll do it. But I can't do it alone."

Larin spread her wings in a great flourish and stepped forward, and Arias half-raised his own, a little confused, thinking that perhaps she'd moved closer to embrace him. Instead, she dipped into a low bow, her beak brushing the stone below her, and one by one, the rest of his friends followed. Roarick was the final one, his great wings filling the space and easily bridging the gap in the circle between Larin and Tybrake.

"You never wanted to be Sire," Brynne said, "and I won't call you that if you don't want the title… but I think I speak for everyone when I say that you are, in every sense but the name. If any of us is worthy of being called Sire, it's you." She straightened up, a glimmer in her eyes. "I've known you since cubhood, so I know you aren't naturally the bravest Gryphon alive. You definitely aren't the toughest, either… I think Larin and I can both attest to that." She gave Larin a nudge, and the black gryphoness gave a hollow chortle of amusement. Brynne continued, saying, "Yes, definitely not the toughest. I mean, sunlight even hurts your eyes—you, a Gryphon, a non-nocturnal creature—"

"I think you've made your point, Brynne," Arias said, ignoring the way she wagged her tongue at him. She settled down again, growing serious.

"Despite anything else, you're incredibly courageous, and I don't think I've ever known a Gryph more resilient than you. You always keep moving forward somehow. I'll admit that you make some questionable decisions here and there, but even so, I've never called your loyalty into question. It's an honor to be your friend, Arias."

The others nodded their agreement with her, refolding their wings in a flurry of color, and Tybrake turned to Arias expectantly. "So what now, not-Sire?" he asked. "You said you had a few ideas. Let's hear the others?"

Arias beamed, feeling a warmth spread through him. Standing there, surrounded by such exceptional Gryphs who trusted them, he knew that he'd found the thing he'd been searching for ever since he'd left Glendale. Could he have known, back then, what the future held? He wasn't blind to the severity of the situation the eyrie was now facing, but, even though it didn't look like it, he knew he had everything he could ever need right here.

"Alright," he said. "We'll begin with the

Barbagryph, but there's plenty that needs to be done around here, as well."

CHAPTER THIRTEEN

As Roarick had postulated, the bulk of his old flock had returned to Hollowcrypt. The pit in the mountain lay open like a great wound, its hollow tunnels and caverns transformed into silent catacombs. As Arias, Tybrake, and Roarick approached the mountain, it came to life with movement as the portion of Hollowcrypt that was still inhabitable came to life with fleeing Barbagryph.

"Wait!" Arias cried to the departing flock. "I only want to speak with you!"

"Then do so," a voice roared out. Talia stalked forward from the remnants of a tunnel, and upon seeing her bold approach, some of her flockmates landed again, their ears raised as they watched her. Roarick avoided the Matriarch's gaze, and Arias immediately understood why. It was hard to meet a gaze so firm and unyielding, but he forced himself to stand tall before her. Here was a gryphoness who, like many in Sandrift, had lost more than one lifetime could account for.

"Is it not enough that you've taken our home from us?" Talia snapped. "If you mean to kill me as you did Swiften, then get on and be finished with it. All I ask is that you leave my flock in peace to salvage what little of their lives they have left." She glowered at Roarick. "This is, after all, my fault, and I will accept the full weight of the repercussions. Had I dealt with you properly from the beginning, Roarick, we could've stayed out of the affairs of these strangers. Hollowcrypt would still stand, and my honor would be intact."

"You shouldn't blame your mercy for everything that has occurred. If anything, blame it on my own cowardice. I came here to beg for your forgiveness, Talia, and to see if there is any way I can begin to atone for my past mistakes, Roarick said."

Talia pinned her ears, looking him up and down. "Ah, yes. It's very brave of you to come to give such a speech when your fire-spitting friend is standing right next to you, isn't it? What are you, keythong? Are you even a Gryphon?"

"I am," Arias said. "Please understand that I have no intention of using my abilities against you. Swiften and Canik were planning to kill innocents, the same as Jance was. I couldn't abide by that; they left me no choice but to kill them."

A gasp of shock rose up at the words. Talia actually took a step back, looking horrified.

"Jance was guardian to this territory. He may not have been the most amiable of creatures, but he provided a service to our flock that no other could. He warded off far more dangerous foes, and he was capable of healing our sick. Not once did he ever threaten to raze our eyrie. Not until you came. Have you ever seen a basilisk in the prime of its greed and bloodlust, searching for a new home? Or a Cockatrice that decides to inhabit your best hunting territory, leaving destruction in its wake? We Barbagryph may be mighty warriors, but against many of the dangerous creatures of this land, we are little more than defenseless peryton. I'm sure Jance was after you for a good reason, Gryphon, but now you've doomed us beyond what I believed to be possible. You should have given yourself up."

Arias shook his head. "You're wrong. Jance may have served an important function for your flock, but he was far from the savior you've made him out to be. Even if his presence kept you safe, how can you disregard that he was willing to destroy your eyrie and kill your flockmates without a second thought, just to achieve his own selfish goals? If you'll remember, I did try to give myself up. I tried my best to escape so that the rest of your flock would be safe when he started to attack the mountain, but you wouldn't let me go." He noticed that he'd started to bristle, the fur along his back starting to rise, and he forced himself to remain calm. "This is all irrelevant, Talia. I'm not here to fight, I wanted to come here to say that what happened to you all is terrible and unfair, and I'm sorry for the part I played in it. I can't undo what has already transpired, and I can even understand why you turned to the Pale for help, although I don't condone it. Please, hear me out… I'd like to show good faith toward you and your flock. Is there any way we can help you?"

Talia's expression darkened, her talons curling into the ground beneath her feet. "You come prancing up to what is left of my home to make yourself feel better by making me look weak? I'd sooner take my flock into the unknown than to accept any help from you or those with you."

"There's nothing weak about caring for those around you," Arias said. "Your flock looks to you. If you leave here, they will absolutely follow you, even if it ends up being to their deaths. You don't have to make that choice. You can stay at Sandrift until we can figure out a better home for you, and, who knows, we may even be able to fix Hollowcrypt so that it's livable again. I know some creatures who are knowledgeable about living underground. I do have the ability to breathe fire, but I won't use it as leverage to get what I want. Instead, I'll do what I can to keep our flocks safe. I don't want anything in return, just the promise that the members of my flock are respected and no harm comes to them. I'd like an end to the animosity that has sprung up between our flocks, though, in all honesty, I have to add that the Pale will remain an enemy to Sandrift. Its individual members are welcome to the same offer I just gave you and your flockmates, but their frequent use of violence to achieve their ideals has run my patience thin."

Talia didn't answer immediately, though her gaze shifted from furious to just a bit more thoughtful. Eventually, she flicked her eyes over to Roarick.

"You always had a way of wriggling out of trouble, and today is no exception," she said. "It would seem that you've found friends with ideas just as blasphemous as your own. I've already decided that to kill you now would be meaningless, so you can stop looking at me like that."

Roarick dipped his head to her. "Thank you, Matriarch."

Talia stood silently, looking to Arias, and he stooped into a shallow bow and said, "Thank you for allowing me to speak. I hope that you do consider the offer, and that, with a little effort, we can put any ill-will between our flocks to rest. On the night of the next full moon, I'd like to have a meeting along the coast. You and any others who come won't be attacked, I give my word on that." He turned away then, and Tybrake and Roarick followed after him, hurrying to fall into step behind him.

"She didn't seem very convinced," Tybrake mumbled once they were out of earshot. He looked over at Roarick. "What kind of demented mindset were you in to get on the bad side of a hen like her in the first place?"

"I've known Talia since we were cubs," Roarick said quietly, "and she's always been that scary. She always wanted to lead, and I always wanted no part of it. She *knew* that, and she tried to pick me for her pair bond anyway, which would have automatically given me far more responsibility than I ever want to see. I guess I'd rather have died than to have others look to me as some sort of authority." He shuddered, and Tybrake chuckled.

"You're a strange one, Roarick," he said.

Arias turned to Roarick. "You're fairly sure that the Barbagryph at Hollowcrypt won't try to attack Sandrift again, right?"

The other keythong nodded.

"And if the Pale were to attack," Arias said, looking to Tybrake, "it's likely that Sandrift could repel them, right?"

"Without a doubt," Tybrake answered. "You're with us, after all."

"I won't be with you. But it's best if we keep that part quiet," Arias amended. Tybrake and Roarick both turned questioning gazes to him.

"We're still missing part of the flock," Arias said, "and it's long past time that they were brought home."

Tybrake held out a wing to stop Arias from walking, frowning. Roarick looked between them, confused.

"If you're talking about the island, then there's no way you should be attempting that on your own," Tybrake said. "You should send one of us. Even Roarick would probably do a better job of flying that than a Gryphon, his wings are made for soaring."

"What about me and soaring?" Roarick asked. "What are you two talking about?"

"There's an island a long way off the coast," Arias explained. "We left some of our flock behind there, because we weren't sure they'd manage to fly across the ocean. And I'm not going the way that you think I'm going, Tybrake. Or at least, I don't think I am. This pendant around my neck was given to me by a Mermaid, the one I rescued from that lake with the Kelpie in it. I think that I've been trying to use it the wrong way. Either way, if it works, I shouldn't be gone long." He paused. "You two can't let Larin know about it."

"What?" Roarick cried, flattening his ears. "I don't need two scary hens mad at me instead of just one. No way am I lying to Larin."

"Yeah, what do you expect us to tell her if she asks about you?" Tybrake asked. "Either way she's going to absolutely kill you when you return. You may as well just tell her."

"She'll try to stop me if she finds out," Arias said. "You know she will. And you guys don't have to lie to her, just… well, I don't know. Avoid her."

Tybrake snorted, but said no more, and Roarick looked doubtful, but Arias persisted. "It's going to work, you'll see. I know that it will."

✳✳✳

Tybrake and Roarick had insisted on heading
to the coast with Arias, far enough away from
Sandrift that they wouldn't be spotted. If his plan
didn't work, they both informed him that he'd be
dragged back to Sandrift until they came up with
another plan. He hadn't argued, and besides that,
he was glad to have them with him. He peered
out at the vast expanse of open ocean, shifting
and monstrous, the hungry waves lapping in a
way that seemed to reach for him. He was close
enough for some of the surf to splash against his
talons, and he took a step back at the chillness.
He imagined it all around him, beckoning him to
his doom, clawing him down into dark, choking
depths –

"Are you going to do it?" Roarick asked,
snapping Arias from his terrifying reverie.
Roarick tilted his head a little, his tail giving an
impatient twitch.

Arias meant to nod, but he didn't move.
Couldn't move. Tybrake gave him a nudge, and he
jumped.

"Yeah," he said, shaking out his feathers. He
stood for a moment longer. "Hey, if this doesn't
work, will you two help me back to the beach?"

"Of course," Tybrake said. "We can fly
overhead."

That made Arias feel a little better. He took a
deep breath, ran to get some speed, and then
launched off over the sea. One didn't have to fly
particularly high to see where the friendly water

of the shallows fell away into the darker, more sinister—at least in Arias's mind—part of the ocean. He swallowed hard, thinking of his friends back on the island, and stooped into a dive. He knew how to swim, he'd done so many times before. He wasn't far enough out that he couldn't get back to land with ease; the waves weren't too high today.

He folded his wings all the way, dropping into the water with a splash.

The salt water closed in around Arias, and then he struggled toward the surface again, paddling furiously. Roarick and Tybrake circled overhead, watching him with curiosity, and he wondered what to do next. He swam in place there for a while, marveling at the fact that he wasn't drowning. He felt a little bit of panic if the waves went over his head, but aside from that, this wasn't so bad.

Something moved beneath Arias. He tried to look down, but it was too hard to discern what it might have been. Maybe just a wriggler, or maybe… his mind immediately turned to the sea serpent, and alarm jolted through him. Tybrake called out in alarm and dove for him, but before the keythong could close the distance between them, something wrapped around Arias, pulling him under.

***

There was a gigantic beast of frightening proportions hanging eerily beneath the waves. It was black and had several long tentacles, and it held Arias so tightly that he couldn't pry himself free. He drew on his mana and tried to summon fire, but he only succeeded in wasting precious air. Frantic, he bit down and twisted, but the creature's rubbery skin was too tough to pierce with his beak alone. A figure swam up to hover in front of him, and Arias stared at the Mermaid with wide eyes; her black and green finnage undulated like a live thing, and her scales shimmered brightly in the light filtering down from above. She gestured to the creature holding Arias, and it released him. Then she pointed up, grabbed Arias, and propelled him back to the surface. Arias gasped, and the Mermaid popped up next to him, eyeing him with a sharp gaze.

"Arias!" Roarick yelled. "Get out of there! That thing is still below you!"

The Mermaid, unperturbed, frowned at Arias. "How did you get that?" she asked, pointing to the shell pendant around his neck. Tybrake hissed and swooped at her, and she scowled, disappearing below the waves. When she resurfaced, she had a long, sharp branch of some sort in her hands.

"Wait!" Arias cried. "It's okay guys, don't attack her." He looked down into the waves again, worried that he'd be grabbed again, but the Mermaid let out an annoyed sigh.

"Orchu, my Kraken, will not attack. Now, answer my question."

"Naia gave it to me," Arias sputtered, and the Mermaid's annoyance seemed to deepen.

"Of course it would be the work of my ridiculous half-sister. So you're the one who brought her back here." She didn't sound particularly happy, and that concerned Arias further, but she didn't give any indication of real hostility. "The necklace was a creation of mine that mysteriously went missing when she was sent to the lake," she said. "I should have expected she was behind it, but there was no time. My name is Fio, guardian to Naia of the Coastal tribes. So, winged one… why have you come here to the sea?"

"I was hoping Naia could help me with something if I could talk to her," Arias said.

Fio was silent for a moment, her huge, black eyes unblinking. "This I suppose I can arrange, as it is only fair. You provided a service to her, however misguided it was. However, you must ask your irritating companions to leave."

"Why?"

Fio narrowed her eyes. "Because I said so. I have better things to do than to sit here chattering away with you, land walker, so if you want to see Naia, you'll hurry up. It's for their own safety, if you must know. Or, you can let them continue circling around up there and see what might happen to them…"

Tybrake and Roarick glanced down with uncertainty. The Mermaid hadn't been particularly quiet in her comments, though

Tybrake and Roarick wouldn't have been able to understand her. The shells around Arias's neck granted him the ability to understand and speak the Mermaid's language, which differed from the common tongue he spoke with others. He debated briefly. What would she have to lie about? He was already entirely in her element… if she'd wanted him dead, he would have been dead already. "It's alright, you two," he called up. "You can leave."

"Are you sure?" Tybrake called down. The Mermaid rolled her dark eyes.

"Yes," Arias said, "it's fine." He hoped the fear didn't come through in his voice. It must have, however, because Tybrake and Roarick lingered a while longer before finally flapping toward the shore.

"Good," Fio said. "Hold your breath. And *don't* panic."

Arias would have wondered at her cryptic words, but he followed her command instead. It was a good thing that he did so, as no sooner had he done it than he felt one of the tentacles coil around him again, dragging his helpless form into the depths.

***

The sea was alive with movement. A huge school of wrigglers circled in a massive swam, their bodies packed so tightly together that they appeared to be one being. The behemoth that held Arias studied him with huge eyes set atop its head, its horizontal pupils scrutinizing him with

256

an uncanny sense of intelligence. There were other wrigglers too, much larger ones, with many, many sharp teeth, that were circling around and below them. Whenever some of the school tried to escape from the loose circle formed by the toothed wrigglers, they were chased back into position by their much larger counterparts. Those that managed to get past them were hunted down and eaten.

Fio seemed unconcerned by all of this, and appeared to be orchestrating the entire event. At a wave of her hands, the toothed wrigglers and Orchu departed, the latter releasing Arias and swimming down into the inky blackness below. Free from their imprisonment, the school of wrigglers broke for freedom, and Fio pointed her strange branch toward them. Then she pointed to Arias, and what followed was a burst of dazzling light.

Arias closed his eyes as all of his senses seemed to be assaulted at once. There was a brief, sharp pain in his throat, as if he'd been cut with something very sharp, and he tried to scream, but no sound issued forth, and instead sea water rushed in. He contorted, trying to regain his bearings enough to swim upward, and then he was flying through the water, his talons scooping at the water as he'd never known they could before. He halted his ascent, feeling that something was off. He wasn't drowning; in fact, he felt as if he'd just taken in a huge gulp of air. He hesitantly sucked in some more of the water, and the process repeated. He looked at Fio in wonder, though she wore her characteristic look of irritation.

"Gills," she said, "and fins. You'll need them to see Naia, but they're only temporary, so *come on.*"

Arias stretched out his wings, finding that instead of feathered appendages at his shoulders, he had long, sleek fins instead. His talons and paws were even webbed.

"Come on!" Fio shouted from up ahead. "You're such a hassle. Hurry up!"

Arias started after Fio, finding that his new fins worked nearly the same as they did when he flew in the air. "How did you do this?" he asked Fio, experimenting with the best way to paddle. Watching Fio stream through the water with powerful strokes of her tail, he looked back hopefully, wriggling his tail stump. He was a little disappointed to find it still missing.

"A whole lot of practice," she said, descending further. "And a little gift from those wrigglers."

Arias looked in the direction the wrigglers had fled in, and, despite the distance, he could see that they were no longer swimming. He paused, startled, realizing that their lifeless bodies were drifting in the tide and slowly sinking down into the water column. The much larger, toothed wrigglers had returned and were quickly consuming them, darting through the mass of small creatures until the only thing left were a few glittering scales.

It was clear that Fio was done waiting for Arias, so he kicked hard to catch up to her, but he felt a nagging at the back of his mind as he did so. He closed the distance between them, managing to match her speed with a bit of effort. He side-eyed her.

"Can all Mer use magick?" he asked.

For the first time since meeting her, surprise displayed across Fio's face.

"Not all, but it runs strongly in us and is easily reached. Naia does not possess the gift, and so it was fitting that I became her protector when it was discovered that I do."

"What you did to those wrigglers just now… was it dark magick?"

Fio stopped abruptly, turning to him. "I didn't expect your kind to have a presence in the ether, and yet you do. What creature are you that you know of these things?"

"Most Gryphons can't use magick, no," Arias replied. "I'm an exception in that regard." He wasn't sure how much to tell her, and decided that less was more. "You didn't answer my question."

Fio paused. "It isn't dark magick, but one might say I practice a close sibling to it. It is… expedient. If you can use magick, why did you not save yourself when Orchu grabbed you?"

"I did try, actually. But it turns out that fire doesn't seem to work in water very well."

Fio continued to swim again, more slowly this time. "Fire?"

Arias supposed it made sense that she wouldn't know what fire was. He thought of how best to describe it, and then said, "It's bright and hot. And evidently doesn't like water."

Fio nodded and regained her previous speed, seemingly done with the topic, and Arias decided that it was probably best to let it drop. He was, after all, down here due the magick she'd just performed, and angering her seemed unwise. He noted that they were coming up to a huge swathe of green, and, as they grew closer, he realized that it was a mass stretching off into the distance, made up of some plant. The closer they got, the darker it got; the fronds stretched up so thick and tall that they blocked out the light from above.

"Stay close," Fio ordered. "I can find my way just fine in the dark, but I'm not so sure about you. To get lost in this kelp forest is not a trivial occurrence."

Arias felt a chill run down his neck as he pressed his way through the waving mass of plants after her, entering into the near-immediate darkness beyond. Fio wasn't kidding about the lack of light; he caught her outline a few times, but more often than not, he was following the sound of her moving through the water ahead of him. His mind began to transform movements in the kelp and strange sounds into the rustlings of horrific creatures, and, at the thought of the sea serpent, he pressed to stay as close to her as possible. "You said you're Naia's protector. Protector from what?"

Fio snorted. "Herself, mostly. She's too naive to be the last true heir to the Coastal tribe waters; have you ever seen the way that she holds a spear? It's an embarrassing and pathetic sight to see! And she's always sabotaging her own safety. I arranged to have Naia taken to the lake you rescued her from to *protect her*, and she found a way to place herself right back in the midst of danger. I have few connections beyond the sea, and simply finding the means to transport her to that lake was an undertaking in itself." She shook her head. "She wants to be a mighty warrior, but she just isn't cut out for it. No, there is a whole world of conflict here that I wouldn't expect you to understand, land walker. Selkies have been causing us issues for many pulls of the tide, and Naia is one of their main targets."

"What's a Selkie?"

"They look like us," Fio said, "only without scales. In fact, they have fur like you do, and spots… lots and lots of spots. And teeth sharper than the hook of your bill. Lots of those, as well, and they aren't shy about using them. They've tried to claim the land my kind have lived on for generations, as this area is bountiful in food. They have plenty for themselves, mind you… they know no limit to their greed, however.

Historically, Mer have given way to their demands for the most part, but finally the king and queen were willing to take a stand against them. Both died that same night."

"I'm sorry to hear that," Arias said. "Is Naia safe now?"

"You can ask her for yourself in just a few murms," she said, and Arias squinted as they burst out onto the other side of the kelp forest, daylight spilling down in long sheets. A huge coral rose up like the largest tree Arias had ever seen, its boney protrusions rising high to cast shade on the myriad of smaller corals surrounding it. Arias thought he saw plants all along the ground here, but some of them moved on their own or even pulled away when he got near enough to them. He'd never seen a plant do that before. A few of the big, toothed wrigglers that Arias had seen earlier took notice of him and Fio, and swam toward them. Remembering how quickly they'd consumed the wrigglers earlier, Arias backed away, and Fio waved a dismissive hand at them, sending them away. Arias watched as they slowly swept the area, their pointed fins hardly moving as they glided just above the ground, and their beady black eyes fixed on nothing in particular.

"What are those?" Arias asked, keeping a watchful gaze on them just in case.

"We call them Daku," Fio said. "They're guards, and good ones at that. Your instincts are good; Daku are fearsome to face. They work for a mere exchange of food, which we make sure they never run out of. No one sees Naia without them knowing about it."

Arias kept that in mind as he followed Fio past the smaller coral structures and into the big elaborate one, ducking through a gap that led to the hollow interior. A fleet of more interested Daku came to investigate Arias, and were subsequently sent away by Fio. There were other Mer, too, all in varying arrays of splendid finnage and scale patterns. Many stopped to stare at Arias, but none spoke or acknowledged Fio and him. Arias found that to be odd, as he expected that Fio would command some level of deference. Then again, maybe he was just too used to the ways of his own kind.

There were many corridors within the massive coral, none completely divided from the rest, but seemingly arranged with different levels, similar to the Kirin temple. Arias couldn't tell if the structure was something the Mer had created or something that had already existed here, like a cave. There were no lights, either, only what filtered in through the many openings in the walls. He supposed it wouldn't be pleasant to be here at night, though the Mer seemed to see just fine in the absence of light.

The corridor Arias and Fio were traveling through widened slowly, ending at an open space. The ground was covered in layer upon layer of something green here, and at its center lay Naia. The younger Mermaid lay prostrate on a particularly thick clump of the stuff, tossing a few stones around, and to her side sat a smaller, pinker version of Orchu. Arias landed briefly to touch the green stuff, and recoiled as he found it was squishy. He kicked off to resume paddling above it, and Fio actually chuckled. "Not a fan of seaweed unless it's all dried up on the beach, huh?"

Naia turned sharply at the comment, noticed Arias, and immediately gave a shriek of joy. He pinned his ears against the piercing sound, and braced himself as she sped toward him, dancing across the space with such exuberance that even Fio took a step back. Arias grunted as she threw her arms around him and squeezed him tightly, displaying her sharp, white teeth in a huge grin. And then he yelped as her pink companion slinked over to him to suction a tentative tentacle to his side. Naia laughed, giving him a little shake.

"Arias, meet Grom! He's pretty curious about you. He's already heard all about you and how you agreed I shouldn't have been trapped in that scummy lake! He missed me a ton! Say hello, Grom!"

Grom pulled his tentacles closer to his body, covering his eyes in a way that seemed to signify embarrassment. Arias was a little unnerved by how big the creature was, and the way he moved. All those legs… it didn't look like anything he'd ever seen before. Orchu was gigantic, of course, but in the open sea, it had been harder to realize his sheer size.

"You never told me exactly why you were in

that lake," Arias said, and Naia froze.

"It *was* a punishment to be put in there!" she sputtered, causing Fio to roll her eyes and turn.

"I'll be outside if you need anything," she called. "He has until sunset before he goes back to being a land walker, and I will not be going through the trouble of performing that spell again, so I suggest you conclude whatever you need to talk about as soon as possible."

Naia stuck her tongue out after her departing form. "My sister is so… stiff," she said, returning to swimming on her back. "And she never listens to my ideas. It's, 'stay here' and 'do that' all day long. You're lucky you get to be up there."

Arias cocked his head. "Fio calls you her half-sister, and you call her your sister. Do those words mean the same thing?"

"No… but it doesn't matter to me. She's the only family I have left. Mermaid rule follows the father's side, and I was daughter to both the King and the Queen. Fio was born to the Queen long before she joined forces with the King to rule the Coastal tribe lands, so officially I'm the heir whether I want to be or not. Fio would do a much better job of ruling than I ever will, but in ten more changes of the seasons, I'll be forced to accept the title of Queen." She blew bubbles at the prospect. "I want to be out there, Arias, fighting the Selkies. Fio doesn't think I'm capable, though."

"I think Fio just worries about you," Arias said.

"Yeah, she does. Way too much. Anyway, enough of talking about this boring stuff! What do you think of the ocean, Arias?"

"I'm happy to see you, but I'm not sure being down here is something I'm excited about," Arias replied with another look at Grom. The creature had so many limbs that it was confusing to know where he began and where he ended. Grom suddenly flushed to a shade of green, almost matching the seaweed below him, staring back at Arias with unreadable eyes. Arias found himself moving backwards to put more space between him and the creature.

"Oh, don't be worried!" Naia said, reaching out to hug one of the Kraken's tentacles. "He can change color whenever he wants! He just knows that I think he's particularly beautiful when he's pink. Isn't that right, Grom?"

The Kraken immediately returned to being pink upon hearing this, and Naia giggled. "You're much better at changing colors than you used to be, Grom! That was almost exactly seaweed-green."

Arias watched the two with curiosity, deciding that maybe Grom wasn't quite as disconcerting as he originally had thought he was. "Naia, does it bother you how Fio is able to use magick and you can't?"

"Hmm," the Mermaid said, looking thoughtful. "Not really. Not anymore, at least. I really wanted to help out after what happened with mother and father, and when it turned out that she had the gift and I didn't… well. There wasn't anything I could do about it, and I accepted that. I wanted to join the guard, but everyone forbade it since I'm the final heir or whatever. I'll find other ways to fight the Selkies, though." She said the last bit with a note of defiance in her voice that made Arias tilt his head again.

"Have you ever been in a fight, Naia?" he asked honestly.

Naia fiddled with the tip of Grom's tentacle. "Well, no, not really. But that doesn't mean I can't. I've practiced the spear with some of the guards before, back before everything changed. Fio won't let me even do that anymore, because she's afraid it'll give me ideas or something."

"Are spears those branch things? Fio had one when I met her."

Naia nodded, dropping Grom's tentacle and propping herself up on her elbows instead.

"Well, I can't speak for everyone," Arias said, "but if I never had to fight another day of my life, I'd be a happy Gryphon. Some of the others live for it, but I'll never understand them."

"We'll see," Naia said. "Anyway, how are you, Arias? And the rest of your flock? I'm happy to see you, but I have to admit that I wasn't planning on seeing you quite so soon! Is everything alright?"

"I hate to ask you for a favor so soon after meeting you again," Arias said, "but there's something I was hoping to see if you or any of the other Mer could help me with."

Naia's eyes grew serious. "Of course, Arias! Anything. I told you I'd be willing to help you if I could. What is it?"

Arias gave the abbreviated version of his story regarding his flockmates and the island. He wasn't sure how much time he had left to be down under the water, but he didn't want to risk running out. When he got to the location of the island, however, Naia's gaze darkened.

"I'd love to help you, Arias," she said, "but if this place is where you say it is, that's bordering with Selkie territory."

"Can you think of any other ideas?" Arias asked, desperate. He really didn't know of any other way to help his friends if the Mer couldn't help him.

Naia dropped her gaze and started to shake her head, but then she frowned and instead looked up at him with a determined gaze. "I'm going to ask Fio what she thinks. I know she'll probably not want to hear anything in regard to me going anywhere near Selkies, but if there's one Mermaid who could come up with a plan, it's her.

Maybe she and Orchu would be a better choice to help you with this, anyway." She smiled at him. "Give us the night to come up with a plan?"

Arias nodded, relieved.

"Do you remember where you dropped me off when you flew me back here to the sea?"

Arias nodded again.

"Meet us there tomorrow long before daybreak. If the stars are already gone from the sky, it'll be too late."

"Alright. Should I bring anyone with me? I have Ardeigryph flockmates who are good at flying long distances."

"No," she said quickly, "less will be better. We don't want to attract more skyward or seaward attention than we need to." She paused. "You're a good friend, so I'll find a way to help you, Arias. What you did for me is more than most really close friends would even consider, so I'll do my best!" Her eyes sparkled, earnest and bright. "It really is good to see you again! I'm hoping Fio lets me visit you at the shore sometime. I really do enjoy talking to you."

"That would be nice," Arias agreed, stretching his wings—well, his fins—out to embrace her. "I enjoy talking to you, too," he said, which was true, even if she did talk a little *too* much sometimes. "Your sister said the Mer don't have many connections up on land, so I wish I could give you something to call me if you need help with anything that I or the others could do for you."

"I'm sure we can work something out," Naia said, pulling away. "And besides, I already know where your kind live. I can just come close to the beach and scream your name until someone notices and tells you."

"You know where Sandrift is?" Arias asked.

"Well, yes of course I do! And if I hadn't seen it, I certainly would have heard it… you guys are loud."

Arias chuckled. "You clearly haven't heard the way you shriek, Naia."

"Whatever," she said, giving him a shove. She looked up, her mirth fading. "You'd better get ready to leave. Fio will see you back to shore and tell you what to do then. I'll see you tomorrow morning?"

"Yeah."

"Alright, then." She smiled, though it didn't quite touch her eyes. "See you soon, Arias."

CHAPTER FOURTEEN

Arias's return to being a winged, non-gilled creature of the land and sky had been spontaneous and a little stressful, but otherwise uneventful. Fio had explained exactly what would happen, and had suggested that he stay in the shallows and wait out the physiological changes that would signal an end to the effectiveness of the magick she'd used on him. Roarick and Tybrake failed to hide their immense relief upon seeing his return, and Arias tried his best to ignore the meaningful looks they tried to send his way. Brynne and the others had done a great job of recruiting back their flockmates who had fled during the Barbagryph attack, and Arias gave the growing group a summary of what was going on, as well as explaining his intentions and showing them a demonstration of his abilities. Some were clearly unnerved by the display, but most were just happy to be home again.

Larin and the others had obviously expected answers about where Arias had been, but he deflected them by instead going into great detail about the trip him, Tybrake, and Roarick had taken to Hollowcrypt. He resisted the urge to tell anyone about his underwater trip to see the Mer, though he itched to do so. Getting feedback of any sort, even negative, would have helped to ease his mind about whatever Naia and Fio happened to come up with.

That night, Arias purposefully slept near the mouth of the den he and his friends shared. It was nice having everyone together again, though he would have enjoyed this more if he hadn't been worried about what the immediate future held. He rested with his eyes closed, listening to everyone slowly fall asleep around him, his ears pricking at the occasional calls the night guard communicated back and forth with. The moon seemed to take particular care in making its journey across the sky tonight, every murm feeling slow and ponderous.

Arias did not dare to sleep—he couldn't risk missing Naia's deadline. Before the sky showed the slightest touch of light, he carefully lifted the wing he'd had spread over Larin and refolded it. Then he rose on soft claws and crept out of the den, freezing as he heard the black gryphoness, an extraordinarily light sleeper, shift and ruffled her feathers against the cold. Arias remained as he was, waiting to see if she'd awaken, but she did not. He breathed out a quiet sigh of relief, and padded away to return to the shore.

Arias's own nervousness regarding being late meant that he arrived at the shore much earlier than Naia had asked him to, but he'd only been pacing the sandy beach for a short while before he saw her head pop up in the shallows. Even in the darkness, he could make out the pointed dorsal fin of one of the Daku swimming nearby her, and the bright pink of Grom's body just beneath the waves. Naia waved to him and called out,

"Hey! Fio said she'd meet us closer to the island. It's pretty safe in these waters, but she went on ahead to make sure we don't end up getting ambushed."

"Alright," Arias called back, spreading his wings to take flight. "So I'm going to be flying the whole way there?"

"Not necessarily," Naia said. "Grom can give you a break if you need it, but I've asked a friend to tag along with us just in case. We have to remember that Selkies are nocturnal, so we don't want to end up in their territory after the sun sets. If we keep our speed up, we should be back into safe waters before that ever happens."

"Is your friend already here?" Arias asked, scanning the water.

"No. He likes hanging around deeper water. But he'll be there, don't worry. And he's big enough that I don't think your friends will have to worry about making the flight back to here. I swim fastest underwater, but I'll come up to the surface every now and then so we can stay in contact."

"Alright," Arias replied. "Ready?"

Naia nodded in answer, then dove back underwater with a small splash. The Daku fin that had been next to her vanished as the creature followed after her, and Arias turned and flew off in the direction of the island, easily tracking Grom as he streamed along near the surface. Arias took in a deep breath of air, excited despite everything. He was finally doing it; he'd finally have a chance to bring the rest of his friends home.

***

The sun rose above the horizon, painting the sky in warm pink and gold colors. Naia matched Arias's speed with ease, and he had to admit that he was surprised by her silence. He'd expected that she'd be surfacing every other murm to try to have some sort of conversation, but neither exchanged any words as they journeyed. It was only in the growing light and from above that Arias caught sight of the spear she gripped close to her body as she swam. He felt a prickle run down his spine, but he didn't comment on it when she did finally surface again.

When the sun hit its zenith, Arias started to lag behind. The air thermals he'd hoped to be lucky enough to find didn't reveal themselves. The waves had grown to massive proportions now that they were out in the open ocean, and Naia had to yell to be heard above the roaring of the surf. Arias avoided dipping down too low to hear her; he didn't want to risk being caught in one of the waves, and regaining altitude would be difficult now that he was tiring.

"Heylen isn't too far ahead!" she yelled. "He can take you the rest of the way. He just called out to me, he'll be waiting for us!"

"Alright, but where's Fio?" Arias called back down, angling his wings as he started to ascend again.

"I'm sure she's probably up ahead with Heylen!" Naia yelled back, diving back beneath the waves.

Arias pushed onward, his eyes watering under the harsh light of the sun. He was so focused on flying that he almost missed Naia trying to signal him. She finally leaped up from the sea in a fantastic arc, her amber scales glittering like hundreds of small jewels. A murm later, a most interesting creature arose from the depths to join her small processional. The shadow of four flippers moved on either side of it, and it had a mane that ran from its huge, blunt head all the way down to its muscular, forked tail. "Go on!" Naia urged. "Hop on! He won't hurt you, and his skin is too thick to be harmed by your claws. You'll probably want to hold on with how turbulent the water is today."

Arias's skepticism only grew as the creature surfaced a little more, two distinct nostrils appearing atop its head as it blew up a pillar of air and water, then turned sideways to glance at him with an eye that seemed too small for the rest of it. It made a high pitched, sing-song sound, and Naia stopped swimming to look up at Arias. "We can't waste time, Arias!" she said. "And you're flying too slowly. Heylen doesn't like Selkies either, so we need to make sure we make it to and from the island before nightfall. He'll leave if he detects any of them.”

Arias banked to hesitantly land on the creature, its smooth skin odd and rubbery under his talons and paws. Naia gave him an approving nod, then called out, “Now, hang on!”

Arias quickly learned that Naia had meant it when she’d told him to hang on. He was nearly thrown free as Heylen used his massive tail to propel himself forward with surprising speed, drenching Arias in salt water. He instinctively dug in to keep from losing his grip on the creature, feeling the wind whip around him as they went faster and faster. He noted that Naia had decided to catch a ride as well, as she was hanging on to one of Heylen’s pectoral fins as he sheared through the water. Heylen’s swimming became much smoother as he leveled his speed, and Arias was able to release the death grip he’d been forced to take, instead staying low against Heylen’s back. He tried to stay alert as they went along, though anything below the surface was undetectable to him. He still remembered how quickly the sea serpent had come upon him and his flockmates, and he shuddered at the thought that it could be anywhere below them and he wouldn’t know it.

The sun started on its downward course, and the island solidified into sight in the distance. Arias perked up when he saw it, though it immediately brought a realization to mind. Naia hadn’t surfaced since they’d come into Heylen’s company, and Arias decided that it was probably because Fio wasn’t coming to meet up with them.

In fact, he doubted that she'd told her older sister anything of this little quest. That didn't bode well for them if the Selkies attacked, but he decided it would be best to just hope it wouldn't be a problem. He stretched his wings, excited, and used Heylen's speed to help him to take off, pumping hard for the island. He was so eager that he pulled ahead of the group with ease, and soon he was soaring over the island, eyes scanning for any sign of his friends.

Arias descended to land at the spring he and the others had drank from in the past, relieved to find it was still flowing with an abundant supply of fresh water. As far as he knew, it was one of the island's only sources of drinkable water, and the many fresh tracks pressed into the damp earth around it suggested it was still heavily used. So where was everyone?

Arias hurried to the beach, following more tracks inland to where he found the entrance to a peculiar hole in the ground. It was lined with feathers and fur, and, remembering the tunneling habits of his Strigigryph friends, he called into the darkness.

"Hello? Anyone down there? It's Arias."

There was a shuffling and a scraping, followed by the sound of rapid movement. Alissi launched herself from the den to take him in, her already wide, yellow eyes widening further as she confirmed that it really was him. "Bless the night and everything within it!" she cried embracing him. "It really is you!"

Nanchu, Ratina, and the other Strigigryph tumbled out of the den and gave him a similar reception, and then he was being smothered by questions and updates.

"How did you get past the sea serpent? Did you fly the whole way back here?"

"What's that weird pattern on your shoulder?"

"You and the others were right, Arias."

Arias made the voice out to be Alissi's. The formerly plump Strigigryph hen had lost a lot of her original rotundness, but she was still a healthy weight.

"There's no way the entire flock could have survived here. Not for long," she said as the others quieted. "We still take peryton and tusker here and there, but it's more of a special treat than anything. Nanchu was an amazing teacher for casting, though! I bet that I'm a better caster than most Ardeigryph now… I caught a huge one just the other day!"

Friendly argument bubbled up regarding whether the wriggler in question was just as huge as Alissi had made it out to be, and Nanchu, the blind Ardeigryph hen who'd taught her, curved her neck and uttered a modest thank you. Arias tried to stay focused. Time was of the essence, and introductions and conversation could wait.

"It's good to hear that you've all done well for

yourselves with what you had," Arias said. "I came here because I've found a way to bring you all back to the mainland, though it's a little odd. We need to go now, though."

It was only after he'd said the last sentence that he noticed Ratina's gleeful expression fall. The slate gray hen looked away from him, crestfallen. Arias knew her predicament wasn't an easy one, and while he didn't have the answers, he didn't want to leave her behind, either. Ratina had killed her old Sire—the leader of Oceanside eyrie before Bala—as a show of loyalty to the Sire of Arborochre, a Strigigryph keythong named Shadowbane. Arias didn't have to ask to know that most of the Ardeigryph back at Sandrift would see her as a traitorous enemy if they knew she still lived, and he knew that the fact that she'd gone out of her way to help him when he'd been in Arborochre with her wouldn't sway their opinions about her.

"Ratina," Arias said, "I'm sure that if you want to come back, there's a way that we could—"

She shook her head. "No, Arias. I know what I did. It wouldn't be fair to ask the others to accept me after that. It's okay. I don't want you to try to vouch for me. In fact... being isolated on this island seems like a worthy punishment for what I've done. The other Ardeigryph would tear my throat out if they saw me alive, and rightfully so. Honestly, being able to live on this island is more than I deserve."

"You did what you thought you had to do to

survive, dearest," Alissi said softly. "I'm sure the rest of the Ardeigryph could be made to see reason. And if not, well… I'd like to see them try to get to you through me."

Many of the Strigigryph nodded to that, and Ratina took a step backwards, shaking her head again. "No. I don't want more fighting, especially not over me. If you all have a chance to leave here, you should take it. I'll be just fine. I always preferred being alone, anyway." She said it with a touch of humor, but Arias could see the somberness in her eyes. Alissi and the other Strigigryph had lived beside Ratina since long before they all ended up on the island, and they had always been sympathetic to her plight. They'd been among the many who'd been trapped in Shadowbane's eyrie, unable to escape the ever-present eyes of his many sentries and guards.

Arias took a deep breath, feeling that he should try to argue with her, but deep down he knew she was right. Suddenly, he knew how Sheba had felt all those moons ago when she'd tried to force her flock at Skyhaven eyrie to accept him as a cub. Her sister, Kayane, had nearly ripped the flock apart by inflaming the divisions that sprung up around it.

Arias's ears flicked sideways as he thought he heard something. He nearly dismissed it, but then it sounded again, and this time the others craned their necks to try to catch it better as well. Arias frowned, opening his wings and taking off to fly in the direction he'd heard the disturbance, and the others followed after him. He landed on the other side of the island, on the far beach, and found Naia signaling to him urgently. Heylen was nowhere to be seen.

"We have to go!" Naia screamed. "*Now!*"

Arias didn't ask questions. He wheeled around, finding that most of the Strigigryph were hesitantly looking to Alissi for guidance.

"I'm not sure what's going on," she said, "but if Arias says that he has a way off this island and that we need to go now to do it, I believe him. What do we need to do?"

Arias locked eyes with Ratina in desperation. The blue hen gave a stout nod.

"This is what I do, remember? I survive. Goodbye, Arias. It was good to see that you're alive and well."

"I'll stay as well," Nanchu suddenly said. "I can't just let my memorization of this island go to waste. I haven't felt this at home somewhere since Oceanside… its home to me, now. You won't have to worry about us, Arias, because we'll be together."

Arias felt as if words had drained from his mind. Naia screamed his name one last time, then turned and dove underwater with a huge splash of her tail.

"Go!" Ratina said. "We'll be just fine. Hurry, now."

"Promise you'll come to the mainland if you ever need to," Arias said. "We'll figure something out."

"Of course," Nanchu said. "But I'm sure we'll be just fine."

Arias spread his wings and launched off from the island alongside Alissi and the other Strigigryph. He cast one long last look backward as he went, watching Ratina and Nanchu become small specks on the beach. Then he turned his gaze toward the task at hand, searching for Naia down below.

Naia was swimming much deeper than she normally did, and was tearing through the water at speed; the only reason he'd spotted her at all was because she surfaced once to search for him. The Strigigryph read his unease and peered down into the waters nervously. Alissi tried to get information from him, but he didn't know enough to tell her anything, which set him even more on edge. The sun seeped lower on the horizon. Nothing happened… at least, not until the island was left far behind. Arias saw a swath of water than didn't seem to fit in with the rest of the blue around it, its liquid a cruel red instead of crisp blue. Arias hadn't noticed before that Naia hadn't been swimming with either Grom or the Daku, and now the latter made sense. The slain body of her Daku guard had been left to float in a patch of its own blood and viscera just up ahead of them.

"Naia!" Arias screamed despite knowing she couldn't hear him. He couldn't figure out how to get her attention, either, but they were headed directly toward whatever had caused *that*.

Alissi glanced at him, fearful. "Arias?"

"I don't know… fly higher for now," he said. "I'll stay at this altitude so I can try to figure out what's going on."

Arias watched Naia balk upon seeing the Daku. She stopped swimming, twisting to look in every direction. Unfortunately, what had slaughtered the Daku didn't remain a mystery for long. Three Selkies surrounded Naia; they looked like Mer, and yet lacked the scales of the Mer. Instead, their bodies were covered with sleek, spotted fur, and, even from up above, Arias could see that they sported teeth so long and so sharp that they couldn't close their mouths entirely. All three held spears with oddly flat, angled ends. One Selkie sped up as it closed in on Naia, but before it could reach her, Grom set himself upon it. The Kraken had been so expertly camouflaged that Arias hadn't been able to make him out in the water near Naia. Grom grappled with the Selkie, his tentacles wrapping around his victim as he overpowered them a battle that was eerily silent from above the water. He realized that Krakens must have jaws of some sort, because when Grom released the Selkie, it was in two halves. Another Selkie lunged for him, sweeping downward with its weapon, and Grom flashed to bright white as one of his tentacles was sheared free. Grom sped away, trailing blood, and the

Selkie followed him.

Arias dove lower, realizing with a shock that Naia had already been caught by the remaining Selkie. The Mermaid twisted and struggled in the grip of the much-larger Selkie, her spear already lost to her, though the Selkie had lost its weapon as well. Arias watched them wrestle underwater, the Selkie trying its best to land a bite on her while she resisted with all her might. Arias felt entirely useless from above, and he knew the feeling would likely translate to reality if he went down there. He felt compelled to try anyway.

Arias dove down, swiping at the water with his claws, hoping to somehow get Naia's attention or to distract the Selkie, anything to help. Naia tried her best to ascend despite the presence of her attacker, and Arias circled anxiously as she did so, poised for a murm to strike. It came. He tucked his wings and zoomed downward, reaching past the waves to the body of the Selkie below, digging his talons in and lifting it free. The Selkie let out an ungodly shriek, snapping at him furiously with its open mouth full of teeth. Arias felt pain tear through his leg, and he threw the creature away from him. It landed with a crash, vanishing back into water, and Naia surfaced immediately. Grom, evidently having won his battle against the other Selkie, rejoined her.

"Are you both alright?" Arias asked, expecting more Selkies to appear at any murm.

"Grom's tentacle will regrow, he'll be alright. And I'm okay, thanks to you. I didn't expect

them to come out before nightfall, but – oh!
Arias, your leg!"

Arias glanced down at the red that was
growing to spread across the white feathering of
his right foreleg. His initial glance made him
afraid that he was missing toes, but he found it
just hurt to move the toes on that talon. "It won't
slow me down," he called down. "Let's just get
across. I'll keep a lookout from up here."

"We will, too!" Alissi called down from above,
and Arias nodded gratefully. It was still bright
enough that he had trouble seeing well, but
Strigigryph had particularly good vision, especially
at night.

"How far to safe water?" Arias asked Naia as
they took off again.

Naia paused, her tone grim. "It'll be nightfall
at this rate."

"If the Strigigryph need to rest, can they still?"

"Yes, once we get to Coastal territory again."

"Naia."

The Mermaid looked up.

"We need to stay in contact. I can't speak to
you or help you if you're deep under water. Can
you at least come up more often so we can check
in?"

She nodded, kicking hard with her tailfin to regain speed, with Grom staying close to her. Arias flew as fast as he could, worried because the Strigigryph were already beginning to struggle. A collective gasp suddenly ran through the flock, followed by screams of terror. Arias didn't want to see what it was, but he would have seen it even if he'd tried not to. The sheer immensity of the creature that was surfacing from the depths was impossible to ignore, and Arias's heart sank as he made out the pointed, whiskered head, and the white, sunken eyes of the sea serpent. It followed Naia and Grom with the dogged focus of a hunter in the final stages of running down its prey, and Naia pressed ahead as fast as she could. It was useless, however, and Arias watched as the sea serpent gained on them.

"Arias!" Naia shrieked, "Save yourselves! Tell my sister –"

"Climb on!" Arias cried, diving down without thinking. He held steady next to her, trying his best to ignore the monster tearing through the water just behind him. Naia didn't question the opportunity, putting on a burst of speed and cresting the water in a flying leap. Arias grunted as she landed on his back, straining against the sudden extra weight, his shoulders protesting as he flapped hard to rise. The sea serpent turned its attention to Grom, its sinuous body whipping from side to side as it trained its focus on him instead. With a spike of regret, Arias realized it probably wasn't feasible to try to rescue the Kraken—he was probably too large to be lifted— but to his surprise, Alissi and a few other brave

Strigigryph answered the call he'd been too afraid to make.

"How do we help?" Alissi asked. A few other Strigigryph carefully grabbed Naia, and Arias watched as Grom changed the course of his escape, doubling back to try to confuse his assailant. The sea serpent followed him, jaws chomping with frustration, and Arias knew Grom wouldn't be lucky for much longer.

"If we can give it something else to chase, it might leave Grom alone," Arias said. "Fly ahead of me, but I have to stay between you and it no matter what. And I don't want you to get too close to the water."

Alissi hesitated, but she angled her wings to fly directly over Grom, and Arias followed behind her. He'd hoped that two Gryphs within striking distance overhead would be enough to attract the attention of the beast, but it doggedly continued its pursuit of Grom who, despite his extraordinary success at staying alive thus far, had begun to flag. Arias dived down a little lower, swiping at the water just ahead of the serpent with his talons. That got its attention. It tilted its head up above the waves, whiskers questing toward the open air above it. It let out a rattling hiss as it sensed the preymeat hovering just above it, and Arias recalled how it had killed so many on their original flight across the ocean.

"Let it target me!" he called out to Alissi, dropping his speed just a bit. "Get clear of it!"

To her credit, Alissi didn't question him. She banked hard to put distance between herself and it, and Arias watched as the beast opened its mouth and bared its throat, sucking air.

Not if I don't give you the chance, Arias thought, drawing from his mana as quickly as he could and opening his own mouth. The explosive arc of violet flame that issued forth illuminated the water below, striking directly down the serpent's gullet. The Strigigryph cried out at the sight of fire, and the sea serpent bellowed a roar of pain as it snapped its mouth shut, contorting backwards to fall deeper into the ocean. Arias watched the creature vanish back into the depths, a long stream of bubbles rising in its wake, and then he started circling, watching for any sign of its return. He wanted to believe that the serpent had retreated for good, but somehow he knew that it was too much to hope for.

Like a nightmare, the visage of the serpent rising from the depths appeared to Arias. The beast launched itself in a crescent above the waves, its charred maw open wide to receive him, and Arias greeted it with another blast of flame. At least a dozen more times in different locations, the serpent appeared to vanish, and, when Arias and the others moved on, it made its presence known again by rising to attack. Arias warded the creature off each time, but it didn't take long before he realized the dire situation he was creeping toward. Every stream of flame he managed to summon was weaker than the last, and he could feel the fatigue eating at him as he drained his mana. The beast was relentless, shrugging off any pain associated with the burns, and Arias realized that it was only by sheer luck that his tactic had worked this long. Creatures of the sea didn't understand fire, and, just as he hadn't until recently, the serpent would have no notion that its ability to shoot jets of water would render his fire useless.

It grew quiet for a long murm. Naia began to make a quiet gasping sound, and Arias vaguely remembered that she couldn't breathe air, not in the same way as he and other land walkers did, but to bring her back to the ocean would mean death.

Think. Hurry.

Arias tried to fight through his own muddled mind to create some semblance of a plan as they continued toward the safety of Coastal tribe waters, but, even as he tried, he noticed small figures surfacing to look up.

It was impossible to know exactly how many Selkies had congregated due to the shifting of the sea, but the way they took a keen interest in the Strigigryph who were carrying Naia was bad news. Suddenly there was a great spray of water as the serpent burst upward, far enough away from Arias and the Strigigryph that Arias was confused. He didn't think to take notice of the long tail flailing toward him—not until it was too late.

Arias felt as if he could see every detail of every scale on the serpent's tail as it hurtled toward him, and all he could do was to brace for the impact that he knew was inescapable. He was so encapsulated in that murm that he didn't notice Naia wresting herself free of her Strigigryph saviors, launching herself toward the serpent in what would ultimately be a useless endeavor to save him. He closed his eyes, the weight of the serpent's tail colliding with him so hard that bright stars clouded his vision. His wings fluttered uselessly on either side of him as he tumbled, but, even as the sea rushed up to meet him, he caught the barest glimpse of something amazing. A giant, black tentacle had risen from the sea like a monolith, and it struck at lightning speed to coil around the serpent's body, forcing it down beneath the waves And then Arias, too, was claimed by the cold salt water.

***

There were a seemingly endless number of Selkies in the water, all racing forward to meet the opposing force of Mer that were streaming in to clash with them. The Selkies seemed to have some sort of connection to the sea serpent just as the Mer did with their Krakens, but, against Orchu, the great serpent seemed finally to have met a worthy adversary. In the rapidly heating fervor of battle, Arias's presence was ignored. He caught sight of Fio's magnificent black and green finnage spanning behind her as she met with one of the Selkies, her spear drawn, and, as he struggled back to the surface, his sight was drawn to the way that Orchu was slowly coiling his entire body around the sea serpent, its jaws crushed shut by Orchu's many limbs. In only a few murms, the serpent's vicious attack became a frenzied attempt to escape. Arias paddled harder,

longing for the fins he'd had when he'd visited
Naia, but, suddenly, he was being grasped and
buoyed upward.

"Arias!" Naia cried as soon as they reached
open air. "Are you alright?"

Arias shook the water out of his ears and tried
to focus on her; her image fuzzed a little when he
tried. He nodded anyway.

"Can you fly? It's not safe for you down here.
The guards will keep me safe, but I don't want
anything to happen to you. Grom can help you to
take off from the waves, but you'll first have to
hold your breath for a little bit. Can you do that?"

Arias didn't like the sound of that, but there
was no time to waste. He drew in as deep of a
breath as he could, and Grom darted for him and
grabbed him before dragging him under. Without
communicating with the Kraken, Arias somehow
understood what he was trying to do as he
stopped his descent and started instead to ascend
at speed. Tucking his wings in close to his body
as they rose, Arias closed his eyes as Grom
crested the waves in a brilliant arc, throwing Arias
up into the air with his tentacles before crashing
back down into the waves. Arias spread his wings,
shedding droplets of water in a great spray, and
tried to use the momentum of his ascent to
continue upward, but he could feel himself
sagging despite his efforts. A Strigigryph
keythong darted down to grab him by his scruff,
straining upward to try to combine their wing
power, and, although it hurt, it worked. Before

long, they were flying comfortably above the sea. The Strigigryph rejoined his flockmates, and Arias let out a long, slow breath of relief.

As the group started to head further into safe waters, Alissi drifted over to fly next to Arias, her wide eyes concerned.

'I'd hoped that we left all of the crazy happenings back on the mainland… and I see now that I was very wrong."

Arias simply nodded, half listening, his eyelids heavy. Lying down and not moving for a long time seemed enticing.

"Arias?"

Arias meant to say something like, 'It's alright, don't worry about me,' but whatever came out of his mouth wasn't really close to words. He was already beginning to drift downward slowly, and while the Strigigryph tried to help him keep airborne, there was only so much they could do. Everyone would have a good chance of making it to the mainland now, though. That was all that mattered.

Arias thought he heard Fio's voice call up from down below, saying,

"I'm sending Orchu to make sure that you get back in one piece. I knew that you were trouble, Arias, but you kept my sister safe, so consider this my gift to you."

The words only barely made sense. He didn't really process one of Orchu's massive tentacles curling around him, carrying him aloft in the direction of home.

Home, he thought tiredly as he slipped into nothingness. *We're finally going home.*

CHAPTER FIFTEEN

It turned out that Naia's decision to enlist Heylen's help in traveling to and from the island where Arias's friends had been had saved them all. Fio hadn't known where to start looking for her sister, but some of her guards had noticed the direction of the creature's hurried return to Coastal waters, and had called upon all the help they could get. Naia was, of course, in quite a bit of trouble, but there had been good things to come of the situation.

The Mer of the Coastal tribe waters had struck a serious blow to the Selkies in the surprise battle, and, while it was unknown whether the sea serpent had been vanquished, it had only managed to flee after Orchu had dealt heavy damage to it. Aside from the outcome of the skirmish, Fio had started to view Naia less as a liability to protect and more as what she was; the future ruler of their underwater civilization. Fio had arranged for Naia to be more equipped as a leader, and the last Arias had heard when he'd met with Naia again was that she was enjoying training in proper spear-wielding technique. She was also allowed to roam her kingdom freely, though she always had Grom and at least a few Daku guards with her, and Arias realized that the real reason Naia seemed happier wasn't necessarily because she got her way, but because her older sister finally took her more seriously.

After spending a few days recovering, and with the night of the full moon looming, Arias hadn't missed an opportunity to invite both Fio and Naia to the meeting he was planning. The difficulty in inviting aquatic Mer to attend a gathering that would occur on land turned out not to be a huge issue due to the location Arias had chosen, though there was still the problem of translation. No one else in attendance would be able to understand the Mer, and so Arias offered to translate. Fio had hinted that the shell pendant he wore hadn't been easy to create, and that there likely wouldn't ever be another.

Arias had known that avoiding Larin's fury wouldn't save him from it, though returning with Alissi and the others had certainly lessened the outpouring of it. His explanations and apologies only went so far with the black gryphoness, and he ended up feeling quite foolish, as it was only after everything had drawn to a close that it struck him how selfish his decision not to tell her had been. He knew that behind her anger at his secretive departure was concern for his well-being, and he was quick to promise her he'd never do such a thing ever again. She seemed to understand his candor, because she grew much softer then, and most part of her anger abated.

Almost all of the Sandrift Gryphs had gathered at the eyrie by the time of Arias's return, and seeing that the Strigigryph had successfully

made the trip across the sea had put the eyrie into
a festive mood. Those who had made the journey
across had all agreed not to mention Ratina; the
only other Gryph Arias told about the Ardeigryph
gryphoness had been Larin.

Larin had been there with Arias and Ratina in
Arborochre when everything had gone bad, and
she comprehended more than most that life
didn't exist in absolutes. When Lue, Tybrake, and
the other Ardeigryph had asked about Nanchu,
Arias and Alissi had repeated what the blind hen
had told them herself. They'd emphasized that
she was comfortable on the island since she'd
memorized its layout, and that it was safe there as
there were no other predators. As a last resort,
they all knew that Nanchu *could* leave the island if
she'd really needed to, as she knew the direction
of Sandrift and could make the distance. Even if
the sea serpent lived, she was capable of flying
high enough to avoid its attacks. Of course,
Arias's knowledge that Nanchu had Ratina
alongside her made him feel much better about
leaving Nanchu on the island. He knew they'd
take care of each other, and he also knew it
wouldn't be the last time he saw the pair.

The threat of the Pale had dissipated as the
days had drawn on, with quite a few of its
members deciding to join Sandrift. Perhaps
remarkably, none had caused any trouble after
their assimilation, and most seemed quite happy
to be in the company of other Gryphs. Both
Hilda and Canik had found the very notion of the
flock Arias now led to be a distasteful aberration
of the traditions of their kind, and yet the ready

acceptance shown by the members of the Pale who'd joined Sandrift made Arias question just how much of Pale membership was based on coercion and fear. Arias treated them the same as he did any other Gryph, and he remained open about his ability to breathe fire, though he refrained from doing so in the presence of anyone other than his close friends. The flock's fear of such a capability was understandable, and he also understood that there was nothing in place to keep him from going against his own words and using his ability to force his will onto others. He was aware that his word as testament wasn't really enough. He found himself wondering whether Jance or Mati-jai or Shadowbane started out with good intentions. Over time, had they garnered enough power and influence that no one dared tell them otherwise? Such thoughts preoccupied him more than he would have liked, and he feared coming to the same ruin as Mati-jai and the others had. He realized that it was as To-shin had warned him earlier... His life, whether he wanted it to be or not, would be different from the others of his kind.

***

Arias's foreleg healed nicely from the bite he'd received from the Selkie, but not without a little help. He'd been surprised at how deeply the wound had torn, as he'd hardly felt it when it had happened; a testament to the needle-sharp teeth of the Selkie that had wounded him. Aside from the pain and the annoyance of having to limp everywhere, he'd started to grow concerned that the wound would become infected, but thankfully Brynne's great aptitude for finding the blackroot he needed meant she was able to supply him with some of the last viable herbs of the season. With daily administering of blackroot, the tear had finally started to heal, but not without leaving a nasty scar. Arias did take notice of Brynne's talent with finding herbs, and he invited her to come along with him on his trip to the Kirin temple to reconnect with Kail and to inform To-shin and the others of the upcoming meeting at Sandrift. Arias secretly hoped Brynne and the Kirin would strike an interest in each other, as the Kirin's knowledge of plant life in the region was nonpareil, and he hoped there was something Gryphkind could give the Kirin in return for their extensive knowledge.

Under a light coating of snow and with the trees bare of leaves, the forest around the Kirin temple looked almost normal. By the next spring, it would be almost as if Jance had never blighted the land. Kail was clearly growing much faster than her peers, an indication of their vastly different lifespans. It was something that couldn't be helped, and something that Kail didn't quite understand or care about. She had many, many friends in the temple, and the Kirin were quite taken with the little hen and seemed not to mind hosting her indefinitely, but she'd missed the presence of Larin and the others, and begged Arias to take her to Sandrift.

Arias and Brynne had both paused as they considered what complications bringing Kail back to their eyrie could cause. Would the cub's presence at the meeting cause issues if the other Barbagryph truly did attend? And aside from that… neither said it, but Kail was just as much a part of the flock as Roarick had become. The idea of giving her up was something that neither of them wanted to consider, but both decided that bringing her along was the right thing to do.

***

Word of Arias's proposed gathering spread quickly. Even the Primal group that had split off from Sandrift earlier had shown interest in it, and, as the night of the full moon marched ever nearer, Tybrake and Roarick informed Arias that Talia had sent a messenger to accept his invitation. It was an exciting time, and, while it wasn't without its stresses, Arias found himself feeling cautiously optimistic about the future. He was so excited, in fact, that he posted himself at the beach and went over everything he hoped to bring up at the meeting long before it actually happened. Seeing creatures slowly trickle in from far and wide was a sight to see, and he thought to himself that next time he'd take the time to invite the Minotaurs and the Pegasi to any future meetings.

The full moon rose high and clear above the horizon, the sky cloudless as if even it wanted a clear view of the interesting sight congregating on the beach below it. Barbagryph, Ardeigryph, Strigigryph, Gryphons, Kirin, and Mer all gathered on the stretch of beach, and Arias was in awe of just how many had cared enough to come. Even Tybrake's leaf Fae had managed to seek him out, and they clung to his neck in the darkness. Kail clambered up to view the assembly from Larin's back, and one look from Talia let Arias know that a conversation regarding the cub would not be skipped... But that would come later.

Arias took a deep breath, thanked everyone for coming, and then described the ideas he had: new, unheard of ideas, but proposals that he hoped everyone would see some merit in.

And to his great jubilation, they did.

***

Spring was one of Arias's favorite times. He liked to observe the tender breeze that was neither cold nor hot, the abundant greenery, and the way the treetops and undergrowth seemed to explode with life. All seemed to sing out with their own song, and he loved it after the long silence that was winter. He sat perched on a piece of driftwood, waiting for the signal to fly, ignoring the loud screeching of a Mermaid who was clutching desperately to the back of a young Ardeigryph keythong. The Mer had taken to challenging one another to the experience, offering any Ardeigryph who would listen a hefty wriggler in return for a few murms above the sea. Arias was sure that Naia had started the whole thing, but of course she'd denied all connections to the odd pastime, claiming that she was much too busy with her new duties to be bothered with such silliness.

Larin sat next to Arias, her sleek tail waving, ignoring Kail's ardent efforts to pin it down. The young Barbagryph hen had lost most of her down, and when she wasn't harassing Arias and his friends, she was trying her claws at learning to stalk and hunt. The Kirin temple wasn't so far away that she couldn't regularly visit her friends there; Arias planned to take her at least once a season to spend time learning and seeing the bucks and does she'd come to know in the territory.

Talia had decided to take Kail back to Hollowcrypt to search for her parents after Arias's meeting, and Arias had felt he was in no position to stop her. But for better or worse, none had claimed the young hen, and Talia had elected to let Kail stay at Sandrift in light of the unusual circumstances. The cub clearly had developed a strong bond with Arias's flock and with the Kirin, and, fundamentally, it set a good precedent for both flocks going forward. Both Strigigryph and Kirin had been involved in helping to restore the shattered structure of Hollowcrypt eyrie, and, while it was now nowhere near as large as it had been originally, what had been fortified would easily house Talia's flock for years to come. Some of the Barbagryph had taken to frequenting Sandrift, even if for the most part it was only to raid the bone pile that now sat next to the communal preymeat. Arias had already gotten to know a few of them, but it was slow progress. Rightfully so, as a whole they were exceedingly reserved around those not from their own flock.

Arias squinted as a strong wind arose. The breeze rustled his feathers, tugging them out to their full length as he breathed in the warming air. There was a storm coming, one of the first big ones of the season, and Bala had promised everyone he'd show anyone who was willing how to 'ride the storm'. Evidently it was an Ardeigryph rite of passage, and something Larin had thought would be fun. She had encouraged him to try it with her despite his misgivings, and had rallied a number of others to come along as well.

Bala had become surprisingly bold since passing on the title of Sire to Arias, and would be among those leading the group on this unusual flight. He'd returned to Sandrift and had taken a place alongside Tybrake, Lue, Seale, and a few others, and Arias was surprised at how the nervousness he'd associated with Bala's personality had been cast aside. The keythong was charismatic and agreeable, and Arias was grateful to have both his council and his friendship.

Kail had been upset that she didn't have her flight feathers and couldn't join them on the upcoming flight, and Arias had found himself wishing he'd had a similar excuse not to go. Still, he stood and opened his wings as he heard Bala shrieking overhead; the sign that it was time to depart. Kail stopped her game of chasing Larin's tail and drooped into a pout, and Arias gave her an affectionate nuzzle.

"You'll be up there with us soon enough," he said, and her ears pricked at the prospect.

"You really think so?" she pipped.

"I know so," he said, gesturing to Larin to take the lead. "Alright Larin. You're the one who thought this would be fun, so I'll follow you up."

The black gryphoness rushed past him, touching skyward and climbing her way to the upper reaches of the stormy clouds. Arias pumped his wings hard to stay in her wake, the unfamiliar wind currents buffeting him to and fro. The Ardeigryph and Barbagryph seemed to hold steady a little more easily than the others in the turbulent breeze, and a few eager Strigigryph rose up to meet with them in the heights, their broad wings flapping twice for every sweep of their larger counterparts'. Roarick seemed just as unsure of the whole ordeal as Arias was, but he stayed close to Brynne even as she broke formation to dart down toward the ocean below them, her talons almost touching the white caps before she caught a thermal back up. Together, the group rose so high that the waves of the sea below hardly seemed to be moving, and Arias stared down in wonder, partly in awe, partly terrified.

"Here we go!" Bala shouted out. "Fly as fast as you can, and let the wind take you! Let's go!"

With a raucous cry, the other Ardeigryph joined him, and everyone else rushed after them, the wind tearing at their coats, the sound of distant thunder shuddering through their very bones. Arias streamed after Larin, riding the gale ever higher until even the clouds were beneath them. Larin cried out with glee, and in a swift motion she reached out and took his talons in hers, tucking her wings. Arias mirrored her movements, uncertain but trusting her nonetheless, and they plummeted together in a maelstrom of black and white, streaming down toward the waves.

The last shred of fear left Arias, and exhilaration as he had never felt before rose in him with wild abandon. He breathed out a fantastic arc of flame that the wind snatched away just as soon as he released it, his heart slamming against his ribs as the great sea rose up to meet them. He and Larin broke away from one another, careening toward the land, their calls intermingling as they flapped hard to rise again. Arias caught Larin's brown eyes glittering despite the gray, stormy sky as she fell in beside him, and he knew that everything within her eyes was reflected in his own.

In that murm, Arias realized that there was no place he'd rather be. Despite everything, he'd been fortunate if only because he'd ended up here, in this murm, surrounded by those he cared about and who cared about him. If the sun set on his life in that instant, he would have died a fulfilled creature, with no care for his legacy or any other such thing. For right then his life was whole; he knew it to be so more than anything else he'd ever experienced, and he wished it to continue to be so for many, many more turns of the seasons.

Thank you for reading! If you enjoyed this book, please consider leaving an honest review for it. Also, consider joining the mailing list:

https://www.kathrynobrown.com/

Read them all!

The Quill and Claw Series

Book One: A Gryphon's Journey

Book Two: A Gryphon's Trial

Book Three: A Gryphon's Mercy